RUNNING GRAVE

RUNNING GRAVE

RICHARD DENHAM

www.blkdogpublishing.com

Other titles in the *Citizen Survivor* series for your consideration:

Citizen Survivors: The Red Book

Citizen Survivor's Handbook

Citizen Survivor Tales

There are a terrible lot of lies going about the world, and the worst of it is that half of them are true.

- Winston Churchill

THE BEGINNING?

Then ...
  He took a swift snorter before he started, ruffled his papers and adjusted his glasses. The cabinet room had never looked so lonely. The Prime Minister's chair, the only one with arms, had its back resolutely to the fireplace. No need of a fire in the sweltering heat of June 1940. Around him were the functionaries of the BBC, in ties and suits because this was Downing Street. Brendan Bracken, the PM's attack dog, stood beside him, all blond wavy hair and attitude. The PM glanced at the photo of his darling wife on the table. Then a green light popped on and one of the functionaries raised a finger.

'I am speaking to you tonight from the cabinet room of Number Ten Downing Street.'

The millions at the other end of their wireless sets wondered whether this was actually the PM or the actor the BBC wheeled in occasionally to fake his speeches. *Everybody* could do his voice. The Mr Impediment of the Commons.

'... And I have to tell you that the situation vis-à-vis the Channel is extremely grave. I spoke to His Majesty the King this morning and have been in all-night sessions with my cabinet. Mr Attlee and I are at one ...'

He couldn't hear the jeers in homes around the country.

'... in the belief that our only hope against the enemy

and their aggression is to close our borders entirely. The bomber may still get through, but there will be no invasion by sea. We brought a number of our brave boys back from Dunkirk and, as we speak, our troops further afield are on their way home from overseas.'

There were no jeers in living rooms now, no cynical sniggering in pub snugs. All there was, across a stricken nation, was a deadly silence.

'As of today, every beach will be defenced, with barbed wire and machine guns. Every city will be rigged with anti-aircraft guns and barrage balloons. If you have friends or relatives overseas, prepare to bid them farewell now as long as the international mail service lasts. Telephone lines to areas outside Britain have already been disconnected. Now, God defend the right. And God save the King.'

The finger came up and the green light went out. The Prime Minister leaned back from the microphone and Brendan Bracken patted him on the shoulder.

From that moment, time stood still.

Now ...

The mirror was becoming increasingly inaccurate, that much was obvious. The Announcer declined to look closer at the reflection – the greenish cast on his once-black tail coat and the frayed edges to his lapels would not be improved by more detailed examination. Nevertheless, he shrugged his shoulders, tweaked his bow tie and slicked back his hair with his all-but-toothless comb. He still had half an hour or so before he had to step up to the microphone, but he always liked to be ready. He sipped his black-market gin – a man had to look after his tonsils in his game and gin did have herbs in it, so it counted as medicine – and looked around for his script. He said the same thing, night after night, but it didn't do to cut corners. This may be the tenth year of the war but he had been trained by the BBC and there were standards.

The door to his miniscule dressing room crashed back on its hinges and all but sent him flying. He had a robust exchange of words with the powers that be approximately every six weeks, on the subject of Jack Jones' dressing room being five times the size of his and with all the trimmings, such as a gas ring and kettle and a chair. But this wasn't the time for that argument – he could feel the bruise coming up on his shoulder blade before he even turned around.

One of the Lads stood there, panting, his flat cap awry on his tousled head. The Announcer had started as just such a Lad, back in the day, but that didn't make him like them; nostalgia wasn't something he subscribed to. He looked down at him and snarled, 'What? You oik. You could have broken my nose against the wall and then where would we be? My diction and timbre are my living.' Vocal virtuosi like the Announcer were, after all, made in heaven. He swiped the Lad around the head for good measure.

Bouncing back resiliently as all the Lads did from blows of any degree of severity, the boy took a deep breath. 'The Station Director says as how you've got to go on in five, seeing as how Jack Jones ain't here and can't be found.' It sounded like one long, almost unintelligible word. The Announcer wondered if another smack upside the head might make the Lad speak more clearly and administered one.

'Ow. That ain't gonna help none, is it?' the Lad yelped. 'T'ain't my fault if Jack Jones ain't turned up for work today, is it?'

The Announcer nodded to himself. So, he had heard the boy right the first time after all. Even so, it didn't do to let the lowest of the low think they had the whip hand. 'What do you mean, Jack Jones isn't here?' He laid the merest emphasis on the correct grammar, for all the good it would do. His consonants rang like gongs, his vowels came out on a blast of gin. What were they thinking in schools these days? *Were* there any schools these days?

The Lad shrugged, using every bone in his body. 'I dunno. I was just told come and tell you you've gotta be on in five. Three now, prob'ly. Because otherwise, we'll have dead air and you know how that goes down wiv the listening public.' He trotted out the phrase although he had never been really able to picture this many headed monster, the people who listened, not having a wireless at home.

The Announcer's eyes widened. Dead air? Dead air!! That mustn't be allowed to happen. The last time there was dead air, caused by someone inadvertently unplugging the broadcasting equipment, there had been widespread panic, with everyone thinking that Recent Events were on their way again. There could be air-raid sirens, searchlights, the drone of bombers and the staccato answer of Ach-Ack. It was a good few years ago, true, but memories were long in the listening public, and it had to be avoided at all costs. Batting the Lad aside, he leapt for the door and set off down the corridor at a dignified trot which nonetheless still ate up the yards to the studio.

Inside the studio, almost as down at heel as The Announcer, the Producer was pacing back and forth, looking at his watch and running his free hand through his already thinning hair. As The Announcer rushed in, he grabbed him and shook him until his teeth rattled.

'Where have you been? Where have you *been*? I sent that Lad …'

'I'm here now,' The Announcer boomed. 'Where is that idiot Jones? Not only does he have the largest dressing room in the building, but he needs must leave us all in the lurch!' He looked around, seeking back-up and getting none. Everyone knew that Jack Jones was the first in in the morning, last out at night. In fact, there was a rumour many people believed in implicitly, that he never actually left, that he had no home, no family, that all he ate was the sandwiches provided by the company, that all he drank was the stewed tea that seemed to run in an unending stream from the urns simmering in the corner. The Announcer hitched his lapels back into place. He knew that the listeners couldn't see him, but there were standards, after all and Lord Reith cast a long shadow.

The Producer thrust a sheaf of paper at him and The Announcer looked at it as if it were smeared in poison.

'And this is …?' he asked, an eyebrow raised, his nostrils aquiver.

'Jack's script. We found it in his room.'

'His script?' The Announcer took a step back. 'But he doesn't ...' he swallowed hard ... 'he doesn't speak Received Pronunciation!' Once upon a time, that had been known as the King's English, but that sort of talk could bring a world of trouble these days. Who the hell knew where the King even was these days?

'Of course he doesn't. He's Jack Jones.' The Producer was almost screaming now and a technician, his face swimming behind the glass of his booth, was mouthing the dread words. 'Dead Air! Dead Air!' and drawing his sharpened thumb across his throat.

'For the love of ...' It was hard sometimes, without the old words to fall back on. 'Just do it!'

And the Announcer, wild-eyed and desperate, cleared his throat, stepped up to the microphone and began ...

* * *

'I think that went well, didn't you?' the Announcer said anxiously to the Producer. 'I got the right ... timbre, do you think?'

The Producer had not heard much after the first ten words. Incoherent crying will do that to a person. He couldn't say that the words were in the wrong order, or that any had been missed out, or even that the timing was off. It was just ... not Jack Jones. But, despite his hysteria and his temper tantrums and other off kilter behaviour, the Producer was a fair man and generally a kind one. But he wasn't a liar, so he settled for 'Umm.'

The Announcer had stars in his eyes. 'So will I be doing this every night now?' he asked, eager as a puppy. 'Until we find Jack Jones, I mean.'

'I don't think so,' the Producer said, unable to meet the man's downcast eyes. 'I think we should manage some rescheduling from today. Reruns of old tapes, that kind of thing. Something the public will be comfortable with. But *thank* you, *thank you* so much for stepping into the breach like that. It could have been a disaster, but because of you, we

5

only had three seconds of dead air. Better than we could have hoped for. Yes.' He lifted his eyes at last and smiled. 'Yes, indeed.'

The Announcer was crestfallen. He had never sought fame, but he had come so close tonight, he had been certain of it. Alvar Liddell could forget it. The future was his. But he was a professional, to the roots of his slicked back, dyed hair. He pinned on a smile and nodded. 'Well, glad to have been of help,' he said, backing out of the Producer's office. 'See you tomorrow.' There was a tiny hint of a question in the phrase.

'Of course.' The Producer leapt to his feet and clapped The Announcer on the back while ushering him out. 'We can't do without you, dear chap. Tomorrow, yes indeed.'

The Announcer left, not looking back and therefore missed the Producer dropping his head into his hands. After a moment, he started to keen to himself; he knew he shouldn't show any signs of weakness, but he found it did him the world of good.

THE STATION OWNER

The Station Owner sat behind his desk, in itself bigger than the Producer's whole office and carefully clipped the end of his cigar. Most people hadn't had so much as a sniff of a cigar since Current Events had taken hold and if asked – though not many people asked The Owner about his personal affairs – he would tell them that he had had the foresight to stash a lifetime's worth of the things in a vast humidor built beneath his Chelsea mansion, next door to the bomb shelter and along a ways from the underground swimming pool. He felt that good old Winnie would approve, wherever good old Winnie was now. The Owner had never been to Hollywood, but he had seen the Pathé newsreels, back in the day, and he knew how men like him lived over there. Since there was not a cat in hell's chance now that he would ever go there – always assuming that 'there' still existed – he had decided to bring Hollywood to Chelsea and wasn't doing too badly. He looked up at his secretary, hovering there like some etiolated waterbird of the heron family and wished she had a pulchritudinous thigh upon which he could roll his cigar; that's what they did in Cuba, wasn't it? He looked away again, suppressing a shudder. Perhaps not – if the crepey skin and disapproving look didn't put him off, the smell of camphorated oil did. He was taking his time over the cigar because, not being the brightest of men, he needed time to assimilate her news. Finally, he spoke.

'What do you mean, Miss Fitzloosely, Jack Jones has disappeared? He's never been known to leave the studio is what I've always been led to understand. So how can he have disappeared?'

Veronica Fitzloosely drew herself up, tucking in her chin and looking down at him disapprovingly from her rather prominent gooseberry-coloured eyes. 'No one knows how, sir,' she said, with a voice that sounded like someone drawing a fingernail down a blackboard at the bottom of a well. 'He just has. They have turned the studio upside down. As you know, his dressing room is his main residence ...'

The Owner cast up his eyes. How typical of the woman to say it like that instead of in normal language like the rest of humanity.

'... and there were no clues there. He doesn't appear to have taken anything. His few clothes are still on their rail, his wallet, even, is on the bedside table. He has two pairs of shoes, apparently, and the ones not on his feet are still there. But of the man himself, there is no sign.'

'Have you checked with hospitals?'

She inclined her head. It didn't deserve a nod.

'Bus stations? Railway stations?'

'Yes, sir,' she said, wearily. 'I believe there was a train to somewhere unimportant this morning, but he wasn't on it. All in all, public transport was so yesterday, don't you think?'

The Owner was beginning to run out of ideas. He wasn't exactly over-endowed with them at the best of time, but this was really too much. They paid the man more than all the other staff put together. The least he could do was be reliable. Then he got an idea.

'Has he ever done this before?'

'Do you mean before, or Before?' the secretary wanted to know.

'What?' The Owner was confused.

'Do you mean, has he done this before, as in at some time in the past? Or do you mean, has he done this Before, as in before we were in this rather extraordinary pickle we are in?' She mouthed the final explanation silently – 'The War?'

The Owner looked frantically left and right. If Miss

Fitzloosely was not such a wonderful secretary and also, thanks to her unusually repellent looks, acceptable to his wife, he would get rid of her. These cranky ideas she had could get a man into trouble.

He looked at her desperately and she shrugged. 'I mean, Before the country became governed as any rational country should be, alone and the best among nations. Splendidly isolationist.'

The Owner sagged in his chair. 'Either. Both.'

'The answer is the same, anyway,' she said. 'He has turned up for his programme every day, on the dot, for more years than anyone can remember. He is never late. As far as anyone knows, he has never had a cold, a sore throat, a cough … in short, until today, he is as near to perfect as anyone can be.'

The Owner thought for a moment. 'I suppose I have met him, have I? I can't for the life of me picture what he looks like.'

'I've never met him,' the secretary said. 'But his face is all over the newspapers. As you may remember, you signed a contract with every Government agency as well as most food manufacturers, the Home Guard, the …'

'Yes, yes, I know all about that.' The Government contract alone paid for The Owner to indulge in some of his little private hobbies and a fair chunk of the upkeep of the household of a certain famous actress. 'Is that what he looks like, then?' He rummaged on his desk for the latest galley proofs of *Jack Jones Suggests*, a handout which went to every home in the land telling them about any new suggestions on how to behave and how to make a national diet go round. He had called them laws once and nearly had his collar felt, so was now more careful. 'Where … oh, yes, here it is. So, he looks like this, does he?'

The face looking up at him was affable, with a flat cap jauntily over one eye and a cheeky grin. Alongside it, a disembodied hand held up an enthusiastic thumb. The man was winking.

'He's a bit … bland.'

The secretary screwed her head round to look. She

didn't go nearer her employer than she had to. Chosen for her repellent looks she might well be, but she didn't know that; neither did she know what monstrous inner thoughts lay beneath that rumpled waistcoat.

'That's his charm, though, isn't it?' she asked.

The Owner held the page out at arm's length. 'I suppose. That wink makes him look a bit half-sharp. I suppose he's all there, is he?'

'He writes his own scripts,' she said, 'if that's any guide. They're quite clever. Funny, you know. People love him.'

'Funny, is he?' The Owner looked thoughtful. 'Not really a funny sort of person myself. I find jokes a bit wearing.'

Miss Fitzloosely found herself something she hadn't been for a long time, surprised at the depths of her boss's stupidity. 'Have you never listened to Jack Jones?' she asked, the incredulity only just masked.

The Owner shrugged. 'Of course not. Load of drivel. I may own this company, but I'm not obliged to listen to any of it. The missus and I like music, mainly. All the household staff were chosen because of their musical abilities. Currently, we're looking for someone who can play the oboe and is at the same time a perfect pastrycook. It's proving to be tricky. Most of them were Austrian, you see and, well …' He spread his hands expressively.

With a straight face, Miss Fitzloosely commiserated. 'It must be tricky,' she said. She glanced up at the clock. 'If that will be all, sir. I have those letters to type and of course the police will …'

'The *police*?' The Owner almost swallowed his cigar. 'What the hell have the police to do with this?'

She blinked. 'Everything, surely. A National Treasure has gone missing, after all.'

He mulled it over. She had a point, even though he didn't agree with it.

'Have you … got the room ready?' He had the whole house swept for listening devices, both mechanical and human, on a daily basis, but you could never be too careful in his opinion.

'It's always ready,' she assured him. 'When they arrive, I'll have them shown in, shall I?'

'Better had,' The Owner said. 'Better had.' And, unconsciously mimicking his producer, he dropped his head into his hands, although he stopped short at keening. That kind of thing was for lesser men than he was; so he keened inside his head.

Richard Denham

THE PRODUCER
(and The Producer's Assistant)

'Oooh, don't.'

Had her voice always sounded like that? The Producer thought to himself. Had it always sounded like an air-raid siren or was it just his head putting together that feeling of terror the siren always engendered and the odd disjointed feeling which kept sweeping over him as if he was standing under an ice-cold shower? 'Don't what?' he asked, automatically, with a sigh.

'That,' she repeated, wriggling free of the hand on her knee. He hadn't even realized he was doing it. It seemed a bit pointless. It wasn't going to get him anywhere. It never got him anywhere, except into trouble with a suspicious wife, but he did it just the same, almost like ordering a drink or a sandwich filled with Government Cheese. Which was like no cheese he remembered from Before. When he was a boy, he thought with a sigh, cheese really *was* cheese. Different sorts, don't even start thinking about the foreign ones. Cheddar, Caerphilly – his little brother, lost somewhere in the toils of the Church of the Remnant always thought it was called Carefully – Red Leicester. And the blue ones, made in caves somewhere he couldn't go any more, petrol rationing being what it was, in other words, non-existent. He sighed again.

'Oooh, baby,' she crooned, extending jammy lips towards his. 'Don't sigh. Baby doesn't mean to make oo sad.'

13

He slid his hand away. 'Why do we do this?' he asked her, world-weary.

She looked rather startled. 'I always thought you liked it,' she said, the whine and babytalk gone from her voice.

He did a doubletake. If she could talk normally, why did she spend her time sounding like someone with severe mental impairment? 'Not particularly,' he said when the shock had passed. 'It doesn't get me far, does it?'

'I'm perfectly willing to go to bed with you,' she said, whipping out a mirror and examining her mascara, cunningly made each morning from spit and soot. 'You just never asked.'

'I think I had always assumed,' he said, dully, taking a swig of his watery beer, 'that this,' he raised his hand, 'would be a start.'

'You should have made it obvious,' she said. 'It's out of the question now, of course.'

'Is it?' He was puzzled. What had changed? Apart from her voice and that was a question for another time.

'Well … Jack Jones has gone, hasn't he? You're nowhere without him.'

The Producer wiped his mouth with the back of his hand and suppressed a smile. That sounded so like Jack Jones' script it couldn't be accidental. 'In fact, I will be brown bread without him, is that what you're saying?'

She laughed and made a couple at the next table look round suspiciously. 'I suppose I am. Not literally, of course. But you're finished in the wireless business, you can be sure of that.'

'He'll be back. He's just … well, everyone is entitled to a day off, aren't they?'

'Everyone else is. But Jack Jones hasn't had a day off since November 1939.'

'He must have.' The Producer was incredulous and yet … he thought back. 'No, I believe you're right.'

'I know I am,' said The Assistant. 'I checked the clock before we came out. He has got a whole drawer for his punch cards and every single one is there. Seven holes for in, seven holes for out. Every week, day in, day out. Although why he punches out I will never know. He never leaves the building.'

'He must do.'

'Again, I must tell you otherwise,' she said, smugly, making him nostalgic for her childish whine. 'No one has ever seen him in the street. When he does his Meet the Public things it is against various backgrounds for the pictures, but they always take place inside. Last one was in front of a background of the Houses of Parliament,' she said. 'A few readers of the rag that ran it noticed that it was from years ago, no graffiti, no posters, but we just managed to shrug it off. So,' she took a delicate sip of her mock gin and tonic – no gin, no tonic, just some bubbles in water and a slice of plastic lemon, 'where's he gone?'

The Producer chewed his lip. 'There's an address on file, I assume,' he said, crisply. It was time he regained control of this situation.

'There is,' she said, fishing out a piece of paper from inside her brassiere. She handed it over to him and he almost flinched when he realized it was still warm. 'It's a map co-ordinate. From an old Ordnance Survey when they were allowed. Unless you have an old map stashed away somewhere, it doesn't get us very far.'

The Producer had been a Boy Scout when he was a lad, but he looked at the number written on the scrap of paper in confusion. 'TQ298799? How does that help?'

'It doesn't. But I assume you will be calling the police in, so they'll know, won't they?'

'Am I? Will they?'

'You can't just let people *disappear*,' she hissed. 'It's Jack Jones we're talking about here, not just some person off the street. I know *they* disappear all the time. But this is ...'

'I know.' The Producer wanted to put his head down on the table and just sleep the rest of his life away. 'It's Jack Jones.' He folded the piece of paper and slipped it into his pocket. He sighed and gave her the nearest to a smile that he could manage. 'Now then,' he said, wiggling his fingers at her. He put on his best American twang. 'Wanna fool around some?' It wasn't his very best Humphrey Bogart, but it would do.

'Oooh,' she squealed. 'Oo is naughty. But Baby would like vat.' She narrowed her eyes at him and dropped her voice an octave, 'And then some.'

THE POLICE INSPECTOR

'Who?'

The Police Inspector was busy and far too important to get involved with Missing Persons. After all, the population of the British Isles ... well, Isle, he supposed described it better nowadays, unless you counted the Isle of Wight, Anglesey ... wasn't what it once was, what with one thing and another ... He snapped to. He found his mind tended to wander these days. There was both too much and not enough to do. In the filing cabinets around him bulged folders with type-written labels. One said 'Feral', another 'British Union'. A third read 'Black Market / John Bull'. A fourth 'Roundheads'. And a fifth, in small print so as not to offend anybody, 'the Church of the Remnant'. The good old days, of murder, armed robbery, actual bodily harm, arson, larceny, fraud and obscenity seemed to have disappeared into the confused hell-hole of the felonious present.

'Jack Jones, sir.' Constable Robert Harris was standing to attention in front of the Inspector's desk. He had expected a big explosion from the man. Surely, *everyone* knew who Jack Jones was.

The Police Inspector pursed his lips, rolled his eyes, then shook his head, after staring out of the window for a moment or two. 'No. I'm sorry, lad. You'll have to tell me more.' The lad was ... what ... twenty-five? He hadn't finished shitting yellow yet, but he'd obviously read

17

somewhere, probably in an ancient *Police Gazette* about Missing Persons. The Inspector knew full well that since the Current Situation began, missing persons were wall to wall and the police had long ago stopped looking for any of them.

Harris was flummoxed. There was really little more to tell. He tried again. 'Jack Jones, sir. You know. Jack *Jones*. On the wireless. "I'd be brown bread without you, Jack Jones" they go, and everybody laughs. Jack *Jones*.' He stayed polite, but inside he was screaming. On second thought, perhaps his take-off hadn't been good enough!

'No. I know you probably think me very foolish, Constable, but really, I have no idea.'

'Don't you listen to the wireless, sir?'

There was something of an accusation in the man's tone and The Inspector picked up on it, very quickly by his usual performance standard. He racked his brain. Was there a law that he had forgotten, that you had to listen to the wireless? He had all the laws about what music was allowed pinned up in his study at home, just in case. No Brahms, of course. Nothing remotely Beethovenesque. And nobody to play any of it now, of course, now that that arch-fiend Myra Hess had been put in jug for the rest of her natural. But wireless …? He risked it. 'No, Constable. Not very often. Busy man, you know the kind of thing.'

Harris didn't really. He worked. He went home. He listened to the wireless while he ate his supper, such as it was, from a tray on his lap. He went to bed. He got up – and repeat, for ever and ever. His Grandma would have said 'Amen' at this point, but he knew better. But The Inspector was not The Inspector for nothing, so he nodded.

'So,' The Inspector continued. 'This Jack Jones. I'm still not totally sure quite what's going on.'

'He's disappeared, sir.' Harris was struggling to work out quite what was so difficult about that. 'It was his programme last night and he wasn't there. He hasn't missed his programme since … well, nobody really knows since. I was listening in. The Announcer read his lines, but it wasn't the same.'

'So,' The Inspector was beginning to grasp things a

little better. 'This Jack Jones is some kind of performer, is he? Tells stories, that kind of thing?' He looked up at his subordinate, brightly. 'Sort of Arthur Askey meets Tommy Handley.'

'Well, now you ask me, sir, I couldn't quite say what he does. He's funny, tells funny stories, you know ... "I wouldn't say my wife is fat ..." that kind of thing.'

The Inspector was taken aback. 'I didn't know you were married, Constable.'

Harris was beginning to feel that he was in some kind of parallel universe. He had no idea in any detail just what one of those might be, but he had heard his parents, years ago, when he was still at school, say it felt like one and he suddenly could see what they had meant. It couldn't be the world he had woken up in this morning, this world where the man who everyone called sir, the man who called the shots, didn't have a clue who Jack Jones was, to the extent of not recognizing his most famous catchphrase or the content of one of his most hackneyed jokes. He couldn't be bothered, suddenly, to explain and settled for a shrug and an embarrassed little laugh.

The silence in the room grew deafening and Harris was certain he could hear the small bones in his ear creak as they settled into disuse. He was a man who abhorred a vacuum, so he spoke next, though he wasn't certain that it was, strictly speaking, his turn. 'I thought, sir, I might go and look for him,' he said, tentatively.

The Inspector looked puzzled. 'Why?'

'Well, he's a National Treasure, sir, isn't he?' Harris ventured.

'Is he? Well, I suppose he is, with his funny stories and catchphrases and clever things like that. Ummm ... I doubt we can spare you, can we?'

Harris didn't answer. He knew a rhetorical question when he heard one.

'Well, can we?' The Inspector spoke louder. They had stopped mandatory health checks years ago, so for all he knew this man could be as deaf as a nit. Or was he thinking of badgers? Anyway – The Inspector dragged himself back – the man seemed to be speaking.

'I would say so, sir. It would do good for public morale to find their hero. Besides, half the station are twiddling their thumbs.'

'I find that a little hard to believe, Constable ... Errr ... I have booklets of new laws coming through this office every week, if not more often still.'

'Oh, you're right there, sir,' Harris nodded his agreement. 'It's just that none of them are laws that anyone would be likely to break.'

'Is.'

'I beg pardon, sir ...'

'Is. None of them is. None is a contraction of not one, thus is, singular.' The Police Inspector had always thought he had missed his calling. English language was so beautiful and if men like this oik had their way, it would fall in ruins one of these days. First it would be the proper use of none, then who knew? The deluge, most likely. He muttered a line or two of Sir Philip Sidney, to calm himself down.

Harris shifted up a gear. There was no need to make any sense with this man, so he came straight out with it. 'If anyone breaks a law, they disappear. You don't have to be a lowlife criminal either, to have that happen. To my certain knowledge, four schoolmasters and a vicar have disappeared from just one London borough this past month. But it isn't *us*, you see, sir. We hear about it. We go round to feel their collars. They've gone. Sometimes it's just a case of "gone". Other times, neighbours tell us they have been taken away. I think you'll agree, sir, that's a bit different. But ...' he spread his arms wide, 'same difference.'

'I still don't think ...' The Inspector was sure he had signed a whacking invoice for overtime only the day before and he rummaged in his Out tray to find it. Yes, there it was. 'I have this overtime docket here, Harris. Last week alone, this station clocked up over one hundred hours of overtime.' He brandished the paper triumphantly. 'So you can't tell me that we aren't busy!' He slammed the paper down on the desk and then, for good measure, slammed his hand on top of it.

Harris by this time didn't care. He was never the

recipient of overtime pay. You had to be Sergeant or above for that and he would never be a Sergeant – he couldn't lie well enough. 'It's fiction, sir,' he said. 'No one above Constable is ever here after half two in the afternoon. Had you not noticed?'

The Inspector shrugged. 'Why would I?' he asked, reasonably enough. He never left his office except to go home, via the back stairs.

'Sir.' Harris straightened his back and put his arms down by his sides, parade ground style. 'I will be looking for Jack Jones, sir, either as a policeman or as a private individual. This country is going to the dogs, sir, and I can't stand by any longer.'

'Oh, I say, steady on.' The Inspector was quite shocked but also in a strange way rather proud. 'Not the dogs, you know. Not the dogs.' He thought of his two beagles at home who he knew loved him far more than did his wife. Dogs were rather frowned upon these days as being a drain on limited resources, but he would die for them, should it come to that. He looked at Harris standing there, his spit-dampened cowlick standing to attention, his helmet held awkwardly in the crook of his arm now as he got ready to leave, possible for ever. 'If it's that important to you,' he said, 'and picked up the phone on his desk. 'Get in here, would you, Sergeant?' and he clicked the receiver back.

Arthur Baker had been CID back in the day, before plainclothesmen came to be regarded as potential Fifth Columnists, so here he was, back in blue, the silver chevrons glistening on his arm. He looked like one of those jolly Coppers from the Lawson Wood cartoons Harris remembered as a boy, without much hair and a little bristly moustache. He'd only recently been transferred, so neither the Inspector nor Harris really knew him.

'Sergeant,' the Inspector said as he scuttled in, 'Missing Persons case. One … er …'

'Jack Jones,' Harris reminded him.

'Jack Jones,' the Inspector went on. 'He's missing.'

Baker looked blank.

'The Constable here wants to look for him.' He caught

the expression on Baker's face. 'I know,' he smiled. 'I know, but the lad's young. It'll be a bit of an experience for him; you know, old-time Coppering.'

Neither Harris nor Baker knew quite how to take this. Baker had never seen himself as an old-time Copper and Harris resented being spoken about as if he wasn't there.

'Keep an eye,' the Inspector went on; and neither man was sure who he was talking to. 'I expect up-to-the-minute reports.'

Harris was so excited he dropped his helmet and was able to conceal his blushes for a moment as he bent to retrieve it. He wasn't totally amazed to discover that his boss was wearing carpet slippers under his desk. 'Oh, sir, I can't tell you how … I'll start at once, sir. I'll report every day, I promise.' He rushed to the door, eager for the off, then paused before he turned the handle. 'Sir … if I find him and he won't come back, what shall I do?' Then he suddenly remembered the senior man still standing by the Inspector's desk. 'Um … I mean, what shall *we* do?'

The Inspector shrugged. 'It's a free country,' he said, then began to laugh, quietly at first and then with huge, racking hoots which sounded very like sobs.

Harris turned the handle quietly and let Baker go first, nodding to The Inspector's secretary, who was sitting behind her desk filing her long, scarlet nails. Where she got the nail polish was a mystery, but as she never did any typing, her nails didn't get any hard use. Perhaps that was her secret. Although he didn't see it, Baker was already sighing and rolling his eyes to the heavens.

THE LANDLADY

Harris's Landlady was impressed. Imagine, a lodger of hers searching for her idol, Jack Jones. She made him promise to bring back her hero's autograph when he found him and also packed him a paper bag of Mock Spam sandwiches. No one knew quite what was in Mock Spam, but it was off ration and needs must when the devil drives. All that anyone knew was that it was pink and tasted of sawdust.

'Now, don't forget to let me know how you get on,' she called as she waved him off. 'I can only keep the room for two weeks or I'll have them dratted Street Wardens on me back. Cheerio, ducks.' The Rent Lark wasn't what it was in the early days of the Current Situation; the Government were too fly now. After all, careless letting cost lives. She didn't actually speak like that when she was alone with her husband, a strange, grey man who lived mainly in the shed at the bottom of the garden, but she had an inkling that that was how landladies spoke, so she tried her best to conform. Over the years, she had found it was the best way. Before – she called the dear old days 'Before' to herself, to make sure she didn't accidentally speak out of turn in public – she had been a concert pianist of some repute – though never in Myra Hess's league – but choosing the right music had become a tangle of legislation which she couldn't cope with and so she had stripped her house of her lovely things, put a single bed with twanging strings in every room and installed lodgers. She played the old joanna, as she had learned to call it, at the Dog and Duck every Friday, all the old songs, the ones from the other war, the one no one spoke about. But an evening of *Pack Up Your Troubles* and *It's a Long Way to Tipperary* didn't salve the musical wound in her soul, so she played her baby grand, the one tucked away in the back scullery where no one would hear it, very quietly. Some Brahms. Some Liszt. And then, suiting the action to the words, she resorted to the gin. She wiped away a tear as she closed the door. Such a nice young man. She hoped he would come back, but she wouldn't be holding her breath. People went missing all the time.

She had waved off so many young men – and a few young women – from her front door and not a single one had ever come back. They had gone off down the road with so many hopes and she could have told them before their heels cleared the gleaming white doorstep that they might just as well have not bothered. One young lad she remembered so very well, a soldier he was, very handsome. Easily as handsome as any of the tenors, basses and baritones she had accompanied in the dear, dead days Before. She chuckled to herself. Actually, the most handsome had been the counter tenor but the girls hadn't looked twice, because they thought he was too pansy for that. Pansy – now there was a word you didn't hear much these days. Probably banned. But he had proved to her in the props cupboard of Covent Garden how pansy he was and that was not pansy at all. Where was she? Oh, yes. The handsome Soldier. He had joined the Free Corps, very excited he was. She had waved him off from this very door, so happy and proud he was, to be going to do his bit. He had promised to write to her.

'Don't worry, Ma,' he had said – lots of her boys called her Ma – as he turned to go. 'I'll be back, you'll see. And I'll write, to let you know where I am. And he had written. Just the once. She had learned the letter off by heart. 'Dear Ma,' it had said. 'After a long journey, I am at the camp in ███ with some great chaps. One of them, ███████ says he saw you ███████████ That made me so ████. Can't write more, we're off to ███ in ███████. Love, your

Soldier Boy xxx' Sometimes, she filled in the gaps for herself and had him lounging on the Lido in Nice, though common sense told her he wasn't. She sighed. Life could be hard, but it could be worse.

She had used her extra Mock Spam on the sandwiches, so she wandered back into the kitchen to try to think of something for an evening meal for everyone. It was getting harder and harder, she had to admit. She knew that some of the younger women, the ones who had been young when this all began, didn't even try to create a proper meal these days. They couldn't remember sitting down with the family and watching avidly while Father carved a chicken, handing Mother the first slice and waiting to see if they would be the lucky one who got the wishbone. They settled too easily for the biscuits which were off ration and for good reason. The Landlady's husband – and this was his only joke – always said that they weren't on ration because you could neither eat nor wear them, though she had thought privately they would be good for soling shoes. He wasn't much of a laugh, to be honest, her husband, his one skill, first vouchsafed in the props cupboard, having long ago fallen into disuse. But she did still hear him singing to himself in the shed from time to time. He didn't know that she stopped and listened to him sing *I Saw My Lady Weep* by Dowland, when he thought he was all alone. She would weep then, her head back against the rough wood of the shed, the tears running down her cheeks to soak her grubby, worn collar.

But for now, she had to think of something for supper. There was a head of broccoli that hadn't gone too yellow. There was some Government Cheese, which hadn't got too many green bits on. Cauliflower cheese used to be an old favourite Before – could broccoli cheese work, perhaps? She counted in her head – there would only be seven for supper, now Harris had gone. So – she hefted the broccoli in her hand – she might be able to make it stretch. There was a packet of dried egg ... broccoli cheese omelette? Her Father had always said you couldn't make an omelette without breaking eggs but he had not been able to see the future. Not *this* future, anyway. He would be dead now, wherever he was.

He had been taken away right at the start of what she still thought of as all this nonsense. His Old People's Home had been cleared of its occupants, to keep them safe, the Ministry had said. She sighed. He was a difficult old bugger, towards the end. But he didn't deserve that. No one deserved that.

The Landlady sat down at the kitchen table and started picking the worst bits off the broccoli. She looked wistfully at the front door, just visible at the end of the gloomy passage off the kitchen. She sighed. She would give quite a lot to be walking down an endless highway with Harris. She would give quite a lot to be anywhere but here.

THE STUDIO

'You're who?'

Baker was happy for now to let the lad have his head. He was there in an advisory capacity, to make sure the kid didn't put his foot into things. So he let him answer.

'Constable Harris,' Harris said. 'I represent the Police and I am here to investigate the disappearance of Jack Jones.'

The Receptionist looked up for the first time. This person looked very young to be a policeman. 'Why aren't you in uniform?' she asked, her lip curled with derision.

'This is not a uniform matter,' he said. 'This is Detection.'

'I thought plainclothes was Fifth Column,' the Receptionist said.

Time for Baker to intervene. 'That is a myth, Madam,' he said. 'Now, be a good Receptionist, will you, and answer the constable's question.'

'Hmm. What if I said that Jack Jones isn't missing?'

'I would assume you were lying.' Harris was hard to annoy, but this woman was getting mighty close and he sensed that Baker had his back.

'I've been told to tell all callers that Jack Jones isn't missing,' she said, stubbornly.

'But I'm not a caller, am I?' Harris said, patiently. 'I'm the Police. Detection. I told you this.'

'Prove it,' she said, shuffling papers and looking at him

with her head cocked on one side.

He whipped out his police badge. Strictly speaking, the police no longer carried anything which would identify them as arms of the government, but he was proud of the badge, which had belonged to his granddad. Baker carried no such frippery.

'Nice,' she sneered. 'Shiny.'

'I would like to speak to someone,' he said, leaning in. 'Someone other than you.' He remembered his Mother telling him that he must always be polite to ladies, but he was ready to make an exception. He knew raddled old prostitutes down by the docks who had better manners than this obnoxious girl.

'There's the Producer, I suppose,' she said, patting the back of her hair that was sticky with the sugar water she sprayed it with each morning to keep it in place. On hot days, she had her own swarm of gnats. 'Or his Assistant.'

'I'll see the Producer,' Harris said, assertively. 'I need to know more details.'

The girl snorted. 'Details? Him? You're lucky if he knows what day it is.'

'Well, his Assistant, then. Is he here?'

'She,' the Receptionist corrected him. She sighed and pressed a button on her phone, which buzzed back at her. She picked up the receiver and held it languidly to her ear. 'Hmm. Hmm. He says he's the police, looking into Jack … Yes, I know, but he knows he's missing, so … Hmm. Yes.' She put the receiver down and tapped her nails on the desk before looking up. She hated the Assistant with a passion. She could have had the job, but some of the special duties hadn't suited her book at all, so here she was, stuck for ever on the front desk, dealing with idiots all the livelong day. Finally, she looked up.

'She's upstairs, third door on the left. You can't miss it.'

'What's her name, please? For my records.'

'Records.' If she had looked any further down her nose she would have met herself coming back. 'Nothing goes on the record through me, thank you. Who wants to be on a list, these days? She answers to Producer's Assistant. That will do just fine.'

'Third on the left?' Harris knew when he was beaten.

'Correct.' She suddenly remembered her training, such as it was. 'Is there anything else I can help you with today?' She pinned on a false smile that didn't match her lipstick, obtained at great personal cost from the rather repellent chemist from down the street.

'Umm … no, thank you. You've been very helpful.' Harris felt he owed her a lie, to match her general demeanour.

'You're welcome.'

'Have you got a licence for that hairdo?' Baker asked, leaving the girl temporarily open-mouthed. 'Because if not, we'll be back.'

Before the clichés became too numerous, they took themselves off to the stairs beyond the double doors opposite the desk.

'Oh, dear,' the Receptionist muttered. 'Did I say left? Perhaps I should have said right.' And she raised two fingers in the air, before going back to filing her nails and looking vacuous.

Harris had second guessed the Receptionist and had gone straight to the right door, helped enormously by the sign which read 'Producer's Assistant' pinned to it and a quiet nudge from Baker. He tapped and peered round without waiting for an answer. Time spent with the Receptionist tended to take people that way.

The Assistant looked up. 'Ah, you'll be the policemen,' she said. 'I've been expecting you.'

He was taken somewhat aback. 'You have? Why?'

'Why not? A National Treasure has gone missing. The only surprise is that you didn't get here sooner. The Producer and I were expecting you yesterday, to be honest. The Owner has even put aside a room for interviews, I understand.' She gestured to a chair.

'I don't think I need to interview the Owner, do I?' Harris was getting a sinking feeling that he may have bitten off more than he could chew and he glanced at Baker in alarm.

'He'll be pleased about that. I'll let Miss Fitzloosely know. Do you need to speak to the Producer? I will tell you now, he knows virtually nothing about the running of this studio. He just ... well, to be honest, I know him as well as most people and I have no idea what he actually does.'

'That's very direct of you,' Harris said.

'No point in lying to the police, is there?' she said. 'I know you, with your rubber truncheons and shackles.' She looked almost hopeful.

'No, no, goodness me, nothing like that.' Harris looked at Baker for confirmation and he pressed himself back in his chair. He had heard things, of course, but had never actually met anyone who had so much as breathed too hard on a miscreant. Perhaps he was just based at the wrong station. Baker wasn't saying a word.

'Well, what do you want to know, then?' She settled back in her chair and looked brightly helpful.

'Jack Jones seems to be a bit of an enigma,' Harris said, hoping that his small audience would understand the word.

'That's hardly true, surely? There's hardly a week he isn't plastered over at least one front page. After that little blip at the beginning of ... things ... when there was talk of taking him off the air, he has been everywhere. He's the voice of everything from parsnip porridge to what to do if your granny suddenly disappears.'

Harris had had parsnip porridge, perhaps more often than anyone should be expected to, and he had hardly known his granny, but he saw the woman's point. Baker had had his fair share of missing grannies in the time Before, but none so striking as the Great Magico's disappearing act at the Southend Coliseum back in the day; he never *had* worked that one out. Even so, the police needed more information than could be gleaned from flipping through the couple of thin and unhelpful newspapers still being published. 'I need to see his personal file, if that's possible,' Harris said.

'Well, I'm glad you added that rider, because it isn't possible.' Everything she said was said with a smile.

'Why not?' Harris could feel his frustration rise in his throat, like a piece of toast gobbled down too fast at breakfast can come back to haunt you. What was it with the women in this place? Did they want their treasure back or not?

'We don't have one. We don't keep files, as such. Everyone clocks in and out and we keep those cards, but that's about it.'

'I was under the impression that there were laws about keeping records on staff.' He was gratified to see Baker nod.

'And your impression would be right.'

He looked at her quizzically. 'And yet ... you have no records.' He drummed his fingers on his knee, the only way he could think of to stop himself from getting up and wringing her neck.

'Let me show you. How is your eyesight?'

'Pretty good, I think. I always pass the physical.'

'Excellent.' The Assistant leaned down and hauled up an enormous tome from the bottom drawer of her desk. 'Hang on ...' she leafed through it, 'it's around here somewhere ...'

'What is that, exactly?' He had never seen a book so huge in all his life.

'I would have thought this was your constant bedtime reading,' she said. 'It is the collected minutes and declarations from the Ministry. There's a bit in here about record keeping ... ah, yes, here it is. You'll need to come round to see it. This book is too heavy to pass across.'

He went round the desk and leaned over her shoulder, trying not to sniff the mixed scent of lavender and clean skin too loudly. She was pointing to a passage marked XVIII/CP/Rec.q Pt a-c/x. The print was almost vanishingly small.

'Can you see? You can lean in, I won't be offended.'

He peered closer and still had to narrow his eyes to read the words. 'Where the staff (as above in XVII/AR) are creatives, the foregoing pars (XVI/AP/a-z) do not apply and no records are required to be kept'.

'Goodness.' He stood up. 'That is a loophole and no mistake.'

She slammed the book shut and leaned on it, her hands folded. 'You can sit back down, now.'

'Sorry.' He scuttled back round to his chair and sat down. 'Who managed to find that? It's hidden well enough.'

'That's the beauty of the regulations, though, isn't it? As time has worn on, there are so many extra bits and bobs that we are all supposed to take note of, that things get lost in all the bumf. If you're clever and if you can afford to employ someone to go through every single little piece of legislation, you can get away with murder.' She stopped with a gasp as his eyes flashed avidly. 'Not literally, of course. But anyway, the Owner had this brought to his attention and so we don't keep records. Cheaper and better that way.

'But this is dated ...?'

'Two years ago, yes.'

'So you must have records from when you had to keep them.'

She looked at him, expressionless. 'We destroyed them.'

'Seems a bit pointless.'

'We needed the space. Look,' she pushed the book to one side and leaned forward, confidentially. 'I can see this is frustrating for you and I am not putting obstacles in your way just to annoy, I promise I'm not. It's just that ... well, it's Jack Jones, isn't it? National Treasure, all that. We're trying to preserve his privacy.'

'So, you know where he lives and all the rest, then? You could tell me if you wanted to.'

'I could tell you, certainly.' But she didn't move a muscle.

'Will you?' He also could be stubborn. They were like two oxen in the furrow, in what could be a permanent standoff.

She looked at him and sighed. He seemed such a nice boy (although she wasn't so sure about the plump old bloke with him) but this whole Jack Jones disaster was looking as though it might well spiral out of control if she wasn't careful. 'It's not a simple thing, sadly,' she said. 'As far as anyone knows, he lived here, in the studio building, in a little room in the roof. He had his dressing room for the daytime, of course, and he was often meeting people, for publicity, you know. But he ate in the canteen and lived in his little attic and that was it.'

'No family? No friends?'

'If anyone asked, he always said that the whole country was his family and friends. A bit trite, but it worked on the whole.'

'No wife? No ... girlfriend?' Harris hesitated over the word. Like all men – and women for that matter – under thirty, he found the idea of anyone over forty being interested in the opposite sex as being rather distasteful as well as extremely unlikely. Still, when a person was famous, it was probably different. And Baker didn't seem fazed at all.

'No. Never has been, as far as I know. And unlike most men in this building, he knew how to keep his hands to himself.'

There was a story there, but that wasn't what Harris was there for. 'So ... has anyone been round to his proper address? The one he lived in before he took up residence here?'

'That's the problem.' The Assistant rummaged in her top drawer. 'This is all we have.'

She passed over a piece of paper with a number on it. Harris had been a Boy Scout when he was a nipper and knew a map coordinate when he saw one.

'Where is this, do we know?'

'No. I think that we ... that is, the Producer and I thought that you would know. The police have that kind of information, don't they?'

Harris couldn't remember the last time he had seen a map. His walk from his lodgings to his station only involved two left turns, one right and a whole lot of straight ons, so it didn't seem necessary, somehow.

'No, not really. We ...'

At last, Baker cut in. 'The kind of information we have, young lady,' he said, 'is no concern of yours.' He nodded to Harris to continue.

'Well, I'm beginning to realize we don't actually know

much at all. Doesn't your ... oh, I don't know, your weather department, don't they have maps?'

'Whatever for? You know we're not allowed to forecast the actual weather, don't you? If you say the sun's shining, you're overly optimistic. If you say it's raining, you're defeatist. If you say it's going to rain later, you're probably Fifth Column. That Mr Herbert said that back in the day. See?'

His eyes were wide. He had relied on the Weather Forecast since he was nothing but a lad. 'But what about the farmers, the sailors, the people who need to know?' He was having a lot of shocks today but this was possibly the worst.

'What about them?' As she said it, she realized the stupidity of the remark. The farmers were almost a slave people, these days, growing everything they could on any scrap of waste land, working all the hours that the Government sent. As for sailors, who'd seen any of those outside the Naval Dockyards, bracing themselves perpetually for, whatever it was they were expecting? 'Anyway,' she went on, 'is there anything else I can help you with?'

Harris stood up. 'You haven't helped me with anything so far.'

'No, perhaps not. Look, why not take this?' She passed him a headshot of a middle-aged man with a cloth cap and a cheery expression. 'It's one of Jack Jones's photographs which we give out sometimes.'

'Good likeness, is it?' He showed it to Baker.

She shrugged. 'I don't know, to tell the truth. Like most people here, I don't take that much notice of the man. He may be a National Treasure but to us he's just the bloke who fills in an hour every night and doesn't ask for too much pay.'

'I suppose if he lives here and eats in the canteen, he doesn't need much pay,' Harris said and Baker found that comment pretty astute, at least for a bloke who hadn't finished shitting yellow yet.

She smiled and it transformed her. Harris wanted to tell her to smile more, but it seemed too forward so he said nothing more. 'I'm so sorry,' she said. 'I hope you find him soon. Him going off like this has landed my ... the Producer in some hot water. He's found a few tapes of old shows but you have to be so careful with old stuff these days, in case it contains something ... well, you know, something it shouldn't.'

Harris sighed, got up and held out his hand for her to shake. This wasn't going to be easy for anyone. 'I'll do my best,' he said. 'I've had an idea as to how I can trace this map coordinate.' He patted his breast pocket. 'May I keep it?'

'Of course,' she said. 'Anything I can do to help. Will you let me know how you get on?' She jotted her phone number down on a scrap piece of paper and handed it across the desk. 'I know making telephone calls isn't easy these days, but it's working almost all of the time.'

He added the paper to the other in his pocket. 'I'll try my best,' he said. 'If he turns up ...'

'It'll be in all the papers,' she reassured him. 'Don't forget ...'

'He's a National Treasure. I won't forget.'

And the policemen saw themselves out.

At the bottom of the stairs, Harris turned to Baker.

'How did I do, Sarge?' he asked.

'All right,' the man said. 'We'll make a decent Copper of you in ten or twenty years.'

Richard Denham

THE SCOUT MASTER

s soon as he knew where they were going next, Baker sat this one out. Scoutmasters, wooden paddles, horse liniment and General Baden Powell could all be misconstrued these days and this kind of enquiry was best left to innocent young men. He himself would go back and report the nothing they'd found to the Inspector, there may even be time for a spot of quiet contemplation over a pint at The Crown.

Harris hadn't been to this house in years. In fact, the last time he had been, the world had only been at war once and he hadn't been born when that conflict was ruling everyone's thoughts. It was known back then as 'the war to end all wars' which turned out to be a bit of a misnomer, but Harris could see why people were hopeful. They were different days, kinder and considerably less scary, whatever Baker thought of them.

Not everyone in Troop 27 had been allowed to come to this house, oh, dear me, no. Only the most senior boys, the ones who might be running a troop of their own one day, were allowed here. There was always a huge spread, put on by the Scout Master's wife, a homely woman who had no children of her own and so was prone to kissing and hugging. The boys had not been that keen on it, due to her incipient moustache, but they tolerated it for their Scout Master's sake. And the whole thing was presided over by a photograph of

General Baden Powell who should really never have been allowed to wear shorts at all.

The house looked smaller, somehow, the walled garden much skimpier, leaving the grimy door and windows much nearer the road. There was a huge house leek in the middle of a parched bed, surrounded by gravel dotted with calcifying cat shit. There was a notice in the window, faded almost to illegibility but on careful scrutiny it was found to read 'No hawkers'. The bell, a fat button housed in a gleaming brass circle as Harris recalled, had been pushed in at some previous date and there was no knocker, so he tapped gingerly on the glass. It had a crack in it for its full height and he felt it give slightly under his knuckles. He leaned forward, listening. He had heard the old stagers at the nick say they could tell from how a knock sounded whether a house was empty or not and he wished he had listened more carefully when they were talking. Or that Baker was with him. There was certainly no sound of footsteps, the muffled cough of someone elderly making their way to the door. He tried again, on the wood this time, getting a splinter of baked and peeling paint in his knuckle for his pains.

Finally, just as he was going to turn to go, he heard shuffling feet just the other side of the door and a querulous voice asking who was there. When he gave his name, the door creaked slowly open, against a pile of very old newspapers and, by the sound of it, jars and bottles. However much the bent figure on the other side of the door struggled, he couldn't open it fully, so Harris had to squeeze through as best he could. Once inside, he had to stand still for a moment to let his eyes adjust because it was almost completely dark and he could tell that there wasn't a square inch of floor without something on it.

The Scout Master, who had always seemed so tall, squinted up into Harris's face. 'Is it really you?' he asked, the voice the same but somehow quieter, as though it came from a distance.

'Yes, sir,' Harris said. 'I'm in the police now, and I'm on a really big case.'

'A big case?' The Scout Master was impressed. 'Are

you allowed to tell me what?'

'Jack Jones.'

'Who?'

Harris rolled his eyes in the dark. How was it possible that the most famous man in the country disappears and no one he talks to has heard of him?

'He's a … a turn on the wireless.' He found himself automatically going back to the words he would have used as a lad, back in the day at camp.

'And they've called the police in?' The Scout Master gave a rusty chuckle. 'You can't be very busy if they send you off looking for one of them theatricals. Me and the missus put one up one year, do you remember that?'

Harris did. She was a girl from the chorus who had brought a whiff of greasepaint, crowds and cheap gin to the Scout Master's arid house.

'Ran off, she did, with the Missus's granny's ring and a nice lighter I had had from work when my old trouble made me retire early.' He shook his head. 'Theatricals! And you say you're looking for one?'

'That's right. Jack Jones. He missed his programme last night and they're worried.'

'Well, now you say the name again, I do recognize it. Never heard his turn, though. Funny, is he, this Jones? Comedian? Singer, perhaps? Like that Tito Gobbi?'

'He's …' It was proving increasingly hard to actually pin the man down. He had not been gone twenty-four hours yet and already he was becoming fuzzy in Harris's mind. 'He does a bit of everything,' he said. 'I've got a picture. Can we go somewhere with a bit more light?'

In the gloom, the Scout Master looked up at him, puzzled. What did the daft lad want light for? Still, if it would help find this Johnson fella, then so be it. He led the way down the narrow passage, made narrower still by piles of detritus leaning on the walls and spilling from tables and hallstands. Eventually, they stood in the scullery, by the open door which had had to be prised out of the frame by force, more or less.

'Sorry about the door,' the Scoutmaster said. 'I don't

go out much these days.'

In the daylight, Harris could see that this was true. The man was pale and grey, with red-rimmed eyes blinking in the light. He was wearing his old Scout Master uniform, mercifully without the hat, with additional cardigans and scarves which seemed to have simply become attached at some point and they had clearly not been off his body for months, if not years. From below the knee length shorts, his legs, knobbly with veins, stuck out, looking too weak to support the weight of accumulated wool and making General Baden Powell look like an Adonis. His hair was long, but as there was not that much of it, it didn't really give that impression, floating like a silver aureole around his head in the draught from the door. Papers on the top of the multiple stacks whispered in the air and a mouse, thin with the pickings available, made a dash for it, only to be snatched up by the neighbour's cat. All in all, Harris wished he hadn't come, but he still hoped he might get what he was looking for.

'Are you all right for food?' Harris couldn't help but be a carer; he had been one, more or less, all his life. He just wanted to help people, that was all.

'I got some tins.'

As a young scout, Harris didn't remember the man's grammar being quite so rudimentary, but it was probably his wife who kept him up to the mark.

'Next door leaves me bread, if you can call it bread ...' The man's voice faded away as he looked out at the sky. 'I don't much like the doors open, young lad, if you don't mind. Show me the picture and we can close up again.'

Harris showed him the picture and the man took it in shaking and filthy hands. He turned it to the light, held it at arm's length, then right up to his nose. 'I'm not sure he's familiar,' he said, 'but he's got what you might call quite an ordinary face, ain't he?'

Harris looked at the picture. He was glad he had got it, because describing the National Treasure wouldn't be easy. Nose? Yes. Mouth? Yes. Eyes? Two. That was about it.

The Scout Master looked again. 'Although, now I look

again … I think the Missus met him, one time.'

Harris smiled. It was generally the women who were the most avid Jack Jones followers. It was something about him, something which made them think he was good husband material, in the dig-the-garden, walk-the-dog sort of way. 'That's nice. About your wife … ummm …' He didn't know how to put it. 'Is your wife dead?' seemed a little blunt.

'Oh, she's gone,' the Scout Master said, with a dismissive gesture. 'Went, ooh, a year or two ago, could a'bin. Yes, a year at least.' He looked around as if the strata of rubbish could pin it down more precisely.

'Oh, I'm sorry,' Harris said. 'She was a lovely woman, wasn't she?'

'Was? Still is, probably, if that's your fancy.'

'Oh.' Harris blushed to the roots of his hair. When his mother said 'gone', it was usually a euphemism for dead.

'Well, I'm still sorry. You must be lonely, on your own.'

The Scout Master looked around again, as if counting the crowds in his tiny scullery. 'I got me papers,' he said. 'Me memories.'

'Yes, and that's why I've come, really. Do you still have your maps, do you remember, the ones we used to use when we went off on camp?'

'Ordnance Survey,' the Scoutmaster said, a gleam of interest in his eye for the first time. 'That's Ord*nance*, lad, not Ordinance, like most people say. Ord*nance*, lad.'

'Yes, that's right.' Harris remembered this rant, it had sometimes gone on for hours around the campfire. Best to just agree. 'I've got a map coordinate here and I wondered if you might recognize it.'

'Ooh,' the Scoutmaster pulled at his lip and breathed hard through his nose. 'That's a tough one, that is. The old memory isn't what it was, these days.'

'Can you try, though?' Harris was struggling a bit with this fallen idol.

'No harm in trying,' the Scoutmaster said. 'What is it?'

'It's …' Harris wrestled the paper out of his inside pocket, 'TQ298799.'

'Umm, is this a trick question?'

Harris's face fell. 'No. Why do you think that?'

'*TQ298799*? Think, lad. Surely you know that number yourself.'

'I … no, sorry, sir. I don't.'

'Well, I'm disappointed, that's what I am. Don't you remember our cook outs? Our sleep outs?'

'Of course, sir. Some of the happiest days of my life.' Even as he said this, Harris grew a little depressed. Mainly because if toasting a sausage over a fire represented your life highlights, then you really needed to try harder.

'Well, then.' The Scoutmaster looked at him brightly. 'The coordinate is …?'

'St James's Park?' Harris furrowed his brow. 'But … it's someone's address, according to what I have been told.'

'That's as maybe, lad. But St James's Park it is, just by the old hollow tree, if memory serves.' The man's eyes filled with tears. 'Good days, those, weren't they, lad? Good days.'

Harris looked down at the man, his layers of clothes, his ragged woggle lying askew across his adam's apple, his knotted legs and could have cried. 'Yes, they were. Good days. Good old days.'

THE BISHOP AND THE ACTRESS

O utside the Scout Master's house, the smell of mouse, old newspaper and despair still clinging to his clothes, Harris wondered whether to take the Scout Master at his word and make his way to St James's Park. No one had a tree in a park as an address, surely? But perhaps Jack Jones, when asked for the detail, just made up the number off the top of his head and it was, just coincidentally, a tree in St James's Park. As he made his way down the decrepit little street back to somewhere where the sun might occasionally shine, Harris played a little game with himself.

'If I was thinking of a random number,' he muttered to himself to the consternation of the occasional passer-by, 'what would I do? Nothing can be random, there is pattern in everything.' He plucked a daisy growing out of a crumbling wall. He had been good at arithmetic at school and had things turned out differently, he would have liked to do something with it, like teaching, perhaps, or being an accountant. He frowned. Well, probably not either of those things, but something to do with numbers. One thing he remembered was the Fibonacci sequence. He still remembered the thrill of excitement when he realized how perfect and how simple it was. And when he found that it described the inside of a daisy, he had almost fainted with pleasure. Perhaps memory had gilded the daisy and he hadn't got out much in those days.

He had gone in from the garden, where he had been supposedly creosoting a fence, and offered the flower wordlessly to his mother. She had looked up briefly from her ironing and, taking the flower, had tossed it in the bin. She wasn't an unpleasant woman in the scheme of things, just overworked and not too well endowed in the empathy department.

'Aren't you a bit big to come in with a daisy, lad?' she had asked. 'How's that fence coming along?'

Harris had opened his mouth to answer, but had feared that he might cry. So he had just nodded and gone back to his fence. But since that day, he could never resist picking a daisy and counting the spiralling dots at its heart. 'One, one, two, three, five, eight,' he muttered to himself. They would be the first numbers of any 'random' number he was asked to supply.

As for the letters, what would he choose? He had never had much success with girls. It wasn't that he wasn't a perfectly normal-looking young chap, he just was too diffident, too backwards at coming forwards, as his granny would have said. A few too many rebuffs from his mother probably; he had never knowingly met a psychiatrist, but had a feeling that that would be the answer. So a girlfriend's initials would not be his first choice. A famous singer, then; he liked a bit of music. Vera Lynn, she was nice. Or had been, at least, before she made the choices she had made. His father would switch the wireless off when she started warbling, long before the Incident. So, not VL. Something he would always be able to remember. He had had no pets, so that was no good. He brightened up and his smile made a passing woman smile back and for some reason feel much better for a while.

EM112358, that would be a random number he would choose. E for Elizabeth and M for Margaret, the princesses who had managed to escape when they had had a small window of opportunity. There had been one brief broadcast, when they first got away, when Princess Elizabeth had promised that they would be back, that they had not gone forever. But there had been nothing but silence since. EM112358 – he wondered where that might be. His old English teacher would have said it was the land of lost content and he was probably right.

Harris looked up from his daisy and found he was at a crossroads. He gave himself a bit of a shake. He was supposed to be searching for Jack Jones, for the good of the nation's morale, not maundering about his childhood. That wouldn't get him anywhere. He had walked further than he intended and found that his feet had had more sense than his head. He was looking down Little St James's Street and he knew that at the end, if he cut through Catherine Wheel Yard, he could get into the park through a dodgy railing. He had been doing that since he was a boy and his father before him, so he was pretty confident that he could still do it. When he got there, it was simpler than he had thought, as the railings had gone altogether for spare parts and a very cursory fence of unevenly spaced poles and a single strand of rusty wire had taken their place. He was sure that there would be a memo somewhere in the depths of the police station, but if there was, he hadn't seen it.

He swung his leg over the wire and pushed through some sooty bushes until he emerged onto one of the paths which encircled the park. He just let his feet lead him – they hadn't done such a bad job thus far, so it was worth seeing what they could do. The park wasn't how he remembered it. There were more people than before, but they were different. There were a few mothers with children, but they were walking along as though on some kind of treadmill. There were lads kicking balls, but they were few and the ball was so much patched that the original colour was scarcely visible. There were a few soapbox orators, with the usual small gaggle of people around them, but if they were hecklers, they were the quietest ones ever assembled. When was the Current Situation going to end, one man asked. 'What do we want? Snoek!' another chanted. A third was exhorting people to find salvation via the Church of the Remnant. Harris remembered times when the shouting from the man on the podium and the men and women at his feet had been so loud it had drowned out the Scout Master's instructions on how to make a fire with the inside of an acorn and a length of string. Then it had all been about the enemy threat. And where was Wathmere now the country needed him? Harris frowned; perhaps that wasn't quite right, but it was close. But now, the hecklers were silent, keeping out a watchful eye for anyone who might be checking on what was being said, how and to whom. Harris was glad he had chosen plain clothes, not knowing that his very demeanour singled him out in the denizens of the park.

And suddenly, there it was. The old hollow tree under whose fragile branches he had sat with his fellow scouts so many lifetimes ago. It was there, but he couldn't know that this was actually the map reference. The Scout Master was old and possibly more than a little mad; he had almost certainly just assumed that the map reference was the place he had been happiest. It certainly didn't have anything about it that could be described as anyone's domicile. He admitted to himself that he had been half expecting a hut, or a tent; even a blanket on the ground would have been something. But this was just an old hollow tree, with fewer branches than he remembered and a bare patch all around where not even the grass would grow, as if the earth itself was poisoned.

As he stood there, feeling rather silly, an old, old man approached from the direction of Whitehall. He moved so slowly it was like watching a glacier but there was something strangely hypnotic about his progress and Harris instinctively knew that the man was heading for the hollow tree, albeit not in what anyone else would consider a straight line.

Because the man was walking so slowly, it was easy to take in his appearance in some detail. He was wearing what looked at first to be fancy dress, but on closer consideration turned out to be a frock coat of very old-fashioned cut and a pair of satin knee breeches, both items now green with age. He wore a purple shirt under the coat, with a high collar which resolved itself as he got nearer into a clerical dog collar which was yellowed and cracking. He wore no stockings with the breeches, but as his legs were pale and hairless with age, this was not that obvious. Unlike the Scout Master, he was not cursed with varicose veins, but the calves were stringy and the shin bones stood out like knives. Under one arm, he carried a silver salver, smooth with endless polishing. Harris realized with some surprise that the man appeared to be a Bishop, moonlighting as a butler. He knew times were hard, but this was ridiculous.

Eventually, the man reached the hollow tree and leaned against it for a moment, catching his breath. Harris inched nearer and could see that he was extremely old, his eyes filmy with cataracts, his hair thin and flyaway but, unlike the Scout Master's, squeaky clean. Cleanliness in general had gone by the wayside in recent times and Harris would be the first to admit that he was often less than fragrant, but this man almost glowed with polish, like his tray. His face was gentle and almost unlined, like the faces of the dead become, when all strife had passed. As he rested against the sun-warmed, grey wood of the tree, the colour began to come back to his cheeks and after a while, he had the strength to turn around and reach up into one of the broken off branches. He leaned the tray on the tree roots at his feet and leaned with his free hand against the trunk as he rummaged around above his head. His face began to take on a worried expression and his eyes flicked left and right as his fingers failed to find what he had expected.

His strength gave out quickly and he slid down the trunk to sit beside his tray, a solitary tear making its way down his soft cheek.

Harris waited, watching. He hadn't often cried in his life – living with his mother had knocked that out of him before he was weaned, more or less – but on the few occasions that he had, he had been careful to do it in private. He felt the urge to go to the old man, to help him, to make sure he wasn't ill or something, but his natural reticence stopped him. He tried to watch the man without looking directly, tricky at the best of times and in the bright sun streaming through the leaves of the more healthy trees of the Park, not completely successful.

The old man looked up and wiped away his tears and turned his milky eyes towards Harris and seemed to see into his soul. He started to struggle to his feet, in a series of acrobatics which had come of long practice. First, lean forward from the waist and roll the torso to one side. Then, lean on both hands and roll further, letting the legs bend until the knees make contact with the ground. Then, turn round in a series of shuffles until the hands are at the bottom of the tree. Then, using the trunk and any protruding bark and scars of branches long dead, clamber upright. Harris tried not to smile, although a few passers-by were not so kind. The butler – or Bishop – didn't seem to mind, though, and hailed them happily from his eventual standing position. Then, to Harris's consternation, he turned and tottered in a determined if shaky path, straight for him.

'Oh.'

Harris was used to people being disappointed when they finally got up close. He took ordinary to new heights – or was it depths.

'Oh?'

'I beg your pardon, young man. I didn't mean to be rude. It's just that I had thought you would be taller.'

Harris was quite proud of being five feet eleven and a half tall. In his boots. With thick socks. 'I'm quite tall, as the general population goes,' he said, a little hurt.

'Of course you are, of course you are.' The Bishop – or butler – patted his arm and then left his hand there, leaning heavily, because he had already walked his week's allowance and it wasn't even Friday. Truth be told, he had no idea what day it was, having lost track sometime in 1927 when people had complained that the new prayer book was too Popish and never really getting straight. Harris let him stay there; he weighed nothing and who knew, he might know something about Jack Jones. The old man began to droop and Harris suspected he was having a little forty winks but he suddenly woke with a start and carried on as if there had been no pause.

'All it was, I was wondering if you were tall enough to help me.'

'Help you get something out of your hollow tree?' Harris said and the man recoiled as if stung.

'Hollow tree?' he said, his voice breaking with emotion. 'What hollow tree?'

Harris gestured with his head. 'That one. Over there. You were looking for something on a branch.'

The butler – or Bishop – pulled himself up to his full height but quickly slumped down again. 'Were you watching?' he murmured. 'I try to be discreet. Did anyone else see?' The tears were in his eyes again.

'Well, people *saw*.' Harris tried to be truthful but didn't like being unkind. 'You are quite ... unusual. With the clothes and all.'

The Bishop – or butler – looked down, confused. What was wrong with his clothes? He had been wearing them for nigh on twenty years, ever since ... well, just ever since. Even thinking about it made him blush.

'But I don't think they *noticed*,' Harris went on. 'Not to say noticed. They just saw and forgot.' Just like most witnesses, he added to himself.

'Well, I hope not indeed,' the old man muttered. 'It was very private.'

'So ... would you like me to reach it down for you?'

'Reach what down?' The butler – or Bishop – backed away and adopted what he clearly thought of as an aggressive stance.

'What you were reaching for.' Harris was not sure how long he and this strange man had been talking, but it felt like years.

'Ah, you know about that, do you?' The old man laid a conspiratorial finger alongside his nose and nodded, winking. 'Well, in that case, yes, I would very much like you to reach it down for me, if you would be so kind. Follow me.'

Harris decided not to take that totally literally, as the man's balance problems made him cant furiously to the left for about ten paces and then tack to the right for the next ten. So Harris steered a middle path and got to the tree a couple of steps behind, which seemed to be the right thing to do.

'It's up there,' the old man said, pointing. 'I can just feel the edge of the paper but it has slipped down out of reach.' He grabbed Harris's wrist with surprising strength.

'You won't look, though, will you? You will give it straight to me?' A thought occurred to him. 'Can you read?'

'Yes.' The question was so obvious it made Harris blink.

'Only, you seem a nice lad, but what are you doing hanging round the park in the middle of the afternoon? Don't you have a job you should be doing? I would think you would have been scooped up by now, nice strong lad like you. For the work parties, you know.' A sudden thought occurred to him. 'You're not a Roundhead, are you? Or perhaps Fifth Column?'

Harris had heard of these – work parties were everywhere to keep the unemployed busy. The Fifth Column were the hidden enemy trying to undermine the state. On the Roundheads, he had to admit, he was hazier and he wished he'd concentrated more on his school history. He knew that lots of people thought that the police did the scooping for the work parties, but he had never seen it happen, had never been asked to take part. But now he was in a cleft stick. Would the old man run a mile if he thought he was police, or would he feel all the better for it? He decided to tell the truth. 'I'm a policeman,' he said. Keep it simple; there would be time for details later, if they became necessary.

'A policeman?' The Bishop – or butler – stepped back and gave Harris an appraising look. 'Now you come to mention, you *do* have something of the establishment about you. Not a bad thing, not at all. Not a bad thing.' He patted Harris on the arm, reflectively. It was hard to tell who was being comforted by the gesture. 'I feel more confident now,' he said, after a moment. 'If you want to know the time, ask a policeman.' The old man winked. 'You know that song, of course. Before your time, but you'll know it.' He gazed up into his face and Harris scarcely liked to disappoint him so he shook and nodded his head at the same time, as best he could.

'If you want to know the time, ask a policeman.' The man burst into quavering song. 'The proper Greenwich time, ask a policeman. Every member of the force has a watch and chain, of course, How he got it, from what source? ask a policeman.' A fit of coughing stopped him and Harris patted him gingerly on the back. It was like patting a sack of old spoons. 'Ah, there's nothing like those old Music Hall tunes,' the old man said, reminiscently.

Harris decided it was time to find out something of the man's antecedents, why he was dressed like that and ... most importantly ... why he was posing as a Bishop. 'Ummm ... you went to the Music Hall a lot, did you, in your younger days?'

This sent the man into a positive flurry of remembering. 'Oh, yes. Dear me. Once a week. More sometimes. Ah, those were the days. Marie Lloyd. George Robey ...' His eyes grew misty. 'No time for all that now. Not in this world. Oh ...' he chuckled but managed to control it before the cough took over. 'I always say to the mistress ...'

Harris goggled. This man had a *mistress*?

'Madam, I say to her, if the times were different, Master Jack would be on the Halls.'

This was getting complicated, but Harris had heard a word he recognized. 'Master Jack? Would that be ... Jack Jones?'

The phlegmy chuckle shook the man again. 'That's what people call him. I prefer to call him Master Jack.'

'Do you ... happen to know where he is?'

'At the studio, where he always is. He hasn't visited Madam for ...' he cast his eyes up and counted randomly on his fingers '... years.'

'But you know him, though.'

'Yes, indeed. In all my years with Madam, he was the most faithful of the Stage Door Johnnies.' The man smiled. It was clear he was years ago and miles away.

'So ... you are butler to an actress ...?'

'No, sir, I am most certainly not!' The man swept an arm down his bizarre costume. 'Do I *look* like a butler?'

'Well, the tray and everything.'

'Oh, well,' the man became hoity-toity, 'the *tray*, I suppose, yes. The *tray*. But the rest.'

'Well, to be honest, you look a bit like a ... a Bishop.'

'I should think I do! Not that I have a diocese now, of

course.' He brushed off an invisible piece of fluff from his greenish coat. 'But at one time, yes, I was a Bishop.' He stood proudly, clearly waiting for some kind of response.

'I can see that it would be hard these days ...' Harris began.

'It would – damned Church of the Remnant – but these days are not really the point. I stopped being a Bishop long before these days.' He leaned in and beckoned Harris to bend closer. 'Have you heard a joke at any time about an actress and the Bishop?'

Harris had to admit he had.

'Well,' the Bishop spread his arms and dropped the tray with a clang. 'That was *me*! I was the Bishop!'

'Oh.' Harris picked up the tray, which had rolled away across the grass. 'That must have been quite ...' He really didn't know what to say. In all the jokes he had heard on the subject, nothing much ever got specified. For one ghastly moment, he wondered if *all* Music Hall jokes weren't based on real people. 'Take my mother in law' for instance. Was she somebody's *actual* mother-in-law? And was that somebody Jack Jones?

'It's a long, sad story.' He gave another of his life-threatening chuckles. 'It wasn't sad at the time, I have to tell you. I was having the time of my life. But ... well, you see, I chose the wrong actress. She got into trouble, went to the Synod and – poof!' He clicked his fingers with a rheumatic clunk and made Harris jump. 'People equated me with Harold Davidson, rector of the unfortunately named parish of Stiffkey. He had a string of mistresses still wearing gymslips, in Shepherd's Bush. That was it for me. She was only in the chorus, but she was a lovely girl. And my mistress took pity on me and gave me a job as her butler and well, that's how you find me today. Defrocked, defenestrated, defenceless.' He straightened. 'But not yet deaf.'

'Goodness,' was all Harris could think of to say. It was a lot to take in. 'And your job inv ...'

'Not job,' the Bishop interrupted. 'Calling.'

'Ah. Yes. Calling. Your calling involves picking up notes in hollow trees. That must be rather unusual, surely?'

'Not really.' The man was calm. 'It's how we communicate. You can't use the GPO, can you? My mistress has had to leave town and she gets messages to me this way. She pays people ...' he looked vaguer than ever '... I'm not sure who ... but anyway, long story cut short, I leave her messages and she leaves them for me.' He looked wistfully up at the branch. 'So it would be wonderful if ...'

'I'm sorry. Of course.' Harris reached up and fumbled in the hollow for the paper. It was tightly folded and wedged in, but he could reach it easily and, pulling it out, handed to the erstwhile Bishop waiting not very patiently on the dry grass. The old man took it in trembling fingers and unfolded it. He looked at it, then held out his arm as far as he could, squinting. Then he covered one eye. After that, he tried it up against his nose, then turned a tearful face to Harris.

'It's no good,' he sobbed. 'I just can't see well enough.'

'Where are your glasses?' Like all young people with perfect vision, Harris couldn't believe that anyone could forget to carry something so simple.

'I last had glasses in 1938. I remember specifically when it was, because the Football Pools were declared a menace to society and that idiot Chamberlain made a fool of himself over Munich,' the Bishop said. 'I laid my specs down somewhere and they disappeared and I've managed since. Madam used to read me the news until it got too depressing. I know where everything is in the house. I know my way to this tree like I know my own bed. But ...' he waved the note, 'I can't read this.' He broke down completely. 'It could be important.'

Harris knew this would need careful handling. 'Could *I* read it, perhaps?'

The Bishop clutched the note to his chest, shaking his head. 'It's likely to be private,' he said. 'I couldn't possibly. Madam might have written anything ... No.' He tucked it inside his faded shirt front. 'No, you can't.'

'I am a policeman, though,' Harris wheedled.

The Bishop looked at him. 'You *say* you are,' he snapped.

Harris tried another approach. He turned on his heel

and made as if to go.

'Where are you going?' the old man cried. 'What shall I do?'

Harris gave an elaborate shrug. Before everything went wrong, an Italian family had kept an ice cream parlour in his street. He rarely had ice cream, but he would spend hours with his nose pressed against the glass, just watching. And he based his shrug on Mama, fat, glossy, always laughing, stuffed tight into her black cotton dress; it said 'I couldn't care less' in more languages than anyone could count. He kept walking, counting down from ten silently. If he got to zero, he would just have to count this as a failed link in the Jack Jones search. But if …

'All right.' The voice was defeated.

'Four,' he murmured to himself and turned round. The Bishop stood there, head hanging, arm outstretched to proffer the note, like a beaten toddler. 'Is there somewhere more private we could go?' Harris asked. As this was a public park, that would be just about anywhere. He thought perhaps that would be a good idea, assuming the content was indeed very delicate.

'We could go back to the house, I suppose,' the Bishop said. 'There's no one there and so no one will overhear. It's not far.'

Harris was suddenly aware that the sunlight was thinner, the air a touch colder. The day had been pleasant enough but it came as a shock to him to remember that he had nowhere to go, nowhere to sleep. If the Bishop would let him sleep in a chair, perhaps … that would at least deal with the night to come. The others could take care of themselves and anyway, who knew, the answer to his problem may lie in the contents of the note.

'Let's go, then,' Harris said. 'Would you like to lean on my arm?'

The Bishop looked alarmed. 'What would people say?' he whispered.

'They would say,' Harris told him, 'look at that nice young policeman helping that poor old man across the park and back to his house.'

The Bishop looked at him for a long minute, then took his arm. It was a relief to have someone to lean on and, he suddenly realized, he *was* a poor old man. He didn't think he would be making this journey again and he looked around with his clouded eyes, trying to put it all into his memory, the greens of the grass and trees, the few splashes of colour from flowerbeds long neglected.

'Goodbye,' he said.

'Pardon?' Harris was startled. Surely, not another change in direction?

The Bishop shook his head. He hadn't meant to say it out loud. 'Here we are,' he said, gently steering his helper to a small gate. 'Just through here and across the Mews and we're home.'

* * *

Harris had never knowingly been in the home of anyone in the entertainment business and he would have been hard pressed to guess what it would be like, but he hadn't expected this. There were no swags of velvet curtains, no thickly shaded lamps on ornate tables. Instead, the whole interior was wood, with some carefully placed cushions and, in the main room, two enormous sofas that looked as though they could accommodate an elephant each with no bother. The smell was something special too, a mix of sandalwood and lavender, but so subtle that it was hardly noticeable except when a light drapery moved in a draught or a door was opened or closed.

'It's ... lovely,' he breathed. 'Really lovely.' The second thought that occurred to him was that no one should ever be told about this place. He now understood why the front of the building was so run down. As they had approached it from the park, his heart had sunk to his regulation boots. There were overflowing dustbins along the short path to the door. One window was half-obscured by a poster which had once exhorted someone to do something but now was tattered and all but unreadable under its grime. The door itself looked like a close relation of the Scout

Master's, ill-fitting and with peeling paint coming away in shards like razors. But this … he let his eyes rove around again. There was no other word for it. 'Lovely.'

The Bishop suddenly looked shifty. 'You do understand, don't you,' he said, grabbing Harris's arm in his surprisingly strong grip, 'no one must know of this. No one.'

'I do understand,' he said. 'I really do.' And it came to him in a rush that, if asked, he would defend this place to the death. 'But how do you keep it secret?'

'Madam and I gave it a lot of thought. Of course, when it was necessary, Madam had the best blackout system that money could buy installed and I keep that down as soon as it gets dark, all day, sometimes. So no lights show. And I keep myself discreet, no loud clothing – not that that would be my taste, anyway – and no one notices me as I go about my business.'

Harris was not so sure of that, but there was no need to upset the old man; he thought he was doing the best he could and there was no need to disabuse him.

'Madam is the same when she's at home. She got rid of her furs and things a long time ago. At one time, there was a market for that kind of frippery and she sold at the right moment. She only sold for cash and there is quite a bit stashed around the house. That's why this note was so important. I am down to my last five pounds and she will have given me a clue as to where to find more.'

'Isn't that rather dangerous?' Harris could have told him of dozens of cases where perfectly humble homes had been ransacked for the sake of a few shillings. People will do that in desperate times. In the last few years, his fellow coppers told him, there was less of that, but only because no one had anything any more, not because there were no bad uns around.

'Isn't what dangerous? Leaving me a note or having money in the house?'

'Either. Both.'

'Well, don't fret yourself, Bobby – I can call you Bobby, can I? I think no real names, no pack drill is the best thing for us, don't you? What with the Roundheads, the

Remnant, the Black Market and those horrible children swarming everywhere?'

Harris nodded. He was going to need details, if this strange meeting was to lead him to Jack Jones, but going along with the old man would be all right for now.

'Well, Bobby, don't you fret. The money is well hidden. It must be, because I know every inch of this place and I never find it by accident. Madam is as cunning as a load of monkeys, I'll say that for her. And as for the notes, no one knows about them and even if someone found one, they wouldn't understand it. And who goes looking in hollow trees ever since they found that body that time.'

'Did that make the news?' Harris was surprised. They had found a body, sure enough, in Hagley Wood, out Birmingham way. But as it was supposed to be a spy, so as far as he knew, it had only been spread via the *Police Gazette*.

'No, not really. But Madam, she has some very influential friends. Well, she calls them friends, I wouldn't want to think of them as friends myself, but she needs to protect herself, if you see what I mean. So she goes about with these people.' The Bishop's eyelids dropped to conceal his eyes for a moment. It made him look rather sinister and Harris found himself checking for a way out.

'Is Jack Jones one of those friends?' It was worth a try.

'Master Jack? No, no, no. Master Jack and Madam have known each other since they were children, more or less. "Jack and Jill", they were. Novelty dance act. I didn't know them then, of course.' The Bishop blushed a little. 'Chorus girls were my downfall. But apparently, they were quite famous, in that circle. There's a programme here, somewhere.' He rummaged in the drawer of an elegant oak roll top desk. 'Yes, here it is. Look, in the middle, about two-thirds of the way down.'

Harris looked and sure enough, there it was. Jack and Jill, Novelty Dancers. Just under Frick and Frack and the Amazing Maurice and His Syncopated Biceps. 'Do you have any photos of them then?' It wouldn't help his search for the missing broadcaster, but he was intrigued. Did Jack Jones have more personality in his face then, or had he always been totally bland?

'Madam has albums. I wouldn't presume …'

'No, of course not. I understand.' Harris made a little mental note to search for the pictures, if and when he was staying the night.

'If you don't mind, though, reading me the note?' The Bishop ferreted in his shirt front and brought it out. 'Now we're alone.'

'Of course.' Harris took the note and unfolded it. Something about the Bishop made him do this with some ceremony. 'Right. It says …' He held it at arm's length. It didn't seem to make much sense. 'It says "Il fagiano non ha un'agenda".' He looked up, puzzled. 'Did I say that right? It's foreign.'

But the Bishop had already scuttled off, a big beam across his face. 'It's Italian,' he said, over his shoulder. 'Fagiano is pheasant, It means "the pheasant has no agenda".' He was standing in the corner, looking at a bookshelf crammed with leather bound books. 'I must tell you that Madam is not a great reader, but when she moved in here, these books came with the house and she has never moved them.' He was looking at the titles, his nose inches from the calf-skin spines. 'Can you help me? I'm looking for a bird book. But one where the pheasant has no agenda.' He kept peering and Harris had to move him in the end because wherever he looked, the Bishop's fluffy hair was in the way. Suddenly, he saw it.

'Could this be it?' he asked, pointing. He knew instinctively that if he tried to take the book down himself, all he would get would be an elbow in his ribs for his pains.

The old man peered, then nodded. 'That's just the one!' he said. He reached up but his old shoulders wouldn't let him do what he wanted and he fell short. Harris reached over his head and brought down the heavy tome, leather bound, and blew the dust off the top of the pages.

'Bird Portraits by Edward Lear, for John Gould,' he said. 'This must be valuable.'

'It was,' the Bishop said. 'Nothing you can't eat, wear or burn is worth anything these days. In cold winters most people would have burned books like these.' He peered up at the boy. 'But Madam, she always looked on the bright side. Better days are coming, she used to say. What was that old number President Roosevelt's party played all the time? Happy Days Are Here Again! Ah, they don't write 'em like that any more.'

Harris handed him the book and the old man sagged at the knees. He put it carefully on the table in the centre of the room and turned the pages until he got to the contents and there it was – 'Pheasant'. He eagerly flicked through and finally, a Golden Pheasant in all his glory sprang from the page. But, to the Bishop's dismay and horror, there was nothing else. He peered at the margins. 'Madam sometimes leaves a second clue,' he whispered, turning short-sighted eyes on Harris. Can you see anything?'

Harris looked, but the pages were blank, apart from a little foxing. 'But look,' he said kindly. 'If ever a pheasant had an agenda, it must be this one. Let's look and see if there is a pheasant on another page. Just as background, perhaps. Let's pull up chairs, sit comfortably and go through the pages, one by one.'

The Bishop was trembling by this time but did as he was bid. And slowly, patiently, Harris turned each page, scanning the exquisite paintings for signs of a modest pheasant, one without agenda but with a secret message of some kind. And suddenly, there it was. The painting was of a capercaillie, strutting its stuff in the heather. But behind it, a pheasant. And placed carefully to fill the whole page without making it too bulky, Britannia sat proudly, looking out at the two men, her trident aloft. The Bishop swept the money up neatly and before Harris could make even a rough estimate as to how much was there, the notes tucked away in the recesses of his rusty old coat.

'Wait a bit, though.' Harris had had a sudden thought. 'What good is that? You can't spend those any more. I can't remember when I last saw a note with Britannia on it.'

The Butler laughed, his worries over at least for now. 'Of course you can't spend them,' he said. 'Who spends money straight out these days? No, I have ...' he looked under sparse lashes at Harris '… contacts, shall we say? And they give me eighteen shillings on the pound in new money. And then I take that and give some to the greengrocer and the butcher and the baker … everyone I need, really. And, yes, before you ask, the off licence. And what they do with it, I don't know. But it means I have tick for a while and they let me run over, sometimes, when Madam's note is late or similar.' He tapped his chest, which crackled. 'The way I live, this will see me a good few months.'

The change in the man was tangible. He stood a little straighter, his face was pinker, he could see a future where, a few hours ago, he had none to speak of. Harris cleared his throat. 'Where is Madam?' he asked. He had closed an eye to a lot of things in the last hour or so, black marketeering just the least of it. But now he was beginning to wonder about the safety of the nameless actress whose house this was.

'Madam travels a lot,' the Bishop said, a surly look crossing his face.

'What, still?' Harris didn't want to pry, but this was suspicious in the extreme. Trains and boats and planes were a thing of the past, by and large, huge rust buckets rusting on disused lines and puddled tarmac.

'Not as much, no. But she is still famous, you know! Her fans haven't forgotten her.'

'Would I know her?'

'How old are you?'

'Twenty-five.'

'Like romance films, do you? Histories with lovely clothes where they all live happily ever after?'

'Not really.'

'Go to the theatre much?'

'Hardly ever.'

'Then I would say, on balance, that no, you wouldn't know her. And with your calling, that's probably as well. As I think I said, she has a lot of very important friends in high places and those friends have wives.'

'So, she's a pr …'

The Bishop drew himself up and raised two puny fists, boxer-style and took a few tottering steps back and forth. 'I should warn you,' he piped, 'I was featherweight champion back in the seminary.'

Harris raised an eyebrow.

'No,' the Bishop dropped his stance and flopped into a chair. 'No, she isn't ... what you were going to say. Madam is witty and beautiful and men like witty beautiful women, though they rarely marry them. So ... she keeps them company, sometimes. And to keep things discreet, I don't always know where she is.' He glared at Harris. 'See.'

'Yes,' Harris said, pushing down his duty as far as it would go. 'And sometimes, she keeps Jack Jones company, does she?'

'I told you!' The Bishop's voice cracked and broke. 'They're like brother and sister. They were Jack and Jill, Novelty Dancers, before he was out of short trousers. She goes to see him, of course, but not ... not like that.' He looked down at his hands. 'Not like that, not with Jack Jones ...' His head nodded and Harris was astounded to see he had gone to sleep. The stress of the day had told on him at last and he was dead to the world, but only temporarily. This time. Harris gave him a gentle push and he subsided backwards, his head lolling, his mouth open, a snore beginning to build in volume.

Harris had planned to see if the Bishop would let him stay the night, but he was getting less and less happy about the idea. He already had such a list of crimes which he should be writing down and reporting to his superiors that he didn't really want to add any more. So he left the old man sleeping and had a snoop around in the twilit world inside the house.

The desk seemed the best place to find clues to where the Actress – and also, hopefully, by definition, Jack Jones – might be. He looked through every pigeonhole and drawer and found nothing dated after 1939. To all intents and purposes, the woman could have disappeared that summer, never to be seen again. He glanced back through the door into the library to where the Bishop was still snoring and shook his head to himself. No, the old man simply wasn't cunning enough to keep a story running so smoothly for so long, so this wasn't a case of the woman being buried in the cellar. But something was off.

At the back of a drawer deeper than the rest, Harris found a small, leather-bound autograph book, full of impossible to read swirls and old, faded pictures of men and women who were stars at the time but now didn't strike even the faintest chord. Their long dead smiles fell hollow now and Harris could have wept for them. But then, just before the end, a face he knew, though much younger and less bland than it had become. Jack Jones, posing on a dock, had written 'To my Jill, I will love you forever, Jack.'

THE WOMAN

H arris was uncertain whether he should leave the Bishop asleep in his chair. What if he died? His snores rang through the house and Harris had heard from his grandmother and all her gossiping friends – who hadn't noticed him under the table when they had their get-togethers involving tea, scones and not a little gin – that when someone died, their breaths got louder and further apart. He stood in the doorway, counting on his fingers and this old man was set to live forever, if regular breathing was any guide. He turned and tiptoed away, closing the door carefully behind him.

The day had moved into a pearly twilight while he had been helping search for the agenda-less pheasant and he wondered where he could sleep that night. His search for Jack Jones had not taken him very many miles so far and it was tempting to go back to his room; he knew it would still be there, for the statutory two weeks, but he also knew that his landlady would not be expecting him and it would test her rationing abilities to breaking point.

There was the Station House, but he had no bed there and questions would be asked. For all Baker had been detailed to accompany him, the man had absented himself and Harris got the distinct impression that the Inspector was doing all this under sufferance, almost as a personal kindness to him. Perhaps, the thought began to dawn on him, no one wanted Jack Jones to be found. Or, to put it another, more sinister, way, perhaps someone *didn't* want him to be found.

The Mock Spam sandwiches had long gone and he was a little peckish now. He felt in his pocket for his wallet. It was very flat, but that was no surprise. He peeped inside and saw that, as long as he only ate once a day – and today he had had breakfast and some Mock Spam so that was it until tomorrow – he could hunt Jack Jones for a week. Sleeping would sort itself out. He had always been able to sleep on a clothesline and as long as there was somewhere fairly flat and out of the weather, he would survive. Keeping clean he could manage. There were still a few lavatories open, if you knew where to look, and he knew that, Church of the Remnant notwithstanding, some closet Christians would still open their homes to itinerants, if they looked cleanish and unlikely to rob and murder. And he knew that he looked like everybody's favourite nephew. He'd be all right.

He'd be all right.

* * *

The problem was, Harris soon discovered, deciding when enough was enough and the time had come to find that somewhere that was flattish and out of the weather. His mother had not been one for fairy stories, counting all fiction as lying and worthy of a smack upside the head, so he wasn't familiar with the tale of Goldilocks and the three bears. So he didn't know that he was exhibiting Goldilocks behaviour as he rejected doorway after doorway and, as he started to get out into the country, hedge-bottom after hedge-bottom. Because essentially, he was a city boy at heart and nothing that wasn't actually a bed looked like somewhere he wanted to sleep. It came as a shock to him to discover he wasn't a big, bold, ranger scout who could put up with privation. He was a policeman who liked three squares, a dry office and a soft bed to go home to. He slumped, dejected, onto a bench on a small and unkempt village green to the north west of London and put his head in his hands.

There were no road signs to anywhere, of course. Nor

had there been for ten years. If the enemy was to come, he'd have to find his own bloody way. But the enemy had not come and now *nobody* knew the way. Not, with the petrol shortage, that there was anywhere to go. All the billboards in that part of London, the ones that used to display happy families out for a picnic in their shiny new Austin Sevens, had gone or been replaced by Government warnings. Careless Talk Costs Lives. Be Like Dad – Keep Mum. There were no faces now, no happiness, no future, not even everyone's cheeky chappie, Jack Jones.

What there was, Harris noticed, was a badly-scrawled threat – 'West London Ferals. Keep Out!'

'Are you all right, young man?' The voice could have etched glass, but it was kind, as was the hand gently resting on Harris's shoulder.

He looked up into a face so lined and creased it was hard for a moment to pick out the salient features, but, like the voice and hand, it had no malice in it. 'I … was just having a sit down,' he stammered. For a moment, he had dropped off and wasn't sure quite where he was or even if he should have been there.

'I don't think so, do you?' The voice was now not only kind but had a skim of humour to it. 'It's half past three in the morning and here you are, sitting on the green, asleep with your head in your hands. The least that you will get that way is pins and needles. The worst you will get is scooped up by some random patrol and slung in chokey for a little bit of permanent disappearing.'

Harris smiled. He hadn't heard prison called chokey since his granddad died.

'I … I'm looking for Jack Jones.' As a statement, it was a tad bald and direct, but it was all he could conjure up at a moment's notice.

'Aren't we all, my dear,' the Woman said. 'One more evening of those awful Best Of Jack Jones records being trotted out and we may as well shoot ourselves in the head. I like the chap as much as the next person, but that brown bread thing gets a bit wearing in the end.' She looked at him more closely in the moonlight. 'Did you hear the running grave this morning?' she asked.

'Running grave?' Harris echoed. 'What are you talking about?'

'Never mind,' she said. 'Are you in some official capacity?' She fingered the serge fabric of his sleeve. 'This feels a bit ... government issue, am I right?'

It was hard to get a word in, but he did nod and manage a quick, 'I am a policeman.'

'A *policeman*? Goodness. Don't say that too loudly around here, my lad, if the Blue Lampers are about you'll probably get your head stove in.' she jerked her head sideways to the Feral notice. The slang in her mouth sounded odd. 'There are more crooks around here than the parson preached about, when he was allowed to preach, poor lamb.' She looked down at him, dejected and now rather worried, sitting on his bench. 'Come home with me, lad. You'll be safe there and you can tell me a bit about Jack Jones. I bet you know all the gossip, eh?'

He was just standing up, so her nudge in his ribs almost sent him flying.

'My word, you are tired, aren't you? I don't have a spare bedroom, as such, but you are very welcome to the sofa for the night. Then you can tell me all the gossip in the morning. Just one thing ...' she leaned in to whisper '... don't come out of your room until I give you the nod. Some of my ... guests ... are a little sensitive, let's say no more than that.'

Harris let her lead him by the hand a pace or so, then suddenly thought of something and pulled back. 'If it's half past three in the morning,' he said, looking around, 'what are you doing walking around outside? Curfews aren't just for whether you fancy them, you know. It's the law.'

The Woman chuckled. 'Oh, you are a love, aren't you? I know all about curfews and the law. In fact, I may well know a lot more about the law than you do, lad. When you're the wrong side of it most of the time, you have to have a good idea what you're on the wrong side of.' She tossed her head towards a big house, lowering dark against the moonlit sky. 'Are you coming, or what? Do you want a proper lie down or do you want to wake up in the morning with your head stove in? Because they are the only options you've got.'

He looked at her again, at the house, at the bench and, holding out his hand, allowed her to lead him to either the sofa or doom; at this point, he wasn't that bothered which.

* * *

Harris woke to a dim, warm, dust-moted silence and after a short look around, closed his eyes again. He had slept in beds far less comfortable than this sofa, which had feather cushions and arms just the right height for supporting the pillow under his head. He stroked the blanket which covered him; it was so smooth and velvety he couldn't remember sleeping under anything as lovely. There was a sheet as well, crisp and – he sniffed – fresh smelling. His Landlady did her best, love her, but she could never get anything smelling like this in her grimy little back-yard, cooled by the breezes off the Mock Spam factory or, if the wind was the other way, the coke furnace. He sighed and snuggled down. Just another ten minutes … just another ten … just …

The little touch on his shoulder was enough to wake him instantly, but at first he couldn't quite focus. He was on his feet and looked functional, but his eyes were whizzing around independently and he was fetching his breath in short gasps.

'Do calm down, Mr Policeman.' The honeyed tones which were in such contrast to the Woman's appearance washed over him and he felt his hackles go back down, the fight go out of his flight. 'It's only me. Thank you for staying put – I'm not sure my other guests would quite understand why you are here and I wouldn't want any … unpleasantness.'

'I am a policeman, madam,' he said, a little loftily. 'If anything untoward is happening in this house, I would have no option but to …' he paused sniffing. 'Is that bacon?'

'It might be. It certainly might be. What were you saying?'

'I am … a … policeman.' Harris looked her in the eye. 'Is that really bacon? Can I have some?'

'It depends.' She smiled and folded her arms.

'I'm … I'm looking for a friend,' he said. 'I am certainly not a policeman.'

'Now that,' she said, slapping him on the arm, 'is the most sense you've made since I met you. Now, come and have some bacon. Egg?'

Harris nodded enthusiastically.

'How many? One? Two? Scrambled? Fried?'

'Scrambled?' Harris had not had scrambled eggs since before he left school. 'Is that with milk, or just done in the pan?' Harris was no cook, but he knew that there were scrambled eggs and then there were scrambled eggs. A girl he had been sweet on – who knows, they might be married now, if things had been different – her mother had made scrambled eggs with eggs from their own hens, milk from their own cow. He hoped he wasn't drooling. 'With milk and butter?'

'Well, cream, if that's all right for you?'

'Cr … cream? I don't know whether I've ever had scrambled egg with cream before?'

'You'll love it. Follow me. I hope you don't mind eating in the kitchen? Only, the other rooms are a bit … untidy.'

'The kitchen is fine by me,' Harris said. They always ate in the kitchen at his Landlady's house and just thinking about it made him feel quite homesick. 'Is there toast?'

'My word!' The Woman smiled and tutted. 'We are a little above ourselves, aren't we, Mr Not-A-Policeman.'

He was instantly contrite. 'No, I didn't mean … if there isn't toast, that is still wonderful. Just to have bacon …'

She patted his back and led him gently through a green baize door and into a long corridor, ending in a pine door. 'I'm just joking,' she said. 'Of course there's toast. We're not animals here, you know, no matter what you might have heard.'

Harris was suddenly suspicious. Or perhaps that should count as *more* suspicious.

'Would I have heard anything?' he asked, slowing his footsteps, which was hard, now the bacon was clearly just the other side of the door.

'Only if you were listening,' she said, enigmatically. 'Now, let's get you some breakfast and see if we can help you with finding Jack Jones.'

'We?' Harris hadn't heard another soul in the house and wondered who would be on the other side of the door.

'Oh, take no notice,' she said, ushering him through. 'Call it the royal we, if you like. It's just a habit of mine. Anyway, let me introduce Nanny. She was my Nanny and Nanny to my children and I have a feeling she will be Nanny to my grandchildren. Nanny hasn't aged a day in the last fifty years.'

Harris looked at the little woman standing at the stove and she certainly had fewer lines on her face than her former charge. She was almost obscured by an enormous white apron and a mob cap pulled down almost to her eyebrows. Her twinkling eyes peered out from under its frilled shadow and she smiled and gestured with a fish slice.

'Sit down, my lad,' she said. 'Bacon and egg first, or do you want to fill up on toast and marmalade?'

Marmalade. Harris had vague memories of marmalade. Golden strands of orange peel, encased in a translucent gel. His mother had occasionally had it in the house when she had to pay reluctant hostess to a family member or so. The last time he remembered it making an appearance was when his grandmother had been buried and the house was briefly and excitingly full of uncles, smelling of beer, cigarettes and masculinity. 'Marmalade?' He thought he had better check.

Nanny threw a glance at the Woman, who nodded. 'Yes, marmalade. But perhaps a fine set up young chap like you would rather get his teeth around some bacon, eh? Well, sit you down and it's coming right up.' With a few deft flicks, the cook tossed some bacon onto a plate and spooned some unctuous egg next to it. She handed it to Harris who looked at it for a long moment in amazement. Never, not even Before, had he ever seen a plate of food so perfect. From the bacon still sizzling slightly, with perfectly crisped rind and fat gone just the right side of crunch to the golden mound of egg, with a flake of butter quickly melting into its folds, it belonged on a breakfast table far more sophisticated than this bashed and pitted length of pine.

'Eat up,' the Woman said. 'Nanny gets testy when people play with their food, don't you, Nan?'

'Don't you Nan me, young lady,' the Nanny said. 'Or you'll be in the nursery corner for the rest of the day.'

Harris, shovelling in food, looked from one woman to the other but saw only love in their eyes. He wondered if perhaps he could give up his search for Jack Jones and stay here, to be cossetted and fed by the two of them, for no particular reason that he could fathom. If he had been interrogated by the best that the Remnant had on offer he would have been hard pressed to say what had made his life thus far so unhappy, but he suddenly realized that it had been. It wasn't for what had happened to him, it was for what hadn't. No one had called him 'my lad' for a start, because no one had ever cared enough to consider him theirs. And no one, absolutely *no one* had ever given him food like this, though his Landlady, bless her, had done what she could with Mock Spam and Mock Egg. He finally paused for breath.

'That was …' He combed his vocabulary for superlatives but couldn't find one that did it justice. 'Delicious. Simple and delicious.' He had heard someone say that, sometime long, long ago and it seemed to fit the bill.

Nanny beamed. She loved a good eater. 'Toast,' she said. It wasn't a question – she knew that the lad would want toast. 'Marmalade? Jam?'

Harris shook his head to jam. Jam he could have any day, even if it was plum and apple, heavy on the apple. But marmalade – he could taste its golden sharp sweetness on his tongue already.

While he was dealing with the pile of golden toast, curls of salty butter and spoonsful of glistening orange, the Nanny beckoned the Woman to one side. She pinched the inside of her arm, just a little, as she had done when the Woman was a little girl and the sun shone every day.

'What are you thinking?' she hissed. 'He's a policeman.'

'Of course he is,' said the Woman, disengaging the old fingers from her skin. 'What of it?'

'What *of* it?' The old lady could hardly believe her ears. 'What *of* it? The house is full of ...' she waved an arm. Bacon, she could have said. Beer. Champagne. Fur coats. Watches. *Stuff*. And as for the other residents – well! As pretty a bunch of ne'er-do-wells as you would meet in a day's march. Though always polite, she'd give them that. Nice lads and girls. She had weeded out the bad apples, spit spot.

The Woman turned her head and looked at Harris, head down in his marmalade and toast. 'I don't think he is what we might call an *ordinary* policeman, Nanny,' she said, quietly. 'He's looking for Jack Jones, for one thing.'

'Jack Jones? Is he lost, then?' The old lady was an avid listener. She liked a nice polite man who could tell nice clean jokes, even if they were essentially the same every day.

The Woman sighed and patted her Nanny's arm. 'Nanny,' she said, 'they've been playing the Best of Jack Jones records for what has seemed like weeks but is probably only days; haven't you noticed?'

Nanny shook her head. Although she listened every evening, it was background to knitting, mending, ironing to her, nothing that she actually had to take any notice of.

'Well, they have. So this nice young man has been charged with finding him.'

Nanny craned round her erstwhile charge and looked at Harris with eyes still keen despite her age. 'They can't want to find him very much, then, can they? Or they would send a real policeman.'

The Woman smiled. Not much got past Nanny. 'That may be so,' she said, 'but he's very determined. I think he might succeed.'

Nanny humphed and folded and refolded the eternal tea towel she carried. 'He looks like a little lost boy, like a couple of the others. Are you sure you should have him here? He's likely to misunderstand.' She looked anxiously up into her charge's face.

'Misunderstand?' The Woman chuckled. 'I don't think his misunderstanding is what we should worry about, Nanny.

It's if he *understands* we need to think fast. Anyway,' she patted the woman again, as casually as she might a pet, 'I have plans.'

Harris had finished his toast and with the women muttering in a corner, it didn't look as though he was going to be offered more, so he sat back in his chair and waited. There was a pot of tea in front of him, under a garish crocheted cosy. There was a little jug of milk, yellow with cream, and a basin of cube sugar. He didn't know if it was for him, but he poured some anyway, into a cup of such delicate thinness, he could hardly believe it could take the weight of the liquid. He added the sugar, though he never had it in tea as there was never any to be had as a rule. He sipped and closed his eyes. Nectar!

The women moved so silently, he almost swallowed his own tongue when he opened his eyes and found them sitting there, silently, looking at him. He laughed nervously.

'You were peckish,' Nanny remarked.

'I'm sorry,' he said. 'It was all so delicious …'

'Silly boy,' Nanny said, slapping his hand with her tiny claw. 'I wasn't criticising. I was just saying. I love to see lads eating well. Have you had enough?'

Harris could have carried on eating her food all day, but guessed correctly that this was just a rhetorical question.

'We need to plan the rest of your search for Jack Jones.' The Woman came straight to the point. 'Where were you planning to go next?' she asked.

Harris was a little flummoxed. He hadn't really given it any thought. So far, he had just walked, following his nose and from time to time coming across someone who could help. 'I … I don't think I had much of a plan,' he said, embarrassed.

Nanny and the Woman looked at each other and nodded, a secret look between two who had shared a lifetime of nods and winks.

'I was thinking I could help you there,' the Woman said and this time, the Nanny was as surprised as Harris.

'Can you?' they both said together.

The Woman set her lips in a straight line for a

moment, deep in thought. This might be tricky. Nanny was not going to be happy, of that she had no doubt.

She looked Harris squarely in the face. 'I am going to have to have you agree to something first, something which might not fit very well with whatever oath you had to take when you became a policeman. Do you think you could do that?'

The oath seemed a long time ago now, but the essence of it was to do his duty as an upholder of the law. More than that might be tricky but the old sweats he'd met so far in the business, like Baker, for instance, seemed to have had no problem. He'd see how this played out.

'I need to know, first, what it is I have to agree with is,' he said, having a sneaking suspicion he had lost control of the sentence.

Nanny tutted. She did abhor bad grammar.

The Woman smiled. She knew what he meant. 'That's fair enough, I suppose,' she said. 'I need you to promise that, no matter what you see or hear from now on, from the end of what I am saying, in essence, that you will not go to the authorities. That you won't snitch on us, if I may use the vernacular.'

Harris had no idea what a vernacular was and whether its use was acceptable these days, but she seemed kind and she had fed him like a king, although he had a feeling that the king, if he was still even living, didn't eat like that any more. So he nodded.

'I think I need you to say it out loud,' she said.

'Yes, I promise not to tell anyone of anything I see,' he said, paraphrasing.

'Or hear.'

'Yes, or hear.'

Nanny and the Woman exchanged glances and one of their secret little nods.

'I don't know where Jack Jones is,' the Woman said, 'I must make that clear from the outset. But from what I have heard over the years, he has access to some ...' another glance at her Nanny, who nodded and patted her arm, '... features of life from a while ago, which makes it easier for him to make his way about.'

Harris frowned and closed his eyes as he worked things through. 'Do you mean … a car?' he checked. People had cars. He knew that. They just didn't always have any petrol.

'In short, yes. And the fuel to run it, what's more.'

Harris was shocked. 'But that's illegal,' he said. 'No one is supposed to travel unless it is on vital government business.'

Again, the nods. 'Indeed. However, we won't judge Jack right now. I, too, have … vehicles.'

Harris's eyes were out on stalks. More than one? Impossible!

'I need them for my business, though I can't pretend it is government business, per se.'

Harris remembered the bacon. The eggs. The marmalade. He leaned forward. 'Are you engaged in …' his voice became a husk. 'Black marketeering?' He looked from one to the other, his eyes still wide.

Nanny smiled indulgently. Dear boy.

The Woman laughed. 'Are you sure you're a policeman?' she asked.

He bridled. 'Of course I am,' he said, huffily.

'Well, in deference to your role in what I suppose we must still call society, I will neither confirm nor deny, but I do have links to commerce, yes,' she said. 'I'm afraid that that will have to do you, if you don't mind.'

Nanny chuckled. 'Commerce,' she said, wiping her eyes on the corner of her apron. 'That's a good one, that is.'

'Thank you, Nanny,' the Woman said. 'I will explain to this lovely young man any details he feels he needs while we're on the road.'

Nanny was on her feet with surprising speed for one with her dodgy knees and dicky hip. 'On the road? We?'

'Yes,' the Woman said, firmly. 'I know you and the Boys will manage without me and I have a mind to go and look for Jack Jones with this lad. He is a national treasure and … well, in short, I want to go.'

'But …' Harris was unsure. 'Driving and for goodness knows how long. What if … well, we're bound to be pulled over and it will be difficult for me. In my position, you know.'

Nanny was subsiding in a series of creaks back into her chair. 'You won't get pulled over, lad. You can trust me on that.'

Harris was not so sure. He had seen people thrown into chokey for indeterminate sentences for going out for a picnic one mile too far away from their house.

'She's right,' the Woman said. 'Now, if you would like to go and have a nice hot bath, you'll find all you need up the stairs, third door on the right.'

'The room with the bath in,' Nanny said, waspishly.

'Indeed. There are clothes in the airing cupboard, there is bound to be something to fit. Chop chop.'

Harris looked down. 'My clothes are all right, aren't they?' Yes, they were a little institutionalised, a little darned and worn, but they were his and he was comfy in them.

'All right, I suppose,' said the Woman. 'But they are a bit ... well, not to put too fine a point on it, they are a bit Coppery, aren't they? I guessed your calling at first sight, didn't I?'

Harris thought for a moment and nodded. 'But I'm in plain clothes,' he pointed out.

'Hmm. If you say so. I would like you to change, though, if you would. If only because of the smell.'

'Smell?' He was really annoyed now. 'I don't smell!'

Nanny chortled again. 'Oh, yes, you do, lad,' she said, coughing.

'What of?' His feelings were really hurt now.

Nanny put a little hand over his and gave it a squeeze. 'Despair, lad. Just despair. Now, off you go. The water's hot. The soap's scented. When you get back here, I suppose you'll be ready for the off, will you, Missy?'

The Woman laughed. Only her Nanny was allowed to call her that and she dropped a kiss on her balding little head. 'Ready and waiting,' she agreed. 'Now, push off and don't come down until you're smelling of roses.'

Richard Denham

THE BOYS

As soon as they heard Harris' feet on the stairs, the women began the argument which they both knew could lead nowhere.

'What are you doing, you stupid, stupid thing?' Nanny said, dealing a feeble slap in the direction of the Woman, who didn't dodge. She hardly felt it and it almost made her cry – once upon a time, a slap from Nanny could send her reeling, now it was like a fly alighting.

'I told you,' the Woman said, with a hint of schoolroom truculence. 'Jack Jones is a National Treasure and I want to help find him.'

Nanny humphed, with the special humph they taught at Nanny School. It could say anything the humpher and the humphee wanted it to and between these two, it needed no repetition.

'That's all very well for you to say,' the Woman said. 'And actually, you're wrong. If he was one of my Gentlemen Friends, I don't remember him especially and even if he were, I wouldn't hold it against him.'

'That's a good one, Missy,' Nanny wheezed. 'I thought holding it against people was something of a speciality.'

The Woman laughed. 'Oh, Nanny,' she said, getting up and stacking Harris' discarded plates to take to the sink. 'I love it when you talk dirty. I would like to know where we would all be if I hadn't done precisely that when we were on our last five bob.'

Nanny flapped her hand again but this time not meaning it to land. She covered her eyes with her apron and began to rock. She hated to be reminded of those times, when her beloved Missy had had to go out of the walled garden, into the World, where she would be mixing with all sorts. But needs must when the devil drives and finally, she had come home one night with a rather portly gent in tow, wearing ill-fitting tweeds and an unfortunate pork pie hat. She had introduced him only as the Spiv but after he had appeared, life was back to how it had always been, or how Nanny remembered it, bacon every morning and nice young men coming and going at all hours. But Missy wasn't young any more. And Nanny got confused. She frowned, trying to remember.

The Woman knelt down by the side of the old woman's chair. 'I'll be back, I promise,' she said. 'This is just something I need to do. The Boys will look after you, you know that. You can have some fun, spoiling them when I'm not here to stop you. And they'll bring news.' She pulled the apron gently away from the tear-soaked face. 'Don't cry.' She dried the soft apple cheeks. 'Come on. Turn that frown upside down.' They both smiled at the reminder from the nursery.

Nanny put out a hand and cradled her charge's face. She had brought up more children than just this one, but she loved this one the most. She smiled to see that some of the lines which etched the beloved face had softened, how her eyes were glowing, how she was ready for the off. 'Are you going to tell the Boys?' she asked.

The Woman shook her head. 'No. You can, if they ask. And of course, as soon as we change horses at Denham, whoever is on return duty will know and tell the rest.'

'Oh, you're heading that way, are you?' Nanny had never lived more than ten miles from where she was sitting, but she knew her geography. As far as the coast, at any rate. She couldn't be doing with foreign parts.

'It's as good a way as any,' the Woman said. 'And unless I have remembered it wrong, there are two vehicles there, a lorry and a little Austin. So we can choose, depending on how things go.'

'What are you setting off in?' Nanny was suddenly all business, taking the stacked plates to the sink and running them under the tap.

'Not sure. We need to be as inconspicuous as possible. I must remind the lad to call me Mum. A boy and his mother travelling somewhere isn't as suspicious as … well, I don't know what else we would look like.'

Nanny stuck out her tongue. 'It's not for me to say,' she said, shrugging. 'I think the mother story is the one to stick to. If the lad will do it.'

'He'll do it,' the Woman said. 'I think he's rather enjoying a bit of cloak and dagger.' She opened a cupboard door. 'Do you have any plans for this bread?'

Nanny sighed and flapped again. 'I'll make you some sandwiches. Go and pack what you need. Quick, now, he'll be down soon. You'll need to be away if you plan more than one change today.'

The Woman kissed her forehead. 'No plans, Nanny, thank you. One step at a time. Just one step at a time.'

* * *

Harris sat in the cab of the lorry and watched with horror as the road came up to meet him at frightening speed. He hadn't been in that many vehicles in his life and wondered if he would ever get used to it. He gripped the edges of the seat and brought his knees up and together in his distress.

'Are you all right?' the Woman asked. 'You appear to be trembling.'

He toyed with saying he was cold, but that wouldn't do at all. If anything, he was feeling a touch on the warm side. 'I'm not really used to going fast,' he said.

'Fast?' the Woman chuckled. 'This old heap can't go fast. If we're lucky, we might get a change into something a bit nippier before we catch up with Jack … Jones.'

Harris wasn't sure if he heard a pause or not, but decided to let it go.

'Anyway, aren't you a policeman? Surely, you're used to speed. Car chases and so on. Those Railtons can do a hundred miles an hour, or so they say. Catching people breaking curfew, that kind of thing.'

'I'm foot patrol,' he said. 'We never chase cars.'

'Well, no,' the Woman said, tartly. 'That wouldn't be very much good, would it? Although, to be honest, you might catch this one, if you had a reasonable turn of speed. I like this one, though. I don't believe she has ever been stopped.'

'But surely,' Harris was still not absolutely sure how illegal the Woman's lifestyle might turn out to be and if that could last, he would be more than happy. Even so, he was almost compelled to ask questions, now and then, for his own self-respect. 'Surely, she isn't out much, is she?'

'As much as the rest, I suppose.' The Woman put the E in Enigmatic. 'But she blends in, that's her skill. I think the dead sheep is a master touch, but we swap it for other things every week or so. I don't think even the most careless farmer would leave a dead sheep in his truck for ever.'

Harris looked behind him, into the flat bed of the truck and sure enough, there was a dead sheep, lying on its back, legs in the air, head askew and tongue lolling. He turned round to face front again, feeling queasy. He didn't like dead things.

'There ... there is a dead sheep,' he said, almost under his breath.

'I prefer to think of it as meat,' the Woman said. 'It didn't go through the usual channels, I admit, but it is, as the saying goes, as dead as mutton, so it serves two purposes. Camouflage for me, Sunday dinner for a few discerning diners. Apparently, the sweetbreads are delicious, but I am not really an offal person.' She deftly swung them round a sharp right hand bend and Harris stifled a cry. 'My word, you *are* a nervous nelly, aren't you? I must teach you to drive. They say drivers aren't as nervous as non-drivers.'

'That's ... that's very kind of you,' Harris said, through clenched teeth. 'Umm ... do you mind if I ask you something?'

'It depends on what it is,' she said, reasonably.

'How far will we be able to travel like this? As I understand it, you have ... staging posts, I suppose I would call them ... so you don't get reported for driving too far. Is that right?'

'Absolutely right, yes,' she said. 'Mostly, they shuttle back and forth between two stages, but sometimes they go further. That's rare, though and we have been caught out a couple of times. We lost a valuable contingent, once and, of course, the safety of the Boys is paramount.'

'The Boys?' Harris couldn't help himself. He was nosey and that was the end of it. Perhaps it went with the territory.

'Yes, my Boys. I'm not sure how many I have now, it must be in the hundreds, but it doesn't matter – every man Jack of them is as important as another, to me.'

'Hundreds?' Harris was staggered. 'What do they all do?'

'Oh, a little bit of this, a little bit of that. You'll meet some soon and I don't want you asking awkward questions. Just act normal, if you can. Oh, by the way,' she reached out to slap him on the thigh and the lorry lurched worryingly, 'when we're with other people, not the Boys, of course but members of the public, police or Roundheads, pray God not them but still ... call me Mum.'

'Mum?' It was a long time since Harris had even called his own mother Mum and it sounded odd to his ear.

'Or whatever you're familiar with. Ma. Mother. Not Mummy, surely – you don't look much like a Mummy sort to me.'

'No, Mum is okay with me but I just ... well, it'll take some getting used to.'

'Another way is to not speak when we're out and about and that could also work, but sometimes you'll have to speak. If you want to know where I am, for example. You can't say "Have you seen that Woman, you know, the posh old bint with a face like a contour map and an arse as big as the great outdoors" really, can you?'

Harris laughed and realized he hadn't done that much lately. Not even when listening to Jack Jones.

She smiled at him and grated up a gear. 'Well, that's good to know. I wondered if you knew how to laugh, lad.'

He nodded and looked at her solemnly. 'I'm out of practice,' he said.

'I can see that,' she said. 'But I would be derelict in my duty as your Mum if I didn't try to cheer you up. Have you heard the one about the Actress and the Bishop …?'

Harris was tempted to say yes, he had, only a day or so ago – could it really be that recent? – but decided to say nothing. Instead, he shook his head, unclenched his fingers from the edge of the seat, lay back and decided to just take every day as it came from now on, just like his new Mum.

They passed a police car idling at a kerb. Instinctively, he ducked a little, which he realized immediately was pointless. The Woman laughed. 'Whose side are you on?' she asked.

'Sorry,' he said, grinning at his own stupidity. 'It's just …'

'I know,' she said. 'It's infectious, isn't it?' Her eyes were fixed on the driving mirror, just making sure the police car wasn't following them.

They passed a garage too, one of the few not locked, bolted and barbed-wired. Two uniformed coppers stood, arms folded, at the entrance, one of them with a tommy gun in the crook of his arm. 'I can remember a time,' she said, 'when you blokes managed to survive with a hardwood truncheon. Look at it now.'

'Can't be too careful.' He tried not to stare at them as they passed. 'With petrol, I mean. Where do you get yours?'

He caught her wide-eyed look.

'Sorry,' he said. 'Don't ask, don't tell, yes?'

'No,' she laughed. 'I get mine from the petrol fairy who brings it all the way from the little petrol mine in Dingley Dell.'

Harris didn't know how much of a lawbreaker this Woman was, but he realized, for the first time in a long time, that he was enjoying himself.

* * *

Harris was asleep. He had only meant to rest his eyes. The windscreen was old and smeared with the grime of years since the wipers had given up the ghost in a squeal of perished rubber. He slept silently and still, in the time-honoured tradition of those who got far too little sleep, through accident or design.

'Wake up, sleepyhead.' The Woman poked him in the ribs as she hauled on the handbrake, for all the good that it would do.

He woke with a start and looked around wildly. For a minute, he couldn't remember where he was, who he was or what he was doing and then it came back in a mad rush. The Woman had scrambled down from the cab and was scurrying off, in the gloom of what appeared to be a barn. Sunlight filtered through gaps in the walls and dust motes danced madly as they settled back down again after the lorry had thrown them up in a flung festoon. She turned her head and looked back.

'Come on. Spit spot.' She clucked to herself. She was turning into Nanny, without a doubt.

He gave himself a shake and dropped down from the cab – the drop seemed longer than when he had clambered up an unknown amount of time ago – and hurried after her.

'By the way,' she said over her shoulder without stopping to wait for him to catch up. 'I'm going to introduce you as Bobby, is that all right with you?'

'There's no need for that,' he said. 'My name is …'

She spun round. 'No. No names, no pack drill here. We all have noms de guerre, no matter what guerre we think we are fighting. So, Bobby, let's get you introduced.'

She pushed open a door and he was in another world.

There were more people gathered there than he had seen in one place for a good many years. Even the middle of London wasn't this full of scurrying busy activity. He had expected the door from the barn to lead him into the great outdoors but in fact it had just led him into an even larger indoor space, an aircraft hangar of a place. He had never actually been in an aircraft hangar, had only the slightest memory of even seeing an aircraft in the sky, but he imagined that this would be how it would feel, just immense space and a roof so far above your head you almost expected to see clouds between you and it. He wasn't to know, but this place did sometimes have its own weather — a fog outside would creep in and would be very spooky. However, on this visit, it was airy and cool, well lit and full of life and movement.

The Woman broke into his thoughts. 'It takes some getting used to, doesn't it?' she said, smiling at his amazement. She nodded up to a balcony that ran the length of the building. Guards patrolled there, but not like any guards Harris had seen before. They were no more than kids, in rough trousers and hand-me-down jumpers. They had fags in their mouths and rifles slung over their shoulders. The fact was stated with no emotion, no attempt to scare or shock. It just was what it was — necessary protection for her Boys and her business. 'They might be hazy on their times tables and their parts of speech, but they can shoot the head off a cockroach at a hundred yards. And that's with a Government-issue Lee-Enfield.'

'Oh.' There seemed nothing else to say.

'Don't worry your little constabulary head,' she murmured. 'Anyone getting that close is doing it on purpose. There are many other stages first. A socking great wall like something out of China — courtesy of a commando training ground. A dense plantation. Dogs. We've introduced wild boar, specially imported from the estate of some mad old Scottish laird. They're strictly speaking illegal of course but as vicious as any dog and also damned fine eating when the occasion requires it. I believe some of the locations have dug pits, but I try to dissuade them from that. Too labour intensive and really too cruel, if you can't patrol at least twice daily. We've had a few deaths from thirst and exposure and we're not vindictive.' She glanced round and caught the expression on his face. 'We're really not. I hope you will believe that, before we've done with you.'

She stepped forward and clapped her hands. In the cacophony of work, somehow it worked like a clarion call and everyone turned to face her. Harris could immediately see that the 'Boys' were not all boys, although the smattering of girls was small. Suddenly, Music While You Work was over.

A box miraculously appeared and two Boys stepped forward to help her up onto it.

There was no doubt about it now. These Boys were Ferals, the dregs of society abandoned by their elders. They'd run away from Dad's bolthole and Dad's slipper, left Mum with their nappy-wearing siblings, or, more often than not, their parents simply weren't there anymore or there was no home to go back to. Harris knew all about them, at least on his manor in what used to be the Met. Their mug shots, measurements and faces stared defiantly out of the walls and filing cabinets at the station. The lads who picked pockets with the ease of a conjuror and fought other Feral gangs with knuckle dusters and coshes. The girls who smoked for England and bought their fags by selling their bodies on street corners when London went even darker than usual. If Harris had ever wondered what the younger generation were coming to, he had his answer now.

Raised slightly above their level, the Woman's creased face broke into a delighted grin.

'It's so lovely to be back,' she said, her cultured tones cutting through the space like diamonds. 'I don't come West half often enough. This ...' she extended a hand towards Harris, 'is Bobby.' She smiled down at him encouragingly

'Hello, Bobby!' The massed greeting almost blew him off his feet, followed by a dozen or so 'Wotcher, cocks' and 'All right, me ol' mucker.' They even *sounded* like Jack Jones.

'Bobby is in transit with me at the moment, but I am sure he would like a break from my driving for a while ...'

The gust of laughter was quieter than the greeting, but even so, it brought dust down from the distant rafters. 'You got that right,' somebody shouted. 'Get that man a chair. He must be terrified.'

'... so if any of you who are on a rest break would like to take him somewhere quiet for a cuppa and perhaps a snack, that would be very pleasant. I just need to do a bit of business and we will be back on the road in ...' she flicked back a cuff and looked at the slim gold watch on her wrist '...

half an hour at the most.' She looked across the raised faces. 'Gladys, can you do the honours? Thank you.'

Gladys. Harris's heart sank. He had never known anyone called Gladys who wasn't built like a wardrobe and had a face like a smacked arse.

The crowd was melting away, back to their allotted tasks. Soon, Harris was alone with a slim girl with chestnut hair falling over her forehead in a silky wave. She looked like a poor man's Veronica Lake. Like everyone else, she was wearing a blue boiler suit, but it seemed to have been cut to order, clinging just where it should and skimming a slender waist and perfect shoulders. Her skin was like cream and her eyes sparkled blue as the sky behind dark lashes.

He looked around for Gladys.

'Hello, Bobby.' The voice sounded like birds singing. Harris hardly dare look – if Gladys-the-wardrobe sounded like that, it would be a particularly cruel trick on the part of mother nature. He looked around.

'Gladys?'

She raised her eyebrows. 'Was you expecting someone else?'

He could hardly say he was expecting an elephant who had been rejected at birth for being too ugly and felt himself blush.

'Ah, I see your problem,' she laughed. 'It's the name, isn't it? Not my favourite, either. Everyone knows an ugly Gladys, don't they? When I come here, I thought of changing it but then thought why the … on earth should I? I'm striking a blow for Gladyses everywhere.'

'No, I …' He looked into her eyes and laughed as well. 'Yes. I sat next to a Gladys at school.'

'Enough said,' she said. 'Let's go and get some tea. You've missed lunch, which is a shame because it was salmon. We had a bit of a glut.'

Harris was still steeped in the memories of bacon and wasn't that much of a fish lover in any case. But a *glut* of salmon? He wasn't strong on the niceties of the food chain, but that didn't sound plausible in these straitened times. He suspected that even a snack here would be something

86

wonderful.

'Our staff room is through here,' she said, moving through the toiling crowd like an eel. She tapped away a roving hand and blew a raspberry in a Feral's face, just because she could. 'It shouldn't be too crowded. You can tell me a bit about yourself. Like, where are you going ...'

Harris gulped. He had never been good at lying. It made his ears go red.

'... or not, whichever you prefer. We've all got fairly chequered backgrounds here. I, for example, used to be ... well, no need for you to know that. Suffice to say, I prefer doing this to doing *that*.'

Harris put her down as twenty, though it was difficult to tell. How many months or years she'd been at the conveyor belt, providing hooky gear for those in the know was anybody's guess. He wanted to know more about her, but he wanted her to know *nothing* about him

Harris looked suitably sympathetic and understanding, or at least he hoped he did.

She laughed. 'No, not *that*,' she said, 'though I can't say I didn't think of it, when I was sleeping rough under a hedge! No, I was in the Church of the Remnant and I'm not proud of it. I was kicked out in the end.'

Harris was surprised. 'I didn't think they ever kicked anyone out,' he said.

'Not as a rule. But I'm afraid I was an undesirable influence.' She put on a hoity-toity accent when she said the last two words. 'When we were out evangelizing, I was telling people not to bother, it really wasn't that good an idea ... in retrospect, I'm lucky I was only thrown out – people have disappeared for less. You know what they're like. Up their own bloody arseholes – excuse my French. God this, God that. When you ask the elders about anything, it's ...' She assumed the nasal tone again, '"If the Good Lord wishes us to know that, he'll tell us in due course." Well, I'm still waiting and I ain't heard a dickey bird yet.'

Harris nodded. He had heard about the disappeared from the policemen, still white-faced and green around the gills who had found the bits. There was a common denominator, at least in his neck of the woods, that too many corpses found on wasteland had been found to have a Remnant background. The Remnant didn't just pinch the old churches for their services, indiscriminately nicking Anglican and Catholic buildings, synagogues and the one mosque in London; they came knocking door to door, like the disciples of Doomsday that they were. And they always had a kid in tow, usually a pretty one, with dimples and curls, like something spawned by Shirley Temple. Harris could just see Gladys in that role, without the sleek hair and the sultry pout, looking up at the Remnant's latest prey with eyes to drown in.

'So, I was sleeping under hedges,' Gladys went on, 'as I said, when one of the Boys found me. I didn't believe it at first. The Ferals were just gangs, layabouts who shouted in the street and kicked balls around – anybody's. they used girls like mattresses and didn't give a monkey's about anybody. But this one told me about this place – Shangri-la, he called it – where they all worked. Yeah, I know, Feral and Work don't really hang together, do they? But the work was for all of us, to have a better life. They didn't have all the posts then, so I am a fair old way from home, but ...' she spread her arms and spun round on her toes '... this is my home now and I couldn't be happier.'

She pushed open a door.

'Here we are. This is us.'

The room they stepped into was as different from the main space as it was possible for a room to be. It was furnished in the same general fashion as the Woman's house, old and comfy with a touch of faded elegance. Nothing matched anything else, but it didn't matter. He drew a happy sigh.

'It is lovely, isn't it?' she said. 'It's all just stuff that we've picked up in various places.' She went quiet, aware that she had almost said too much. 'It's nice to relax in.'

Harris was looking round the walls. He wasn't much of an art lover, but he was sure he had seen that picture of the lad in blue somewhere before. And that cart up to its axles in water.

'Tea?' she asked. 'Coffee? Something stronger?' She

had never experienced her boss's driving, but had heard it could be life changing.

'Tea,' he said. 'I'm not a coffee person, really.'

'Ah.' She wagged a knowing finger at him. 'That's because you've only had coffee *essence*, isn't it? Everyone knows that isn't real coffee. Dandelions. Chicory. And they are just the ingredients I dare tell you about.'

'How do you know what goes into coffee essence?' He was surprised enough to ask her – it seemed an odd snippet of knowledge for this frankly gorgeous girl to have.

'We make it in one of the other posts,' she said. 'But we don't drink it – it's horrible stuff, though ours is marginally less horrible than most. No, we have real coffee here.'

'What's "real" coffee?' Harris was puzzled. 'We can't grow coffee here – can we?'

Gladys laughed nervously. 'I don't know,' she said, with a girlish laugh which sounded oddly forced. 'I expect we can in some parts, can't we? Somewhere warm. Cornwall, perhaps. The Isle of Wight, why not.'

'I thought the Isle of Wight was uninhabitable these days,' he said, trying not to sound too much like a policeman.

'Probably because of all the coffee plantations,' she said, turning her back. 'What tea do you want, then? Chamomile, dandelion or hawthorn?' She thought it probably best not to mention the Lapsang Oolong or the Darjeeling.

'Dandelion.'

'Sugar?'

It didn't surprise him that they had sugar still. He just hoped the dandelion tea would taste like this room smelled, a bit smoky, a little bit like dried grass, but not in a bad way. 'No sugar, thanks. And just a splash of milk.'

The girl stood there looking at him. He looked like a teenager trying to pretend to be a man, though she guessed he was probably in his twenties. In the sunlight from the skylight, there was a faint fuzz of stubble on his chin and she wanted so much to press her face against it – fraternization amongst the Boys was strictly forbidden, though not unknown. That Jerry Bolton took some watching. It was just that there wasn't anyone she had met, even with all the comings and goings, who she could be bothered to break the rules for. She made a decision and poured the boiling water onto some Orange Pekoe Tips which were really only for Grade IIIs and above. She doubted he would recognize it – he would just think she was brilliant at making dandelion tea. She cut a hunk of carrot cake and passed the cup and plate across.

Harris's face fell. Carrot cake? He was expecting something more ... or perhaps he meant less like normal life. Gladys saw his expression.

'It's only *called* carrot cake,' she said. 'It's not actually made from carrots. What was that Government bloke's name? Lord Woolton, wasn't it? I can hear him, now, on the wireless, sounding a hundred and banging on about carrots and parsnips and ... God, how appalling! This cake's got all the things the carrots were replacing. Like walnuts, sultanas, raisins, dried peel, eggs, sugar ...' she ran out of ingredients. She was not on a cooking rota, not since the steamed pudding incident, which few would ever forget.

He took a bite and had to close his eyes. He had never tasted any cake so delicious. 'This is ... is ...'

'I know.' She had a slice for herself, even though her tea break had been less than an hour before. 'It's the icing, isn't it? There's a secret ingredient, but I can't put my finger on it. Nutmeg, do you think?'

Harris shook his head, lost in a world of sugar. 'Dunno,' he murmured. 'Don't care.'

'That's the ticket!' The Woman's crystal tones sliced the air. 'Drink up. Eat up. Time we weren't here.'

Harris sighed. Somehow, it would have been better almost to have never met Gladys, never eaten this sublime cake, never drunk dandelion tea like no other. Memories were all very well, but you couldn't eat or drink them, imagine snuggling up against them ...

The Woman caught Gladys's eye. She had been young once, young and in love though in her case, sadly, not with the man she was married to. She remembered a young beater once, on a 12 August made more glorious than usual by his tanned biceps and his ... she gave herself a shake. She was of mature years, that she would grant, so perhaps that was why Harris looked like a rather bemused boy scout to her, but she could see that to someone more his age, he might have been considered good looking. She blew down her nose, thinking. She couldn't let them go off just the two of them, that would be asking for trouble. A young couple driving any vehicle would just attract attention, both official and unofficial. Three people travelling would be the same ... but she could give them more time. Something for them both to have as a memory, when they were as old as her. She came to a decision.

'Okay, Bobby,' she said, making him jump. He had forgotten his new name. 'I am a bit weary and our next hop is longish. Night's coming on as well. So, we'll set off tomorrow. First thing, mind. Before breakfast, so sorry, no bacon. Gladys.' She fixed the girl with a very beady stare. 'Can you amuse Bobby until dawn, do you think?'

Gladys looked at her, startled. She had heard that the old girl was a bit frisky, but had never had a direct example of it. 'Amuse? You mean ... amuse?'

'I mean anything you're comfortable with, my dear,' the Woman said. 'Tiddlywinks. Chess. Cribbage ... Whatever takes your fancy.' She gave them a benevolent look, turned on her heel and walked out.

The two stood looking at each other. 'I don't play chess,' Gladys said at last.

Harris looked crestfallen. He had been tiddlywinks champion three years running between seven and ten years old. He could beat about half the people he had ever played at chess and all of them down at the nick. He had a working knowledge of cribbage as long as his opponent went slowly. But he had a feeling that Gladys had chosen the unspoken option, the one that took her fancy, and he knew just as certainly that humiliation was bound to follow. He had a general impression of what went where. It was when and in what order which had always eluded him. He cursed himself; he really hadn't got out enough.

She took a step nearer. 'I can tiddle a wink, on a good

day,' she said, reaching up and pulling his face down towards hers. 'I've never tried cribbage.' She fastened her mouth on his and he almost passed out.

'We … we can't do this here,' he managed, pulling away.

'No,' she said, letting go and pulling her jumper straight. 'But we can do this here.' And she pulled him by the hand to a door in the corner. 'Come on, it's vacant. No one will bother us here.' She turned the sign to say 'Engaged' and led him to his doom.

THE POST

'Oh, hello.' The Denham Post Manager looked up from his ledger. 'I thought you were off.'

The Woman shrugged. 'I couldn't bear to do it, in the end. Young Gladys seemed to have taken a shine to the lad and he ... well, I don't think he ever has much fun.'

'Who does?' The Post Manager pushed the ledger away and rubbed his eyes.

The Woman smiled. 'You do. Look at you, there, with all your lovely columns all adding up like nobody's business. I believe you would rather do an hour of double entry book-keeping than have a bit of fun with Gladys.'

'Bit young for me,' the Post Manager remarked.

'Well, any woman, then. It occurs to me, I know nothing at all about you.'

'Isn't that the idea?'

'Yes, but there is a limit. Are you married?'

'Not now.' There was no emotion, nothing to give a clue.

'Dead, is she?' The Woman, since the beater, had not given her heart to a single human being.

'Perhaps. I have no idea. She went out for milk in 1942, and I have never seen her since.'

The Woman, hard as nails as she might be, was a little shocked. 'You tried to find her, though.' It was a statement which could also be a question, depending on taste.

'I put in a report,' he said, looking longingly at his

ledger. 'I don't remember if I got a reply or not. You know what the police are.'

'Surely …'

'Really.' He pulled the ledger a touch nearer, so he could just run a finger up and down its columns. 'I don't mind. I don't miss her. She was … we were never really that close. It was a convenience, really. I needed a home. She had one. She needed … well, I'm not sure I could ever provide what she needed. So when she went, I wasn't that surprised. She got more pleasure from listening to the wireless than ever she did from me.' The Post Manager looked surprised at himself. He wasn't generally that forthcoming. Even getting him to say what he wanted for his tea could take ten minutes and more.

'Jack Jones?' the Woman asked, on spec.

'As a matter of fact, yes,' he said, surprised. 'I could never see it, myself. Bland and boring, I thought. And if I never have to hear anyone say "I'd be brown bread without you, Jack Jones" again, it will be too soon.'

'He can be a little repetitive, perhaps. But his heart's in the right place, don't you think?'

The Post Manager shrugged. 'Maybe. Anyway, no wife. No intention of getting friendly with Gladys. But you probably did the lad a favour. He looked a bit … peaky, I thought, when I saw him earlier.'

The Woman had never heard of that as a cure for peakiness, but you lived and learned in her experience. 'I'll need a bed for the night, if that can be arranged. Gladys's would do.'

'She's in a dorm of six. I'll arrange something.' The Post Manager jotted down a note. He found if he wrote things down, even something to do in the next five minutes, it got done. Otherwise, it wasn't so certain.

'Are you in a dorm of six?'

The Post Manager's hand froze in the middle of writing a word. 'No.'

'I'll bunk up with you, then,' she said. She saw his expression. 'Not everything is as wrinkled as my face. And even the bits that are still work.' She looked him in the eye. 'If you're interested.'

'I ...' She was technically his boss, though all Post Managers had more or less autonomy over their kingdom.

'I hear there's another way of double entry book-keeping around these days.'

His eyes lit up. 'Really?'

'No. But perhaps we could discuss it later. With the lights off, all kinds of entry could be possible.'

'All right,' he said, 'but can we leave the double entendres to Jack Jones?'

'Suit yourself,' she laughed.

With a sigh, he closed the ledger and heaved himself to his feet. He had heard that such things went on, but they had never happened to him. No matter. There was a first time for everything.

* * *

The work of the Post went on around the two couples otherwise engaged. Eggs were counted into cotton-lined tins in sixes, tens, dozens and any number upward, depending on their final destination. They were then packed in boxes marked 'Glass – With Care' and sent on conveyor belts to the vehicles outside, which could be anything from a boy with a barrow to a tarpaulin covered lorry. Wines of every vintage were laid with care in between shredded rags and packed in wooden crates marked 'Rags' and addressed to fictional paper mills. No one but the Post Manager knew everything – only he knew where things came from and where they went and currently, he didn't really care. A fleeting thought went through his mind that if he had known then what he suddenly knew now, his wife might not have skedaddled after a fictional bloke on the wireless, but coherent thought was not presently a skill he had, so it wasn't something which he bothered about much. The Woman was much more limber than he had expected and, in the dark, she felt much softer than her face had led him to expect. He sighed a heartfelt sigh and she smiled to herself. Spread a little sunshine, she thought to herself. Spit spot. A spoonful of sugar made the medicine go down and similar trite sayings; Nanny would be proud.

* * *

Dawn broke over the Post and to all intents and purposes, nothing had changed. It was still discreet and inconspicuous to the naked eye, a clump of trees in the quiet countryside, it was still humming its quiet industrial hum. The Woman and Harris moved through the crowd with very conflicting ideas going through their heads. Harris found it hard not to grin all the time and although he knew the chances of ever meeting Gladys again were slim, they were agreed that some things were just meant to be memories and this was just one such. He had found that actually, things were much simpler than the boys at school had led him to believe. Or perhaps – and he gave himself a mental pat on the back – he was simply naturally good at it. He had a little swagger in his step and the Woman looked at him fondly. He might only be her son for the duration of this adventure, but she had done him a good turn and that gave her a good feeling. The Post Manager she had left sleeping the sleep of the satiated; dear man, he was easy enough to please and as far as she could tell he didn't have the acumen to notice that much of her was not quite as it appeared. She also grinned from time to time, two jobs well done; Harris all grown up, the Post Manager's ghost laid – even if she didn't find Jack Jones at the end of this, she could chalk up these at least.

'Good evening?' the Woman asked as they clambered into the bullnose Morris waiting for them in the barn.

'So so,' Harris said, glad that the light was dim. Even he was beginning to see that the grin could get annoying. He'd noticed that the vehicle had changed, but said nothing.

'That's good,' she said. 'Now, shall we head North or West?'

'South,' Harris said, reminiscently.

'Now, that's enough,' she said, tapping him sharply on the leg. 'Don't make me sorry for doing you a favour.'

'I'm sorry,' he said. 'I just feel I'm a different person

this morning.'

'Well, you are,' she said. 'But can you put the different person back in the box for now and concentrate. North or West?'

'But why not South? Seriously.' Harris's geography was as bad as his Human Biology had been the night before.

'Because ...' She looked at him as she double declutched for all she was worth. Could it really be that he had no idea? She thought of the journey ahead and even if they ended up in Aberdeen, there were still not miles enough to explain. 'I have a gut feeling,' she said, 'that he won't have gone South.' Gone South to be shot at worst, to be interned at best, to starve while waiting for either. South raised its problems. All across the Weald, the Roundheads had their quarters, scattered villages, small towns, farms with affiliations. Further south still, the Government held firm, with pill boxes, barbed wire, road blocks. It was from the South and East that the invasion would come, whenever that would be, and the Government were known to shoot people on sight. Regulars, Home Guard, the sleeve badges hardly mattered. A bullet from one was as decisive – and final – as from another. No, gut feeling it would have to be.

'Well, North, then.'

'Straight up or veering right or left.' It struck her that perhaps points of the compass wouldn't do the trick with Harris, whose grasp of direction seemed a little rudimentary.

'I think Jack Jones might be heading for a coast,' he said, surprising her mightily. 'But I don't know which one. To the left ... I don't know where that would go? Is France over there? I don't remember any geography from school. We were only little and the teacher really just kept talking about Stonehenge and things.'

'I think that might have been history.' The Woman would have closed her eyes but they were out of the grounds of the Post now and even with few cars on the road, it would still have been dangerous. How could the education system have gone to the dogs so comprehensively and so fast?

'Oh, was it? I was never sure. I liked maths, though. And some English.'

'*Some* English?' That was an odd concept.

'Poetry. I liked that. And some books, if they weren't too long.'

'Shakespeare?' The Woman was hopeful again.

'Who?'

'Ah. Did you learn any poetry off by heart? We did a lot of that when I was a girl. *Daffodils.* That kind of thing.'

Harris hadn't heard of that. It sounded a bit unlikely. 'I learned one by myself. I found it in an old book and liked it, so I learned it.'

'What was it?'

'I don't know the title. The mice had eaten the tops of the pages. But it went …' Harris tipped his head back and closed his eyes tight. 'It went … Before the Roman came to Rye, or out through Severn strode …'

'The rolling English drunkard made the rolling English road.' The Woman almost burst into tears. 'Chesterton.'

'You know it!' Harris all but clapped his hands. 'It's a good one for us, isn't it? Because we're just going where our guts take us. A reeling road, a rolling road, that rambles round the shire, And after him the parson ran, the sexton and the squire.' He stopped, suddenly solemn. 'Only, there isn't a parson or a squire. And I don't know what a sexton is.'

'Chin up, lad,' the Woman said. 'Perhaps if … when we find Jack Jones we'll have bluebirds over the white cliffs of Dover …'

Harris's eyes were wide. 'I didn't think we were allowed to … not after what she did …'

'I apologize. It just slipped out. Where were we? Oh, yes, A merry road, a mazy road, and such as we did tread the night we went to Birmingham by way of Beachy Head …'

She crashed into another random gear, as was her way, and headed up and a bit to the left while they ate up the miles very slowly, to the cadence of Gilbert Keith Chesterton, of blessed memory.

* * *

The next Post was up and to the left and they got there for

lunch, which was chicken with what the Woman thought of as All The Trimmings and Harris thought of as heaven. Meals were staggered at the bigger Posts, but they ate together here, as this was only small, a unit disguised behind a fake wall, itself behind one of the officially designated pubs, serving warm beer and pork scratchings made of ... Harris had often wondered, but whatever it was, it had never seen a pig. It seemed almost too delicious an irony to be eating such food just feet away from the few men who had both the time and money to pause in the middle of the day to visit the hostelry, but after a mouthful or two, Harris's qualms slid away.

'This is wonderful,' he said with his mouth full. 'It can't just be chicken.' He had had chicken the previous Yule, but it hadn't tasted like this. It hadn't looked like this, either. He looked down the table, at the four dismembered carcasses with their crispy skin peeled back and shredded by eager hands and thought back to the cylindrical greyness which they had shared at the Landlady's, with a small mound of greyer stuffing alongside. Here the stuffing was full of herbs and the crunch of granary breadcrumbs, none of which Harris could recognize; he just knew it tasted like stuffing should.

The Woman leaned forward and said to the chef, who sat at the end of the table, 'This stuffing is wonderful – I must have the recipe. What are these little ...' she made nibbling motions with her teeth '...berries in here?'

The chef flushed with pride. 'It's a little something I thought I'd try,' he said. It was so nice to have someone with a palate at his table. 'It's an idea I got from ...' he suddenly realized he was on an unfortunate trajectory but managed to get back on track '... an old history book. They're cranberries. The American settlers used them with turkey.'

The Woman almost applauded. A first rate catch, if ever she heard one. Now it just remained to be hoped that Harris had no idea where cranberries grew. She glanced at him. He didn't look as if he knew or cared. She smiled at the chef who went pale with relief.

'Well, they're delicious. Well done. It deserves to

become a classic.'

The rest of the meal was less contentious. Spotted Dick, light as a feather and studded with dried fruit that sang of the sun, with custard which had never seen the inside of a tin, finished off a meal which stunned Harris almost into a coma. In the past thirty six hours, about three quarters of the food which had passed his lips had been something he was eating for the first time. New experiences seemed to be springing out of the wainscotting and he was now disappointed if something unique didn't happen every half hour or so. But the rest of the afternoon was uneventful. A map was drawing-pinned to a wall and there was an enigmatic flag stuck in to indicate – Harris assumed – where they currently were. The coastline was sketchy, with few details. The Woman looked at it with nostalgia and put a reminiscent finger on a smooth stretch where she knew there were indentations of little coves with shell-pocked sand, backed by cliffs the colour of a ginger biscuit. There were few roads marked, just some which even the ageographic Bobby knew were main routes for keeping tabs on some of the historically less easily managed areas – one led straight into the middle of Edinburgh; he knew this because some of his colleagues at the Station had been seconded there once when things had got really bad. Another led to the west coast of Wales, but as far as he knew, there was no big city there, so that one was a mystery. The other led down to the West Country – he had always loved the sound of that and equated it in his mind with stories of a king – Arthur, was it? – who a teacher in his kindergarten had told them all about. Knights, dragons, fair maidens; it sounded like a place which Gladys would like to visit. Even the sound of her name in his head gave him a jolt in his loins which he still hadn't quite got used to and he looked around to see if anyone had noticed him jump.

'Looking at the map, eh?' A Boy had joined him and was looking to the West as well. 'The West Country, eh? Ever been there?' The Feral was probably fourteen. He had spots and lank hair and he was still having trouble with his octave range.

'No!' Harris was appalled that anyone would even think it possible. Surely, it was too far away to even contemplate. Then, he remembered the sort of person he was talking to.

'I bin there,' the Boy said. 'It's lovely down there. The sky goes on for miles. Not as much as up here,' he pointed up and to the right. 'Up there, the skies are so big, they ... well, you can't hardly fathom.' He spread his arms and smiled to himself.

'You've been there as well?' Harris was amazed. Surely, people didn't just *go* places. It wasn't allowed, for one thing. He mentally kicked himself, again.

The Feral blew out his cheeks. 'I bin nearly everywhere,' he said. 'Takes a while, of course. You can't just do it in one. One time, we met an old bloke, can't tell you where, and he said you used to be able to go any distance, nobody to stop you nor nothing. You could just ...' his eyes became misty with longing '... drive.'

'You can drive, can you?' Harris was getting a little testy. This Feral, with his more-travelled-than-thou attitude was becoming a pain in the arse. Harris was willing to bet that he had never spent the night with a girl as glorious as Gladys, though, so he kept that hugged to him, as his final checkmate.

'Course I can drive. First thing they learn you when you come here. Driving from Post to Post, they need us all to be able to go out at a moment's notice. So you have'ta be able to drive, and drive anything as well. I learned on an old Morris, like the one you come in. But others learned on all sorts. Him over there,' he turned and nodded to a red headed lad clearing the table, 'he learned on a tractor. But he does all right. He just is a bit slow. Never got used to the speed, y'see. He's from the Isle of Wight, he is. Apparently, they've got a little rhyme down there which sort of sums him up – "I can't read an' I can't write, But that don't hardly matter. Cos I come from the Isle of wight an' I can drive a tra'tor". Good, ain't it?'

Harris was laughing despite himself.

'What about you, then?' the Feral asked. 'Where you

from?'

'Oh,' Harris blustered. 'Here and there.'

'Ah,' the lad tapped the side of his nose. 'I getchya. Nod's as good as a wink to a blind horse.''

Harris shifted the focus. 'So, when you say drive … what are you driving, as such?' He could feel his inner policeman knocking to get out.

'All sorts. Goods. People, sometimes. It depends …'

'They may have taught you to drive,' a crystal voice with a lifetime of cigarettes in it murmured from behind them, 'but they didn't teach you to keep your mouth shut very well, did they?'

The Feral turned and stared in horror at the Woman, standing there with a smile like a basilisk on her face.

'But … I … but he come with you. I thought …'

'No, you didn't. Washing up and spud bashing for you for a month, young feller me lad. This isn't the first time, is it? Your card's marked, sonny, and don't you forget it. There's half a dozen policemen within hailing distance that'd like to hang you out to dry.'

The lad slunk off and started clearing the tables with his ginger colleague.

'I'm sorry,' Harris said. 'I didn't want to get him into trouble.'

'You didn't,' she said, shortly. 'He gets himself into trouble. As I said, it's not the first time. If you've finished testing your geography to extinction, we need to be on our way. Ready?'

He nodded.

'Then let's go.'

* * *

'Where are we going, though?' This leg of the journey was being completed in the back of a limousine, complete with chauffeur in a cap and epauletted coat. The Woman had explained that sometimes, too many cars ended up in one place and so it was necessary to add people without vehicles. Harris had wondered aloud how it was all arranged and she murmured something which sounded like 'logistics', a military term, she explained. Pressed, she told him there was a man somewhere with some phones, a map and a whole lot of toy cars. They probably had similar things in Whitehall, in the War Office, but hopefully, nothing on *their* maps about the Woman's little operations. The chauffeur sniggered. He knew that she had missed out the hundreds of hand-rolled gaspers and a daily gallon of gin. And yet, the system worked.

Harris thought the answer through. He tried a method that had failed him throughout his life; ask the question again. 'Where are we going, though?'

'Persistent little bugger, aren't you?' the Woman said, blowing cigarette smoke at the back of the chauffeur's head. She didn't like smoking and driving, but she did like smoking, so this was a treat for her.

'I only want to know where we're going,' he said, reasonably.

'Up and left a bit,' she said. 'We're going to see a very special lady who I think can help us out. And if she can't, she will definitely know someone who can.'

'With Jack Jones?' he asked.

She nodded.

'Is she a spy?' Harris did hope she was. He had never knowingly met one and surely this should be the kind of person they should be looking out for.

'No,' the Woman chuckled and coughed. 'No, she's not a spy. She's a knitter.'

* * *

So far, Baker had done quite well. When he told Harris that he really wasn't interested in the Scout Master, that wasn't quite true. He had followed the lad to St James's and noted the meeting up with the old bugger who seemed to be all gas and gaiters. He'd followed them across the park to the elegant building behind the hedging. It was just his luck that the rain had started then and he was wet through by the time Harris emerged, annoyingly dry and warm as it seemed to him.

Then the stupid little shit had sat down in the park, as

though to spend the night. For a while, Baker put up with it, keeping moving as much as he could so that the night air didn't get to him. You could have knocked him over with a feather when a Lady of the Night approached Harris and took him away. Nothing about this made sense. For a start, it was far too late for a proposition in the park. He couldn't make out the tart too clearly at a distance, but she carried herself well, though she was longer in the tooth than was usual for ladies in her profession.

Baker had to admit to being a little disappointed. It wasn't that coppers didn't hook up with tarts – that sort of thing had been de rigeur since the days of Sergeant Goddard and Kate Meyrick back Before. But he was a little surprised by Harris; he didn't seem the type.

After that, it was Bedlam. The Woman was leading both coppers – unbeknownst to her – all over the bloody country, moving north-west. He'd kept tabs on their movements via patrols and shortwave wireless, so he knew exactly where they were. All he didn't know, precisely, was why.

THE KNITTER

The chauffeur dropped them off on the corner of a very ordinary street in a very ordinary town. Harris had been asleep when they first arrived, so he hadn't seen the name of the place, but as he had never left London before, it would have meant little to him. He knew that Birmingham was up from London and to the left, he knew that York was up as well, more or less straight. Norwich (which he thought was spelled Norritch) was up and to the right. After that, it was all a bit of a blur. This place didn't look unlike a million other suburbs he had seen so he just had to trust the Woman that it was further up from Oxford (wherever that might be) and a few degrees left. He had seen an enormous bulk of an old building across some water meadows as they had driven in, the grass dotted with very picturesque cows and buttercups. He assumed that this was somewhere in what his teacher had always called Olde England. It smelled good. He didn't know what of, but he liked it, wherever it was.

The Woman turned to Harris. 'Don't be surprised at whatever you find here. My friend the Knitter has numerous projects on the go at once, so it isn't always easy to work out what's what. Just go along with whatever seems to be happening. Accept tea of any kind. Don't ever, *ever* drink her coffee, which is evil personified. Eat the cake. Don't eat the bread – she does something to it that turns it into an instant brick, so it is inedible. You don't need to call me Mum, but don't react to anything she calls me, because it won't be my name. All set?'

He nodded. Tea not coffee. Cake not bread. Sounded like his kind of house.

The Woman rang the doorbell and a cacophony of barking immediately broke out, just the other side of the rather beautiful Edwardian door, complete with stained glass. Harris had been through a lot of front doors in the last week, from decrepit to palatial but he thought this one was his favourite. There were snowdrops so delicate you could almost see them tremble and an oak tree which went high into the top of the door sprinkled autumn leaves through air full of bluebirds. Speaking accurately from the flora and fauna perspective, it was pretty impossible. As a piece of art, it was the kind of thing he liked. He was still admiring it when the door was flung open and a very tall and rangy woman stood there, knitting needles sprouting out of a bush of greying hair piled up anyhow on top of her head. She peered over a pair of glasses perched precariously on the very tip of a long and inquisitive nose. To those who loved her, she looked like a benign aardvark; to those who didn't, she looked like an aardvark who had just seen an anthill she would like to kick the shit out of. Bobby was undecided.

'Darling!' she crowed, throwing her arms wide. 'And who is this delicious young man? Really, Genevieve, you are full of surprises. Come in! Come in! Is this a social call?'

The Woman stepped into the open arms and was engulfed in the Knitter's woolly embrace. She was glad she had warned Harris to just follow whatever might ensue. When the Knitter was in Genevieve mode, anything could happen – she would potentially be rather continental and that was something few were familiar with these days.

Once inside, the noise of the dogs was almost unbearable. They sounded like the Hounds of Hell, baying from the back of the house now, banished by the Knitter when she went to open the door.

'I didn't know you had dogs,' the Woman said.

'Pardon, dear?' the Knitter leaned in, cupping her hand.

'I. Didn't. Know. You. Had. Dogs.'

'Oh, yes. I should have said. I've got a couple of dogs, now. Newfoundlands. A bit big for some tastes, but their hair makes wonderful sweaters. I sit and comb them of an evening and then spin the combings. So warm and also of course, very economical. Anyway, come and meet them. They're very friendly chaps, if a little exuberant.' She had walked as she talked and was now pushing on a door at the end of the hall. Before it was even half open, the barking stopped and two enormous dogs, mountains of black and tan, leapt out and were shimmying around the visitors' legs like a tide of hair and muscle. Harris wasn't much of a dog lover but decided to consider these things as more like horses. He didn't like horses much, either, but they were more to his taste than dogs. One was now licking his ear, without really having to reach up much. The other had descended into a heap of fur and drool at the Woman's feet.

'They're old softies,' the Knitter said. 'Just let them say hello and then they'll leave you alone. Let's go through into the sitting room. They have their beds there and they'll settle down there quite happily.'

The sitting room went from the front of the house to the back, with the stained glass motif repeated in each window. To the rear, the view was stunning. A long lawn sloped down to a thread of river running through a gorge below. The opposite side of the gorge was rimmed with trees but here, on the house side, there were just a few flower beds and a strategically placed bench.

The Woman and Harris went to the window as if drawn by magnets and just drank in the view.

'It doesn't matter how often I come here,' the Woman said, 'this view still takes my breath away.'

'It is lovely, isn't it?' the Knitter agreed. 'When I have a rush job on, I have to sit with my back to it, or I would get nothing done at all.'

The dogs had, as predicted, undulated down onto their beds and were dropping off to sleep, huge heads on gargantuan paws. The sound of their breathing mingled with the birdsong and distant murmur of the river. Harris thought to himself that he could happily stay here for the rest of his life. He leaned his forehead on the glass and gave himself up to the beauty.

The Knitter nodded to him and poked the Woman in the ribs.

'Your friend is very quiet, Gen,' she said.

'He's had a lot to take in, the past few days,' the Woman said. 'We're on a bit of an adventure, Bobby and me.'

'An adventure!' The Knitter's eyes sparkled. 'How exciting. Anywhere nice?'

'Don't know, to tell the truth. We're looking for Jack Jones.'

The Knitter chuckled and a knitting needle fell from her hair. She picked it up and looked at it closely, pushing her glasses up her nose to help focus. 'My ivory Number Ten! I've been looking for that!' She let the glasses slip down her nose again. 'Did you say Jack Jones? They've been airing his best of records. It's getting a bit desperate now, to be frank. I can almost recite it as he goes along. On holiday, is he? I don't remember him ever having one before.'

'He ... well, no one seems to know where he is. Bobby here is on his trail.'

'Oooh.' The Knitter had another moment of excitement. 'Sleuth, are you, lad? I've got all the Patricia Wentworths and a few Ngaio Marshes. I *do* love a whodunnit.'

'In a way,' he said, lowering his eyes modestly.

The Woman looked at him fondly. He was learning to dissemble, bless him. He was a quick learner, quicker than she had dared to hope.

'Anyway, sit down, sit down. Mind out for knitting needles. And dog hair. And ...' there was a yowl and Harris leapt up from his chosen chair '... the cat. She's an Angora, for the hair, you see, and she's a bit temperamental, love her. That's it, that's it. Just pat your knee and she'll come back.'

The fattest cat Harris had ever seen fixed him with a baleful green eye and sat down heavily on his feet.

'There, you see. She likes you.'

'What happened to the chinchillas?' the Woman asked, looking around.

'I've had to move them out into the old stables,' the Knitter said. 'I had the old vicar from the village round, oooh, when was it ... probably a year or so ago now, poor chap; dead now of course. Yes. Mmmm. And they were ...' she glanced at Harris and raised an eyebrow. He looked a little virginal, to her eyes.

'No, go ahead,' the Woman said. 'He's more knowing than he looks.'

'Gladys?' the Knitter whispered.

The Woman nodded.

'Oh, well, then, I don't need to mince my words. To tell you the truth, they were at it like weasels – the chinchillas, that is – and the poor man didn't know which way to look. So, out they went. Then I heard he'd died and well, I must say the whole place smells a bit fresher without them, so they stayed out. I have them in, one at a time, of course, for combing.'

Harris was wondering if she had any pets she didn't comb. He was a little shy of going too near in case she decided to try to harvest any of his body hair.

She looked at him. 'Don't worry, lad,' she said. 'The only human hair I knit with is my own. There is something of me in every garment I create.'

He looked stricken. How did she know ...?

The Knitter laughed and slapped both hands down on her knees. 'Bless the boy,' she said. 'Everyone thinks the same as you, lad,' she said. 'I have no special powers beyond knit and purl.'

'Any interesting projects on at the moment?' the Woman asked.

'Funny you should ask,' the Knitter said, rummaging down the side of her chair. 'I am designing a rather interesting tank top for a neighbour. Here's the pattern, if you want to have a look. Any idea why they're called tank tops, by the way? I went out with a tank commander, back in the day; none of his people wore them.'

She handed over a piece of paper, covered in closely

written lines. Harris craned across to look.

'k1p4k12s1k2togpssocbl3B ...' he read. 'What is that?'

'It's a knitting pattern, lad,' the Knitter said. 'Does your mother never knit? Your grandmother?'

'No.' Harris had to admit that the only thing his mother ever did apart from smoke endless dog ends and work out ways that he had transgressed some arcane rule, was ironing. It wasn't until he had gone to live with the Landlady that he realised that the idea of ironing was to remove creases, not put them in. 'She wasn't much for handicrafts, my mother wasn't.'

'I'm sorry,' the Knitter said, hearing the past tense. 'Has your mother passed away?'

'I have no idea,' Harris said, baldly.

'I see. Well, in that case, let me explain.' The Knitter pulled out two needles from her hair and to the surprise of Harris there was a couple of inches of knitting already done and a small ball of wool attached. It had been invisible amongst the rest. 'K1, you see, is knit one stitch, thus.' She stuck the needle in and wound the wool around it. 'Through, round, through and off, see.'

He nodded.

'Then P4 is purl four. You put the needle in from the other side, but it's essentially the same. Then you ...'

'Knit twelve.' Harris was getting the hang of it.

'Indeed you do,' the Knitter said, beaming at the Woman. 'He's a quick learner.' She quickly did the stitches the pattern required. 'Then you slip one, see, then you knit two together and pass the slipped stitch over. That way, you have reduced the number of stitches on the needle. Then you cable, which means you put the next three stitches forward – some people use another needle, but I just drop them and pick them up – knit the next three and then the dropped ones.' She held out the knitting. 'See?'

Harris looked at the piece of work in her hand. 'It's like a code,' he said. He liked codes.

The Knitter pulled her hand back as if he had bitten it and the Woman, who thought she had seen everything, jumped in surprise.

The Woman recovered her composure first. 'It is, a bit,' she said.

The Knitter soon was calm again. 'Everything in life is a code,' she said, her voice perhaps a tad higher than it had been before.

'Daisies,' Harris said.

'Pardon?'

'Daisies. One. One. Two. Three. Five. Eight. Thirteen.'

'Is he ... well?' the Knitter asked.

'It's the Fibonacci sequence,' the Woman said. 'You just add the two numbers which come before. So zero and one are one, one and one are two, two and one are three ...'

'I see, Gen, but ... daisies?'

'May I go out for a moment?' Harris said, getting up.

'Yes ... of course.' For a moment, the Knitter wondered if he were house trained and then reminded herself that he was a human, not another combable animal.

He was back in a minute, with a daisy. He pointed to the middle and counted the first few rows with her, then stood back, expectant.

The Knitter did not disappoint. With her glasses firmly in place, she looked at the centre of the tiny flower, bright in her hand. 'I see it,' she said, looking up excitedly. 'I *see* it!'

The Woman looked so proud she might have hatched Harris out herself.

'Does everyone know this?' the Knitter asked, excitedly.

'If you mean, does everyone but you until just now know it, no, they don't. It was first described thousands of years ago but it seems to be a well kept secret. Useful?' The Woman put her head on one side.

'Useful? Gosh, yes.' She looked up, her eyes alight. 'It means I can do ... tablecloths. Shopping bags ... it means I don't have to do jumpers all the time. Thank you *so* much, young man. Thank you *so* much.' She jumped up and took both his hands in hers. 'Now, something to celebrate, perhaps. A Pastis, Genevieve?'

'Er, perhaps not ...' The Woman opened her eyes

wide and then nodded in the direction of Harris.

'Ah, no, perhaps not. What about … a tisane?'

'No.'

'Ah … tea?'

'Only if it's dandelion.'

'What about Darj …?'

'Mmmph.'

'Victoria sponge?'

'Perfect.'

'It's real cream,' the Knitter said, apologetically.

'Not to worry. Bobby here knows all about dairies and how we can … obtain things. Good, English dairies. See?'

'Oh. *English* dairies. I see. Right. Some nice sponge cake with cream and jam and a cup of dandelion tea, coming up.' The Knitter bustled out and almost immediately straight back in. 'Be here in a jiff.'

Harris sat there, confused. Who was making the tea?

His question was answered when a girl came in, bumping the door open with her ample backside.

'Put the tray here, dear,' the Knitter said. 'Thank you.'

The girl put the tray down on a low table between the Knitter and the Woman and went out, with a small nod.

'Was she a *maid*?' Harris asked, aghast. 'Aren't they illegal?'

'Maids are, of course,' the Knitter said, without a pause. 'Hester is my lodger, she does work in the house in lieu of rent.'

Harris frowned. That sounded quite like a maid to him. And, another thing, how was it that this house only had the two of them in it? It was *huge*. Surely, it was breaking the law – where were the Street Wardens? He opened his mouth to speak but the Woman was there first.

'How many lodgers is it you have now?' she asked. 'Ten, is it?'

The Knitter was startled then realized. 'Twelve now. Sometimes. They are off on their … holidays?'

'Very wise,' the Woman said. 'All go together. Give you and Hester a bit of a break.'

'That's right,' the Knitter said, grasping at straws.

'Now, Gen, it has been lovely to see you. But I expect you need to be going.'

Harris looked down at his cake and back up, stricken. It was lovely, so light it almost floated away. And he didn't know what they did to dandelion tea outside London, but it was always delicious.

'Finish your cake and tea,' the Woman said. 'I just need to go and …'

'Get measured for a jumper,' the Knitter said.

'Exactly. Be back soon.'

And the women left him to his cake, his tea … and his thoughts.

* * *

When they had safely gone, the Knitter went into her parlour. Hester was a maid no longer but a secretary, fiercely typing away at a battered Remington, lifted from the corridors of power in a quiet moment. The Knitter picked up the phone and got the operator.

'Clackmannon 318,' she said. Not that Harris was there to hear it – or Genevieve – but the voice was harder now, more in charge.

'Putting you through,' the voice said from along the wires.

There was a series of clicks from Clackmannon. 'Clements Biscuits,' a voice said.

'Sir Marmaduke,' the Knitter said.

'Who do you want?' the voice asked.

'Cromwell if he's there. Fairfax if I must.'

'How about Pym?'

'Oh, all right.'

'Who's this?'

The Knitter tutted. 'You're not following protocol, Hampden. The codes. It's Ireton.'

There was a pause. 'Righto. Putting you through.'

The Knitter tutted. Where *did* they find these people?

'Pym,' a dark brown voice said.

'Ireton,' the Knitter answered. 'She's been here.

Genevieve.'

There was another pause. 'Genevieve. She's a long way from home.'

'She is. Had an idiot with her, a lad, probably mid-twenties. They're looking for Jack Jones.'

'Jones?' Pym echoed. 'She told you this?'

'She did,'

'Well, that's fascinating. We hear he's done a runner from his studio but that was days ago and it's all gone horribly quiet since then. I'll brief Cromwell and Fairfax and get back to you. Stay by the phone.'

THE MAJOR

The chauffeur had picked them up at the same corner and dropped them off in a secluded lane which ran through a nearby wood. A small van was parked on the side of the road and the Woman walked confidently up to it and got in. She hit the wheel in annoyance.

'Sorry,' she said to Harris. 'I didn't know it would be this old heap. Good job we don't have to go far tonight. Can you just give it a turn or two with the crank? The handle is under the passenger seat, look.'

Harris was at home with this. The police station where he usually worked had almost no vehicles but the ones they did have all needed starting with a handle. Only Inspectors and above used the Railtons. He spat on his hands, bent his back with knees braced and gave her a couple of brisk turns. The engine caught second time and he got back in, stowing the handle where he had found it.

'You're good at that,' the Woman said.

Harris grinned then his face fell. 'Good to be good at something,' he said and turned his head to look out of the window. The list of things he was good at wasn't very long, if he were honest.

'You're good at numbers,' she said. 'Look how quickly you worked out that knitting pattern was a code.' She decided to throw him a crumb. She knew there was next to no chance that he would remember where the Knitter lived.

'Codes are easy to see,' he said. 'But what are her

115

codes for?'

'She doesn't always know. What she does is knit a pattern and then give the person the key. Then once they know it, they can throw away the paper – most people burn it, as I understand it – and then they wear the jumper or whatever it might be. Then they always have the code by them.'

He chewed on a thumbnail. 'So, she's s spy,' he said.

'Not any more.'

The silence between them grew, broken only by the growl of the engine.

'So … whose side was she on?' To Harris, everything was black and white.

'Spies aren't on anybody's side, when it comes to the crunch,' she said. 'The winning side, for preference.'

'And what is that?'

'You're being very philosophical today,' she remarked after a pause.

'I'm away from home,' he said, simply. 'I'm finding I don't like that very much.'

'Surely, you've been out of London before?' she said, incredulous. She had travelled all over the world, back in the day, and found the confines of an entire country too restricting. To be stuck in one city, even though it was the biggest in the world when counting was last allowed, would be to drive her mad.

'I'd never been out of the borough before,' he said. 'Even in my scouting days, the furthest we went was Hyde Park.'

'Goodness.'

It took a couple of dozen miles for that to sink in. The Woman hadn't been speechless for a good few years, but she was short of conversation now.

Harris broke the silence first. 'So, is your name really Genevieve?'

She looked quizzically at him. 'I told you, don't be surprised by anything she calls me.'

He looked at her. 'You haven't answered my question,' he said.

She drove on, looking at the road, not answering it still.

'So,' he tried a different tack, 'I assume she doesn't have a dozen lodgers, the Knitter.'

'No.'

'Just Hester. Just one lodger in a great big house like that.'

'Did you like her house?'

Harris's eyes lit up. 'I loved her house. Those little flowers in the stained glass – I don't think I have ever seen anything so beautiful.'

To a woman with a Gainsborough in the downstairs toilet, this was something of a surprise, but she let it pass. 'How beautiful would you have found it if we had had tea and cake with another dozen people in that room?'

'No. But it's the law, though.'

'That doesn't mean it's right.'

Harris turned to face her. 'The law is always right.'

'My goodness,' she said, mildly. 'So, you'll be turning yourself in at the next police station we come to, will you?'

'What for?' His eyes were out on stalks. 'I haven't done anything wrong. I'm looking for Jack Jones, that's all.'

She set her mouth in a line and nodded to herself. 'Sorry,' she said. 'I'm just counting up the number of illegal foods you have eaten since we met. Let me see ... bacon, eggs, cream ... and that's just your first breakfast. Then there's ...'

'All right, all right. But I didn't ask for them!' He was red in the face now, like a little boy caught out.

'You didn't turn them down, though, did you?' She sounded very like Nanny at times like these.

'It ... it would have been rude.' It was all he could come up with at short notice.

She gave a bark of laughter. 'It would indeed have been rude. And you a Boy Scout.'

'I haven't been a Boy Scout for years,' he sulked.

'You still see your old Scout Master, though,' she said, quietly.

'Have ... have you been *following* me?' he asked,

rearing up in his seat.

'Not as such. But let's just say I know a bit about you.'

'So,' he was outraged, 'so when you "found" me, it wasn't just chance.'

She laughed again and pushed him back in his seat. 'Don't loom over me, boy,' she said. 'You won't improve my driving that way. No, think what you like, but in fact it was just chance. I knew about you, yes, but when I found you sitting there, you could have knocked me down with a feather.'

'Why … why do you want me?' he whispered.

'You're interesting.'

'No, I'm not. I'm the most boring person I know.'

'You think that because you're biased,' the Woman said. 'You're the only person I have ever met outside a university who has heard of Fibonacci, for a start.'

'You've heard of him and you're outside of a university.' Harris was horrified. He sounded like himself, aged four.

'True. But that is just for now. I have been in universities, here and there, off and on.' She smiled to herself. That had shut him up for a bit.

'Apart from that, then,' he said.

'Look, Bobby,' she said and turned to face him for a disconcertingly long time, given that they were now on a main road at dusk with blackout covers on the headlights, though no plane had gone over the entire country for years. 'Look, don't overthink things. Jack Jones needs to be found and if he can't be found, we need to know he can't be found. *Capisci?*'

'I don't understand what that means.' He was getting testy and was beginning to feel she was taking the mickey out of him.'

'Do you understand?'

'No, I just said I didn't.' He folded his arms and looked out of the window like a grumpy toddler.

'No, I mean, *Capisci* means, do you understand?'

'Oh. I think I do, yes. You mean, we can't just let Jack Jones go off …'

'On his Jack Jones.'

'Yes, that. Without us knowing where he has gone, who with and preferably why.'

'And there you have it, you see. In a nutshell, perfectly understood and shared with me so I understand.'

'Of course you understand,' he said, but he wasn't sulking now. 'You more or less said that to me not three minutes ago.'

'I did, that's true,' she agreed. 'But anyone else would understand it as well, which is the important thing. Why did you decide you wanted to find Jack Jones?'

'I ... I don't know. I don't think I decided at all. I just asked and they said yes and I ...'

'Shit! Shit! Shit!' She was banging on the wheel.

'What?' he almost shouted. 'What's the matter?'

'Use your eyes, boy,' she growled. 'Two o'clock.'

He did as he was told and saw them. 'Home Guard,' he muttered.

There was a barrier across the road with a little hut alongside it and three armed men stood there, in khaki and battle bowlers. 'It's just Look, Duck and Vanish,' he said, trying to make light of the situation.

'That's how it was when they started, yes, but not now.' She was slowing down as the men fanned out across the road. 'Now, they're a different animal altogether. I didn't expect these bastards to be as far north as this. Look,' she shot him a glance, 'You're my son, all right? And you're an elective mute.'

'A what?'

'You can't speak. You can hear and understand, but you can't speak. Whatever I tell them, just go along with it. Are you carrying papers?'

'No,' he told her. 'Regulation Thirty Eight C.'

'Good. At least the Government gets something right.'

She crunched her gears as she brought the van to a halt and she wound down the window.

'Is there a problem ...' she checked his sleeve, 'Corporal?'

Harris hadn't noticed it but suddenly there was a small

119

wad of notes in the Woman's lap. Nobody used money any more, but it still opened doors.

'Papers,' the Corporal snapped.

The Woman ferreted in her handbag slung over the handbrake and produced them. The other two Guards were circling the van, scowling in at Harris and trying to see what was in the back.

The Corporal looked at the documentation. 'Mrs Helen Jenkins,' he read aloud.

'That's right,' she said, smiling.

The Corporal glanced across at Harris. 'And who's this?'

'My son,' she said. 'Bobby Jenkins.'

'Papers,' the Corporal barked.

Harris sat there like a rabbit in the headlights. His first instinct was to talk his way out of trouble, tell them he was a policeman, that they were all on the same side, but as an elective mute for the last minute and a half, he knew he couldn't say a thing.

'He's under my care,' the Woman said. 'Ever since his breakdown. Defectives don't have to carry papers.'

'Who told you that?' the Corporal asked.

'It's the law,' she reminded him.

The Corporal looked as though he was chewing a wasp. If there was anything he hated, it was women with attitude. 'Is it?' he said, with all the venom he could muster. 'And where are you both going this fine afternoon?'

The Woman softened. As if from nowhere, a tear trickled down the side of her nose. 'My dear old mum,' she sniffed and rummaged in her handbag again, this time pulling out a battered photograph. It was the Knitter. 'She hasn't got long.' The Woman's lip was trying not to wobble. 'We got the call last night. There wasn't time to set up the usual travel arrangements. We just got in the old jalopy and off we went.'

'From Hammersmith?' the Corporal was reading Helen Jenkins' papers again.

'That's right. Fontevraux Avenue. Number Twenty-Eight. Just by the bridge. Do you know it?'

He ignored her. 'Open up,' he barked to his men.

The van doors swung wide with a creak and Harris jumped.

'Got a nervous disposition, has he, your lad? Along with his other problems? You frightened of loud noises, lad?'

'He can't answer you, corporal,' she said wistfully. 'We both wish he could. He's never been able to since his dad ...' and her voice trailed away.

'Nothing 'ere, Corp,' one of the Guards shouted and slammed the doors.

'And where does she live, this dear old departing Mum of yours?'

'Wombourne.'

The Corporal's eyes lit up. Got her! 'Well, you're going in the wrong direction, Missus,' he said, triumphantly. 'Wimborne's thataway!' He jerked with his thumb over his shoulder in the way she had come. He had been there once on a dirty weekend with a girl from the ATS, Before, so he knew exactly where it was.

The Woman looked at him with narrowed eyes. He had fallen straight into her trap. She smiled. 'No, not *Wim*borne,' she told him. '*Wom*bourne. It's ahead and to the left. But a few miles yet, so, if you don't mind ...' and she switched on the ignition.

'Uh, uh,' the Corporal said. 'It's above my pay grade, lady, to allow a journey of this kind, whatever the circumstances. You'll have to follow me and talk to the Major.'

'Very well,' she said and took her papers back. 'Oh,' she smiled at one of the Guards. 'Would you be an angel and crank for me? Got a mind of her own, I'm afraid, this baby.'

Grudgingly, the Guard took the crank handle from Harris and got to work while the Corporal straddled his Vincent Meteor and kicked it into action, waving at the Woman to follow him.

For a mile or so, the pair rode in silence. Then she said, 'It's all right, you know, even elective mutes *breathe* occasionally.'

It was true that Harris had been holding his breath and he let it out now, his cheeks fluttering. 'Dear God,' he said. 'How did you *do* that?'

'Do what?' she asked.

'Lie through your teeth like that.'

She laughed. 'Years of experience, dear boy, years of experience. But don't get too relaxed – I've got to do it again in a minute. Alternatively, of course, I could just put my foot down and spread this bastard all over my bonnet.'

She caught the terrified look on Harris's face.

'Just joking, Bobby,' she said, 'Just joking.'

* * *

It didn't look all that different from Bobby's nick. The smell was different, though – blanco and boot polish rather than damp biscuits and stewed dandelion tea. Faded posters on the wall including an absurd amount of 'Keep Calm and Carry On' and 'Let Us Have the Courage to Endure' posters plastered over each other like some sort of mad wallpaper.

The Corporal had flagged the van down inside the Home Guard camp perimeter and had told the pair to wait there. Then they were ordered out and into a Nissen hut, officers, for the use of, where a spotty youth was making tea. They were allowed to sit down.

The Major, when he arrived, was something of a disappointment, at least to the Woman. She had hoped for lantern-jawed, broad-shouldered, perhaps wearing a kilt – she did appreciate a well-turned calf on a man. In fact the *actual* Major looked like an accountant, with thick-rimmed glasses and a battledress that fitted him nowhere. The shoulder strap of his Sam Browne was too short so that the belt itself nestled somewhere under his diaphragm and his pistol butt was under his right armpit. He read the papers the Woman had showed him.

'This is your son, Mrs Jenkins?' he asked.

'Yes,' she said, patting his hand. 'This is Bobby.'

'How old is he?'

'Twenty-five,' she said.

So far, it was going like a routine interview. 'How long has he been silent?' the Major asked.

'Ooh, it must be ten years now, since soon after the Dunkirk disaster. Bobby was just about to leave school when he heard his dad was one of the few who came back from the beaches.'

'Which outfit was he with?' the Major asked.

'Ox and Bucks,' she said. 'Of course, he didn't talk about it much.' Her face darkened. 'And that was the problem, wasn't it, Bobby?'

Harris read the silent signs fast and bowed his head as the Woman squeezed his hand.

'You know what boy are, Major ... oh, do you have children?'

'No,' the Major said, 'My wife and I were not blessed.'

'Oh, shame.' Harris thought she was ladling it on a bit thick, but it wasn't his place to say so. In fact, it wasn't his place to say anything. 'Well, Bobby wanted to know what his dad did in the war, that sort of thing. I told him not to keep on about it,' she dabbed at her eyes with a handkerchief and blew her nose like a foghorn, 'but you would do it, wouldn't you, Bobby, love?'

He hung his head still lower.

'One day, my husband – Alf, his name was – one day, he just snapped. He slapped Bobby across the face and tried to ...' she struggled to compose herself, 'he tried to ...' and she squeezed the lad's hands tight, 'tried to strangle him. Well, it was all those pent-up memories of fighting his way back to the coast, you see. We found out later that his unit had got cut off and they were in a bombardment for two days. Well, Alf was never exactly strong, mentally, if you know what I mean, so he just cracked. It didn't come out until Bobby's questioning.' She shuddered and steadied herself until she could go on. 'I pulled him off Bobby and called the police. I didn't know what else to do.'

The Major realized that the Woman's handkerchief was rather sodden by now and he passed her his own. She took it gratefully and sniffed back the tears. 'They put Alf away. I visited him at first, but he'd become totally unhinged. They wouldn't let me take Bobby and in the end told me not to come either. It was heartbreaking. And from the day of the attack, Bobby,' she managed a smile through the haze of her tears, 'Bobby has never said a word.'

The silence hung heavy in the Major's office until he cleared his throat and said, 'And this lady ...' he looked down at the photograph, 'Your mother ...'

'Yes,' the Woman smiled again, but not for long. 'My dear old mum. To be honest ...' Harris couldn't look her in the face when she said that, '... I don't know how she's kept going as long as she has. We got the telegram late yesterday. And I told your corporal – such a helpful man – I told him we had no time to make the usual arrangements.'

'No, no, of course not.' The Major nodded in sympathy. 'I do understand. Look ... er ... Mrs Jenkins, contrary to what you've probably heard, we're not all heartless martinets in the Home Guard. My own dear mother ...' he caught the look on the Woman's face and immediately changed tack. 'Suffice it to say, you may continue your journey to ... where is it again?'

'Wombourne.'

'Exactly. I'll have my Adjutant telephone ahead and clear any more Observation Posts for you, to save time.' He stood up and extended a hand. 'I hope you make it in time,' he said. 'Goodbye.'

'Goodbye, sir.' The Woman shook his hand. 'And thank you. Bobby, say goodbye to the kind man.'

The Woman knew – and Harris knew – that she was chancing her arm with this one. But the Knitter had been right; he was a quick learner. And Harris just nodded and smiled.

'Corporal,' the Major boomed out of the hut door. 'See this lady back to the road, would you? Cleared for her journey.'

It wasn't the best news the Corporal had heard, but he knew his place. He touched the brim of his battle bowler. 'Very good, sir,' and felt the need to crank the Woman's van again before getting on his bike.

The Major looked at the sodden handkerchief on his desk, sighed and threw it into the bin. Yes, he told himself for the umpteenth time, there were a lot of sad stories in this war.

They just kept on turning up. He looked at the map on the wall, showing just his bit of Merry England, with the camps marked as fake pubs and the roadblocks as halt signs. Suddenly, and he didn't know why, he remembered his schooldays at Marlborough and struggling to read Homer's *Iliad*. A war that lasted forever. Surely, such things were not possible. But that was ancient fiction, the Trojan War. This, he shook his head at the nonsense on the map, this was now. And it was real.

The phone rang, jolting him away from the Trojan plain and the thundering clash of armies. 'Carstairs,' he said, 'Er ... oh, all right. Bring him down.'

Police. Just what he needed after the day he'd had. He straightened his battle-dress blouse. No one had told him you don't wear a Sam Browne with one of those and no matter how often he fiddled with it, it just wouldn't sit right. There was a rap at the door and a stout policeman strode in, bald of head and grim of face.

'Are you the commandant?' he asked.

'I am,' the Major said. 'Major Carstairs.'

Bloody typical, the policeman thought. A sodding crown on each shoulder and he doesn't know what day it is. 'Sergeant Baker,' he said. 'V Division, the Met.'

'The Met?' The Major shook his head. 'You're a long way from home, Sergeant. Can I get you a cup of tea?' He offered the man a chair, too.

'Thank you, sir, no,' Baker said. 'I understood that you have recently had a woman and a man in this office.'

'I have indeed,' the Major said, sitting down. 'A tragic case.'

'In what way?'

'They're on their way to a death visitation,' the Major told him. 'The lady's mother.'

'And the man?'

'He's the lady's son. Poor lad suffered a trauma years ago. He can't speak.'

Baker sighed. 'On the contrary,' he said. 'Sometimes, you can't shut him up.'

'What?'

'He isn't the lady's son. He's Constable V312 Robert Harris, one of us, I used to believe.'

'What? He's a policeman?' The Major had gone quite pale.

'So I was always led to believe,' Baker said. 'What name did she give?'

'Er … Jenkins. Helen Jenkins. Hammersmith address.'

'Jenkins, my arse,' Baker growled. 'Ditto Hammersmith. Where did they say they were going?'

'Wombourne.'

'Yes, well, we can forget that for a start,' Baker said. 'What she said and where they're going will be Black Bishop to White Knight.'

'Wait. I haven't cleared the road blocks yet. My lads'll catch 'em.'

'Don't bother,' Baker said. 'I told you; they wont be following those roads.'

'Just what's going on?' the Major wanted to know.

'You may well ask,' Baker said, getting up. At the door, he paused. 'Tell me, Major, did the woman mention Jack Jones at all?'

'Jack Jones?' the Major frowned. 'What, the wireless chappie? No. Should she have?'

THE SINGER

For half an hour, Harris couldn't hear anything except the growl of the van's engines, the rattle of its back doors and the grating of the Woman's gears. He noticed that after the Corporal waved them off at the outpost, she swung left and doubled back across a rough field that skirted the wood. Whatever road they were on now, it wasn't the one they were on before.

'Now,' she said at last, easing up on the accelerator, 'where were we before that little nonsense? Oh, yes, if memory serves, I was asking you why you wanted to find Jack Jones.'

'Umm ...'

'You walked out of the front door and let your feet guide you. And so far, they haven't really done you a bad turn, have they? No one has beaten you, stolen your money, thrown you into an oubliette anywhere?'

'What's an oubliette?'

'I forget. Anyhow, here we are, toddling along, up and a bit to the right and I think we're getting nearer. Had you had *any* clues thrown your way before you started eating all my food and ...' she glanced sideways at him and decided to go easy on the Gladys references '... becoming very friendly with my female Boy?'

'Well, I met an old man who had been a bishop and was now a butler if that's any help.'

'Ah, the Bishop. Yes, I know him. Was the Actress in

residence?'

Harris had stopped being surprised. 'No. I half thought she might be with Jack Jones. They seem to go back a while. There was a picture of him on a dock somewhere.'

'As for the Actress being with him — you could be right. And as it happens, our host for tonight might know.'

'Where are we going?' It was fully dark now, the van's grilled headlights not making much of a difference on the country roads. Harris's stomach was rumbling.

'Well, here, as it happens.' The Woman took a frighteningly sharp left turn in a gap between two tall privet hedges and drew up what seemed like mere inches from the wall of a house. 'I hope he's in. But if he isn't, I know where the key is.' She got out and then turned and spoke urgently into the dark of the van's interior. 'Whatever you do, and I mean *whatever* you do, don't mention Vera Lynn. He will but when that happens, just change the subject.'

'Why?'

'Always why,' she said. 'Little boys should be seen and not heard.' She tapped his hand. Then she slammed the door and walked round the corner of the house, fuming. She got more like Nanny every day. 'Just don't, that's all.'

'Nobody talks about her anyway,' Harris pointed out, catching her up. 'Not since …'

'Exactly. But it's more than usually important here. It makes my friend … a bit maudlin.' She knocked on the wood of a door set back behind a tangle of twisted roses.

A light popped on and a head appeared in a small gap as the door eased open. 'Who's there?' The voice was like honey dripping on velvet.

'It's me, you daft lump,' the Woman said. 'You got my message, didn't you?'

'Of course I did.' The door was flung open. 'But you can't be too careful these days, can you?'

Harris was more taken aback than he could say. The man who had opened the door had a face even more familiar than Jack Jones, twice as handsome as well. His slicked back hair had its usual mirror shine, his eyes — which Harris always suspected were made up — shone like toffee behind coal-black lashes. His little 'tache, which always looked painted on in his publicity photos, was indeed, at this close quarter, painted on. All in all, it was like looking at a waxwork suddenly come to life.

Before Harris could speak, the Woman turned to him. 'No names, dear, please. The neighbours don't know who lives here and the walls may well have ears.'

This was no odder than his life had been for the past few days, so Harris shrugged and followed her into the house. That it was a short term rental was only too obvious. There was furniture, of course, but bought all of a piece from a department store. Some bits still had the labels on. The sofa had an elaborate network of antimacassars – in this case, just as well – and candlewick spread over it to protect the fabric underneath. The curtains hung with rigid symmetry. Only the wireless looked like a personal possession. The tuning dial was almost worn smooth and the surface behind it had no letters on it, just a swirl of worn bakelite. A chair was pulled up to it and in certain lights it was possible to see the smear of brilliantine where the Singer had leant his head against the speaker. It was a lonely room for a lonely man.

'I thought the message might be some kind of test,' the mellifluous voice said, the head inside a cocktail cabinet. 'Yet here you are.'

'Here I am,' the Woman said, sitting in an armchair that looked as if it had never borne the weight of a single buttock before.

'And with a Friend.' There was a weight of questioning in that simple phrase.

'Yes. This is Bobby. No,' she held up a hand, 'not his real name, so don't get aerated. But I have to call him something. We are on an Adventure.'

'An adventure?' The Singer didn't really join in the excitement in her voice. 'How ... exciting.'

'Well, it is,' she said. 'We are hunting Jack Jones.'

The Singer did a one shoulder shrug. Harris had never really liked him on the wireless, finding him rather oily, and now, in his sitting room, found him oilier still. Especially when it became clear that his head was in the cocktail cabinet just to make himself a very stiff whisky and nothing for his guests.

'I expect you'd heard he was missing,' the Woman persisted. She had heard that the Singer had gone a bit downhill since the incident, but had not expected it to be quite this bad.

'No. Not really.' The first whisky had gone and another had taken its place.

'It's been in the papers and also, of course, his show has been recordings since it happened.' She glanced at the well-worn wireless, the smear of hair oil against the speaker, the worn tuning dial.

'Never listen to him,' he said, then followed her glance. 'I listen to the wireless, of course I do. If you spin the dial often enough, sometimes one of my songs is on.'

Harris looked at the Woman, a little confused. He had heard that the Singer was banned on almost every airwave, not that there were that many to choose from. She gave him a warning look in return.

'That must be nice,' she said. 'A few royalties.'

'Hah!' He spun round and had to hang on to the back of the sofa while the room caught up with him. 'A few royalties. That'll be the day. No, the welching bastards, they only play the songs I did before I knew what a contract should say. So, not a penny piece do I see. I live here,' and he waved a hand to the corners of the room, 'by the kindness of strangers.'

Harris looked at the Woman, who winked.

'Food gets left. Drink. Though I must admit the drink is on fairly short rations. But ...' he gestured widely and slopped some whisky over his hand. 'One survives.'

'One seems to be doing all right,' the Woman said tartly, making a note to herself to halve the whisky allowance.

The Singer slumped suddenly into a chair. 'One survives,' he murmured again and appeared to drop off to sleep.

The Woman sighed. 'I was afraid of this,' she said to Harris. 'I had heard that he is more or less incoherent by nightfall. The Singer knows everyone, on a more or less superficial level. Or at least, he did Before. But he and the Actress ... that was something special, for them both, I think.'

'But ...' Harris couldn't really marshal his thoughts. He had thought that the Actress had gone off with Jack Jones, the love of his life.

'I know what you're thinking, love your little heart. You are thinking that anyone can only ever love one person. That you will love Gladys until the day you die. That you will wait for her all your life, and she will wait for you. Let me tell you something, sonny. Life is all about compromises. Yes, no doubt one day the Actress and Jack Jones were everything to each other. But that doesn't mean to say that there haven't been other people since.'

'It doesn't seem right.' Harris was on a very high horse and couldn't see a way down off it that didn't involve falling flat on his back with his legs in the air.

'Possibly not. But we're not here for the right, are we? Just for the best.' She kicked the Singer savagely on the ankle. 'Wake up. Just for a minute, please!'

The Singer leapt in his chair but didn't open his eyes. She kicked him again, so hard that anyone with working synapses would surely have complained but he merely turned his head and looked at her. After a long pause in which his pupils expanded and contracted several times, independently of each other, he spoke.

'Ow.'

'I'll give you "ow",' she said. 'I'll give you something to say "ow" about. Wake up, you horrible old soak. How could you let yourself get into a state like this? You, of all people.'

He looked wistfully at the wireless and the enormous studio photograph hanging above it, showing him in his prime. 'I was quite something, wasn't I?' he asked. 'Back then.'

Indeed he was. The Clark Gable moustache, the Brylcreem boy hair, the Tuxedo whiter than his teeth. He was Hutch, he was the Ink Spots. He had sung with every band from Carol Gibbons at the Savoy to Jack Hylton at the Piccadilly and Teddy Brown at the Café de Paris. 'Cocktails and laughter – what comes after?'

'DTs, by the look of it,' the Woman sneered. She looked at him regretfully, her face, for a moment, like Helen Jenkins', whose husband had been put away ad whose son had lost his voice. She had carried a torch for him herself, just like every other woman with a pulse in the country and most of the rest of the world. He had had the world at his feet when he made the one wrong decision that ruined his career and his life – he had believed everything that Vera Lynn told him. He would never go into details, but he had never been the same again. The Woman looked deep into his eyes but couldn't find the man who had once made women faint when he sang.

'You were indeed,' she said. 'You still are, under the whisky.'

He smoothed his hand over his hair and then touched the edges of his painted moustache in a gesture so often repeated he could do it in his sleep – and often did, depending on the dream of the moment. 'Bless you. You are an angel.' And suddenly, as if someone else had taken over his body, he was on his feet. His head was inclined upward and to the left – his right was his best side – one hand was on his heart and the other was extended towards the Woman, who looked rather taken aback, not a common occurrence.

'Bless you, for being an angel.' The voice was like caramel running down their spines. 'Just when it seemed, that heaven was not for me. Bless you for building a new dream, just when my old dream crumbled so helplessly.' The last note, pitch perfect and glorious, melted away and Harris and the Woman sat, momentarily entranced. The Singer slumped back into his chair.

'Sorry about that,' he said. 'I suppose you noticed that bum note in the eighth bar?'

The two shook their heads.

'Well, I did, and I can't live with myself these days. Sorry to have imposed that on you. Sorry …'

'It was lovely.' Harris wasn't much for music, but he knew what he liked. 'My landlady is musical. She would have loved that.' Harris was suddenly almost overcome with homesickness and dropped his head in case the tears came.

The Singer did that to people – it had once been his stock in trade.

The Woman shook herself. There was work to be done. 'Did the Bishop call here in the last day or so?' she asked, abruptly.

'The Bishop?' The Singer was suddenly cagey. 'Why do you ask?'

'Just interested, I suppose. You and he used to be such ... friends.'

'But he's of no account. Never has been.' He lurched towards her. 'It was always about you, wasn't it?'

'Was it?' She was serious for a moment.

'Friends. Hah! Yes, friends is what we were. Yes. Then I started to use words like "marriage" and "children" and you were off like a rat up a pope.'

'Pipe.'

'What?' She had broken his thread and made him confused.

'You mean "a rat up a pipe".'

'I know what I mean, thank you. But ... you may be right. The Bishop may have dropped in. I can't remember when, though.'

'Might it have been in the past week, do you think?'

'Hmmm. That sounds unlikely.'

'I think it might have been, though.' Even Harris could hear the Nanny coming through now. She would be saying 'spit spot' in a minute, he was sure.

'Has it rained this week?' the Singer asked.

Harris and the Woman looked at each other. If he was relying on the weather to know what day it was, things were worse that they had expected.

'I don't think so,' the Woman ventured.

'Then he might have done. I remember it wasn't raining when he came. He looked just the same as always. A little dodderier, perhaps.' He cocked his head, listening to a rerun of the last few words. He nodded and chuckled to himself. Dodderier was not an easy word to carry off by this time of night.

'Was there anyone with him?' Harris couldn't help

himself. This was supposed to be his hunt, after all.

The Singer looked confused. 'Anyone? Who, in particular?'

'No one. Just wondered …' Harris didn't know what would send the man down another rabbit hole.

'Let me see, now. I didn't *see* anyone, but there must have been. Unless he's learned to drive, and I can't see him doing that. Bishops have people, don't they? There was an engine running in the road.'

The Woman was surprised. The house was well set back behind hedges and hearing an engine running would have been quite a feat of concentration she would have assumed was beyond him.

He pointed to his ears when he saw her expression. 'These,' he said, 'are just as important as this,' he pointed at his throat, 'for a singer. I have always been blessed – or cursed, depending on your point of view – with hearing like a bat. I can't swear to the make, but it was something quite expensive, I would say. Very …' he ran his hand through the air '… smooth.'

'A driver, perhaps,' the Woman suggested. 'A chauffeur?'

'Might be,' he said. 'Bishops do have drivers, don't they? I'm sure they do. Is he still buttling? I keep calling him a bishop, but was he a monk, perhaps? I don't really remember.'

'Bishop.' Harris didn't have much to bring to the table, but he did know that.

'Bless you,' the Singer said.

The Woman looked at Harris and shook her head. Sometimes, it wasn't worth explaining.

'Anyhow, whenever it was and whoever was in the car, he didn't stay long. Most of the time he was talking bollocks. Something about a brave new world and was I interested? Well, I told him – or at least, I think I did – that Aldous Huxley never really did it for me and anyway, that was just a story, wasn't it? He didn't even have a little drinkie.' Having reminded himself, the Singer looked around him aimlessly for a glass, preferably full.

'So he didn't tell you where he was going?' The Woman sensed that these were the last few useful moments that the Singer had to give. 'Or why he'd called?'

'Going? I thought he might have come just to see me,' the Singer said, a little plaintively. 'He certainly made enough fuss, stroked my sleeve, said how sorry he was and all that. I think he may have blessed me, at some point. Still,' he mimed drinking, hoping that would do the trick, the changed tack again, 'too late for marriage and babies now, I would think, wouldn't you? Woman of your age?'

The Woman shrugged. She was pretty sure she could still just manage a baby if called upon to do so. Marriage, she wasn't so sure about. There was a husband still knocking around somewhere – she remembered putting him down at some society do or another and had forgotten to take him home when she left. So ... she became aware that the Singer was still speaking and pulled her attention back.

'He'll be back in London by now, surely? Even without a chauffeur.'

The Woman sighed and pushed herself up out of the chair. 'Come on, Bobby,' she sighed. 'Say bye bye nicely.'

'Bye bye nicely,' Harris said and the Woman smiled. So this young man had once been a child – what a relief to know.

But the Singer was asleep, his right hand twitching as he dreamed of glasses full of the best that Scotland had once had to offer.

Richard Denham

THE PROTECTOR

Secrecy had been a way of life for the Knitter for so long she didn't give it a second thought now. She still remembered fondly the early days, being wined and dined by Vee Vee Vivian and slobbered over by Rupert Vansittart. There was even a little ops room fumbling with dear old Hugh Sinclair. From time to time, she wondered where they all were now; cashiered, caged, shot? Who knew? Where they were not was still working in the murky Whitehall corridors of power; she was certain of that.

'Well, what can we do, darling?' Hughie had asked her when she had last confronted him, 'We've got no guns, no ships, no planes ...'

She had stopped him with 'Of course we have, but they'll achieve nothing locked up for a rainy day.' It was no use; she might as well have been talking to the Admiral's kettle. Vee Vee was much the same – 'It's policy, darling,' he'd told her with that pompous nasal drawl of his, 'Whitehall knows what he's about ...'

'About as much use as a chocolate teapot,' she had finished the sentence for him, continuing the kitchen metaphor. 'What happened to all that Bulldog stuff, fighting until the end and so on?'

Yes, it had all sounded rather fine on the wireless, when there was still a BBC and everybody thought the war could be won. But now ... now there was only one way to fight a war, *really* fight it, not cower behind the walls of

Fortress Britain. And that way was the Roundhead way.

'Well,' Rupert Vansittart had said, 'if you think you can carry on fighting after Dunkirk, good luck to you. You'll need a better army than we've got. How about the New Model?'

It had been a bitter joke at first, she remembered as she turned into the leafy lane that led to Headquarters. An army of the people. What had Oliver Cromwell said, back in the day? 'Give me a plain, russet-coated captain, one who knows about what he fights for and loves what he knows, above what you call a gentleman and is no other.' Well, the 'gentlemen of Whitehall', the operatives of SIS were silent now, scattered on the winds of indifference and fear. So the Knitter had taken Vansittart's advice. She had not founded the new New Model, but she had found it; like-minded people who wanted to carry on the fight.

She parked Wolseley and nodded to the guard at the side door. Here was a sign that read 'Wot? No survivors?' and she winked at it as though it would wink back.

'Cromwell in?' she asked the guard. Like the Regular sentries who used to change the guard at Buckingham Palace before the royals all scarpered, he ignored her, looking straight through the dotty, middle-aged cow with the knitting needles in her hair. 'Never respond, never explain' – the motto of the Auxiliaries from which the Roundheads had been born. They were the darkest of a dark world. No names, no packdrill, no humour, no survivors. Cross a Roundhead on a dark night and you could kiss your arse goodbye. Whenever she visited Roundhead HQ, the Knitter carried her specially-sharpened needles in her handbag. And a Browning automatic, just in case.

The place was, as usual, a hive of activity, secretaries carrying sheaves of paper, phones ringing and typewriters pinging.

'Roundnay Dom. How can I help you?

'Marston Moor Eight Nine One. Give me your details, caller.'

The Knitter knew where the kettle was, but this morning was too vital for a mere cuppa. Her fingers had just reached the drinks cabinet when a voice stopped her.

'Ireton,' it said. 'We're not made of money, you know. There's a war on.'

She twisted her face into a 'you-caught-me-out grin. 'Oh, come on, Fairfax, you can't deny a woman a little of what the doctor ordered.'

He laughed. 'Go on, then. And I'm counting fingers, by the way.'

She poured a glass for them both and sat down heavily in the depths of the armchair, cradling the glass in her hand. 'Whenever I ask myself what Scotland is for, I have a little sip of this and it all becomes clear. Cheers, m'dears.' She and Fairfax clinked glasses. He was smaller than she remembered, ground down, no doubt, by the effort of it all. How do you keep a war going when everybody's given up? Fight the good fight with all thy might', she had sung back in her Sunday School, when the world was at peace and everybody could come and go as they pleased.

'Cromwell'll be along in a minute,' Fairfax said. 'He's having one of his days.'

'Black dog?'

''Fraid so. We're all a bit on edge, to be honest. There was an execution at Leominster the other day.'

'I heard,' she said. 'How many?'

'Eight,' he sighed, sitting down. 'Usual thing. Defeatism. You know, one of 'em actually said — and to my face, mind you — "What's the point of it all? We can't win, can we?"'

'Outrageous!' she tutted. 'Was there a trial?'

'Kangaroo only. You know, we used to do it properly, defence counsel, traitor's friend, that kind of thing. Nobody's got time for that now. We've got another five lined up at Truro.'

'Truro?' She raised an eyebrow. 'That's dangerously near to Government territory.'

'It is,' Fairfax acknowledged. 'The irony is, of course, that we're doing the Government's job for them.'

'Milksops,' she snorted.

The door jerked open and a larger man swept in,

immaculately uniformed as what would have passed for an officer of the Merchant Navy, had such a thing still existed.

'Ireton,' he nodded to her. 'I see Fairfax is being the perfect host.'

'Ah, the Lord Protector. Cromwell,' she raised her glass to him. Nobody stood up or saluted these days. All that went out with All Clear Sandwiches.

'Pym tells me Genevieve's on the move.'

'She is,' the Knitter nodded. 'Driving West with some simpleton youth in tow.'

'Who is he?' Cromwell poured himself a large one. 'Chauffeur? Heavy? Toy-boy?'

'Perhaps all three,' she said, 'although Genevieve was driving. No, it was the Jack Jones thing that bothered me.'

'I hear he's gone walkabout, as I believe the Aborigines said... say.'

'Apparently so.' Fairfax flicked open a file on his desk. 'Jones's last live broadcast was nine ... no, ten, days ago. Since then, it's been "The Best Of ..." and "As I Was Saying".'

'Couldn't just be ill, I suppose? Pulling a sickie?' Cromwell wanted all the angles covered.

'Our man on the inside says no,' Fairfax told him. 'Jones is a secretive bastard at the best of times, keeps to himself, hides in his rooms. Doesn't seem to have a home life.'

'That's been checked?'

'Yes. Eighty Three Wymondham Street, Maida Vale.'

'God in Heaven!' Cromwell rumbled.

'Quite. We've got a Copper whose beat that is who's sympathetic to the cause. Says he hasn't seen Jones for nearly two weeks, not that he was there that regularly before. But it is unusual for him not to go back there at all.'

'What's Genevieve's angle?'

'According to her, they – the lad and her – were on a mission to find Jack Jones. That's all I got.'

Cromwell humphed into his glass. 'Not helpful,' he said.

'Not at all,' the Knitter agreed. 'Can I offer a suggestion?'

'Be my guest.'

She held up her glass for a refill and cleared her throat. 'You'll fill me in, gentlemen,' she said, 'and correct me if I go wrong. The state of play, as I see if, is that the Government is no nearer to restarting the war than it ever was .'

'That's right,' Cromwell nodded. 'As you know, I have had talks in the shadows over the last two months among Cabinet friends and I might as well have talked to the broom cupboard. It's all "defend and hold" as usual.'

'And I take it our stance has not changed?'

'Of course not,' Fairfax said. 'To use the vernacular, "Get off your arse and take it to the enemy".'

'And who is the enemy?' the Knitter asked, arching her fingers around the cut crystal.

Cromwell allowed himself a chuckle, a rare occurrence at the best of times. 'I'd say we're beyond rhetorical philosophy, Ireton, but I'm not so sure. It's changing every day.'

'Thought it would be,' she nodded. 'And internally?' she quizzed him.

'How do you mean?' asked Fairfax.

'What she means, Fairfax,' Cromwell had to explain quite a few things to his Number Two these days, 'is that this dear of Blighty of ours is falling apart. At first of course, as we all know, it was just Wathmere and his Union plus a few fellow travellers of the Right, Lords like Brocket and Buccleuch. They were all secretly impressed by the enemy. Now, of course ...'

'Now,' the Knitter broke in, 'As I see it, we have a new problem. Defeatists, Doomsters, we're-all-going-to-diers, who spend their time moaning, wailing and wringing their hands.'

'And doing runners,' Cromwell added.

She laughed and wagged a finger at him. 'Precisely,' she said. 'Which is where friend Jones comes in. You were monitoring his wireless broadcasts, back in the day?'

'We were.' Cromwell said. 'They were growing more odd by the day. Oh, still the same "cheeky chappie" nonsense – "Have you heard the one about" bollocks. But between the lines ... Our man who understands the code stuff said he was passing on information to … and that's where, I'm afraid, the Intelligence broke down. We don't know who it was aimed at, but the message was clear enough.'

'Let's all get the hell out,' Fairfax cut in. 'Make a fresh start. Build again.'

'A new England,' the Knitter nodded.

'One with blue birds over it, and *we're* not afraid to use the old lyric. Nothing wrong with Vera Lynn if you're sane and not afraid to speak out.'

'Those codes,' the Knitter got back to Jack Jones. 'Did you hear the running grave this morning?'

'Exactly,' said Cromwell. 'It made no sense in the run of the programme, but he used it a lot. It was a password or an instruction, we're not sure which.'

'Genevieve's sure,' the Knitter said. 'Jack Jones has got to her. How, I don't know, but she was always a rebel.'

'Where does this lad fit in?' Cromwell asked. 'The one travelling with her?'

'I don't know,' the Knitter said, 'and I'm not sure it matters. He's part of her plan and she's part of Jack Jones's. What we have to decide is what to do about it.'

'We've got the roads covered,' Fairfax told her. 'They can't get much further and they're definitely making for the North West.'

'The Lakes?' the Knitter asked.

'My guess would be Liverpool,' Cromwell said. 'The Docks, as was.'

'The States,' the Knitter said.

'Go West, young man,' Fairfax murmured.

She stood up. 'The Home Guard's on the road further east,' she said. 'Stepping up operations.'

'Tell us about it,' Fairfax grumbled.

'So I must be away. You'll keep me informed?'

'Depend on it.'

She drained her glass and saluted them. 'Last one in Downing Street's a cissy,' she said.

'Downing Street,' they echoed and emptied their glasses too. The Knitter saw herself out.

* * *

Fairfax raised the decanter.

'Oh, all right,' Cromwell said. 'I shouldn't, but it's been a week, hasn't it?'

'He won't get away with it, you know.' Fairfax poured for them both. 'Jack Jones.'

Cromwell grunted. 'The Jack Joneses of this world always get away with it, Fairfax. That's why I know there's a God.'

'Tell me,' Fairfax settled into his chair again. 'You've known Ireton for years. And Genevieve. Were they close?'

Cromwell nodded, smiling at the memory of it. 'Like peas in a pod,' he said, 'back in the day. I knew them, long before this nonsense, when we all sang from the same hymn sheet. They could almost read each other's minds.'

'Really?'

'Well, that happens sometimes, doesn't it, with sisters?'

Richard Denham

THE DRESSER

B ack in the car, the Woman had little to say and Harris, who didn't know whether she had found anything out as he had no idea what she had expected to discover, kept quiet too. It was now fully dark and he didn't know where they were heading. He hoped there would be food, because his stomach was beginning to think his throat had been cut.

'Hungry?' the Woman said suddenly, and made him jump.

'Yes, I am. I know I have eaten really well lately and everything and, well, that ought to do, but I am absolutely famished!'

'I'm a bit peckish myself,' she agreed, and turned right suddenly, making Harris gasp and two rabbits leap for their lives. 'I think this is the turning. I haven't been here for years. I may have to talk our way in, so don't say anything. It might be tricky.'

They pulled up in front of a cottage which had seen better days. But closer to, there were signs of life. The knocker, in the shape of the Lincoln Imp, was bright with polish and the roses around the door were tied neatly to a robust trellis. From inside, there was the most tantalizing smell of cooking, but quite what it might be was hard to tell. Harris sniffed. Cake? Bread? It was delicious, whatever it was. The Woman smiled at him in the dark.

'Love her. She does like to bake.'

The door edged open and a single eye peeped round it. 'Who is it?'

'It's me,' the Woman said. Harris was longing to hear her say her name. Genevieve, was that it? Darling? He felt sure she was Someone. Royalty, even. Aristocracy certainly. But she never used it and nor did anyone else. It was all very well to insist on no names, no pack drill, but he was a policeman, when all was said and done, and he wasn't getting the right information. He shuddered to think what he would be able to write in his report and what Baker's and the Inspector's take on all this would be. He'd been gone for days now and hadn't reported back as he said he would. At the moment, he would not manage much more than his name and metaphorical collar badge number. But so far 'It's me' had seemed to be enough.

'Who's me?' The voice and the eye were suspicious. Harris held his breath.

'Come on, dear. You know me. Open the door a bit wider and let me come into the light. Under the wrinkles, I am still the same.'

Reluctantly, the door edged open a little more and the Woman stepped forward. There was a pause and then a shrill, drawn out cry of delight.

'It's *you*!' Harris cursed under his breath. 'Oh, it *is* you! Madam and I were only talking about you the other day.'

The Woman smiled. That was one question she didn't have to ask, at any rate. 'So, she's been to see you?'

'Of *course*! Madam wouldn't pass my door without coming to see me. But come in, come in. Who's this you've got with you?' A pair of shrewd eyes raked Harris up and down. 'He's a bit young for you, dear, isn't he? A bit ingenu?'

The Woman laughed. 'This is Bobby, dear. He's … well, can we come in and have a sit and a natter? We've been travelling a while and Bobby is having a bit of a time of it, one way and another.' She bent her head and whispered in the old woman's ear.

The woman laughed explosively. '*Really?*' she chortled. 'At his age? Why, by the time you were his age, you'd … was it the Duke, dearie, or that dancer in the chorus?'

The Woman laughed as well and swatted her hand at the woman. 'Depends,' she said. 'Either. Both.' She turned to Harris and said, 'We're leaving you out. Sorry, let me explain. This is ...' she looked at the woman, who shook her head, 'this is the Dresser, who looked after the Duchess and me back when we were both treading the boards. I didn't last long, did I, dearie?'

The Dresser chuckled. 'You danced like a baby elephant,' she said, 'for all you weighed next to nothing wringing wet. But Madam, now ... she was like a feather over the stage. Everyone loved her.'

By this time the conversation had taken them into a cosy sitting room, with an overstuffed sofa and two squashy chairs flanking a fireplace. There were knickknacks everywhere and Harris tucked his elbows well in as he made his way to the furthest chair. The other two sat side by side on the sofa and the Dresser held one of the Woman's hands in both of hers. The Dresser peered shortsightedly at the Woman and tutted.

'You've let yourself go a bit, dear,' she said. 'No offence meant, of course.'

'Of course not,' the Woman said. 'And none taken, I'm sure. But look again.'

The Dresser peered closer and then reached out a tentative hand. ''Oh, my,' she said softly. 'But why?'

'You can't be too careful in my line of work,' the Woman said, 'and no one looks twice at me these days. A few wrinkles make you more or less invisible.'

The Dresser laughed and suddenly jumped up. 'Oh, my sponge!' she said. 'I must just go and check my oven. Excuse me, dears.' She turned to smile at Harris, who had thought he was forgotten.

When she was out of the room, he spoke quietly to the Woman. 'Are you in disguise?' he asked, incredulous. 'Who *are* you? Should I be arresting you?'

'To take your questions in order,' she said, 'yes, to an extent; I'm afraid if I told you I would have to kill you and finally, probably, but I would much rather you didn't. We're getting along all right, aren't we? And we are getting closer to

Jack Jones all the time. It would be a shame for you to lose out on the find of the century, wouldn't it? Promotion guaranteed, I would imagine. Picture in the papers. Make your mother proud.'

Harris suddenly realised that he didn't want any of that and that the chances of him remaining a policeman when all this was over were vanishingly small. But he nodded and smiled at her. 'If you would rather I didn't know,' he said, 'then I do respect that. And I do trust you to get us to Jack Jones before it is too late.'

'Too late?' The Woman was startled. How much did this lad know? She had always assumed nothing, but now she wasn't too sure.

'Well, yes. I can't take forever on this case. I'll have to go back and report eventually.'

'Oh.' She hoped her relief didn't show on her face. 'I see.'

'She's taking a long time over checking her oven,' Harris remarked. 'Shall I go and see if she's all right?'

'No, no.' The Woman knew the Dresser of old. 'She will be making a tea worthy of kings. She can't help looking after people. It's what she does. Without Madam to cater for, she will be a bit lost.'

'But surely ...' Harris was confused. 'Madam has her butler to look after her.'

The Woman chuckled. 'It's years since any of us has been quite sure who looks after whom there. It used to be that the Bishop looked after her like a mother hen. He was so grateful, you see. And he tried to turn a blind eye to her little preferences, he really did. But sometimes, she just needed somewhere to indulge her liking for chorus boys and titled gents – she was never really that bothered which – without him praying for her immortal soul in every corner of the house. So then, she would come to me. Or here.'

Harris looked around. Somehow, this cosy little home with its smell of cooking and dusty potpourri didn't seem like a typical love nest.

'I know what you're thinking. In general, Madam brought the nobs here and the chorus boys to my place. The nobs liked it – it reminded them of their childhood, visiting the old retired Nanny somewhere on the estate. And the Dresser loved having them here. She would do breakfast in bed, with her eyes suitably averted, of course. So I'm glad Madam called on her way to ...'

Harris pricked up his ears. 'On her way to where?'

'Salvation, dearie.' The Dresser was back, walking backwards and pulling a laden tea trolley.

Harris and the Woman looked at the old girl, then at each other.

'I'm sorry,' the Woman said. 'The Duchess ...'

'Has seen the light. Isn't it wonderful? None of that naughtiness now, oh, dear me, no.'

'By "seen the light", you mean the Church of the Remnant?' The Woman could hardly believe it.

'There's only one church, dear,' the Dresser said, patting her hand, 'whatever those blaspheming Anglicans and Catholics tell you. Thank you so much for your most recent delivery, dear,' she said, 'it was just in time to give Madam and her friend a nice send off tea.'

'Madam's friend?' Harris's ears pricked up.

'Do you know Madam?' the Dresser asked, with the honey only just hiding the razor blades in her voice.

'I know *of* her,' Harris said.

'Well, everyone knows *of* her,' the Dresser told him. 'But that doesn't mean I am going to tell them every last mortal thing about her. The papers used to be round here all the time, looking for gossip but they'll get nothing out of me, I told them. Nothing about my girl.' She suddenly changed tack. 'Milk in your tea, dear? Sugar?'

'Umm ... yes. Both, please,' Harris said.

'Cake? Scone? Bun? Sandwich?'

The Woman tried to laugh. 'You're overwhelming him, dearie,' she said. 'Let him just cut and come again, eh? So,' she lifted her cup and looked at the Dresser over its rim. 'Madam had a friend with her, did she? Chorus boy? Nob?'

The Dresser chuckled. 'She's over that kind of thing now,' she said, 'although she is still very lovely. She's a new woman. We all are. No, her friend was nothing to look at, really. Not ugly, you know. Just not a very memorable face.'

Harris took out a much-folded bit of newsprint in which Jack Jones was exhorting his public to eat snoek. 'Was this him?'

The Dresser took it and looked at it short-sightedly for a moment. Then she wheezed her way up from the sofa and took it over to a light, where she examined it again. 'Hard to say, my dear,' she said, handing it back. 'It could be, it could be not. Bland face, not distinguished, just like the one in the paper. But I can't imagine Madam knocking about with some common advertiser. He was from the Church too.'

'It's Jack Jones, dearie,' the Woman said, kindly.

'Who?'

'Don't you have a wireless?' The Woman looked around and realized that the sideboard, where most families displayed their wirelesses with pride, just had a dusty vase of immortelles on it. And, although she hadn't seen them at first, a row of inverted crosses. Remnant crosses.

'Oh, no, dear,' the Dresser said. 'I know in the old days they used to have some lovely plays and music – Jack Hulbert, Cicely Courtneidge – and such but now it's all so dreary. Endless commands of what to do and what not to do. I gave it to the gardener, years ago.'

The Woman sighed. So much for gratitude. It had been a top model, in its day. 'Well, if you had a wireless, you would know Jack Jones. The whole country has heard of him, I should say.'

'I always knew my place,' the old girl said. 'I just made sure all you naughty chorus girls had your knickers on before you went on stage. I knew what you was after, all of you bad girls.'

'Anyone with money, in my case,' the Woman said, drily. 'Dear Daddy may have been a duke but we didn't have a pot to piss in, as Nanny would say.'

'I would say she would *not*!' The Dresser was horrified. She had often suspected that the Nanny had a few words she used instead of cursing, but had never been able to pin her down. One of them she almost remembered but couldn't get her tongue round it. More than a dozen syllables, it had, and nobody but dear Mary had ever said it in her hearing. 'How is dear Nanny?' She was suddenly very homesick for old friends.

'She's very well,' the Woman said. 'Keeping us all in check, as always.'

'She always was very good at that,' the Dresser agreed and absentmindedly buttered a second scone.

'So,' the Woman coaxed. 'Was this the man who was with Madam?'

The Dresser bit down on her scone. 'Hmm. Too much bicarb.'

'It's important, dear.' The Woman realized she was holding her breath.

'Let me think for a moment.' The Dresser munched on a scone and reached for a sandwich. 'Have you heard anything of that dreadful Singer chap lately?'

The Woman glared at Harris, daring him to say anything. 'No. You?'

'Certainly not.' The Dresser shuddered. 'Oily little creep. Only, I think Madam had dropped in on him.' She mimed draining a glass. 'Still got his ... problem, I understand.'

'I believe so.' The Woman didn't tap her foot, but was coming close. 'So ... the man ...?'

'Oh, goodness me, dear. You do go on. Yes, it could well have been him. But ...' she waved her hand in the air in front of the Woman's face. 'There's nothing to get ahold of, is there? He didn't say much. She told me he was a Receiver in the Church, you know, welcoming new converts, that sort of thing. Odd that, other Receivers I know hardly ever shut up. The gift of the gab goes with the territory, but he was very quiet. He did say one thing I didn't understand, though. He asked me if I'd heard the running grave that morning. Well, I told him I had no idea what he meant and he just smiled. Come to think of it, I didn't think he was quite all there, you know, not exactly the ticket.'

'Well, thank you anyway, dearie,' the Woman said. 'And thank you for our tea. Delicious as always. Say thank you, Bobby, like a good boy.'

'Bobby? Is that your name? So nice to hear someone not ashamed to say who he is. These days everyone is so ...'

'Sensible,' the Woman said, smartly. 'No names, no pack drill, we always say, don't we, dearie? Don't take me too literally. I just like the name Bobby, don't I, Bobby?'

'Yes,' Harris said, grimly. He suspected that calling her Mum might be a step too far, but at least he didn't have to keep up the elective mute thing here.

The Dresser stood up to show them out. She knew the end of a visit when she saw it coming. 'Thank you for coming, both of you,' she said. 'Two visits from my girls in one week. You're spoiling me. Don't leave it so long next time.' She looked Harris up and down. 'I don't care what you say,' she said, 'he's years too young for you.'

'Don't come with us to the door,' the Woman said. 'It's chilly when it gets dark and I don't want you catching cold.'

'All right, dear. Make sure the door slams to on your way out, won't you?' The old woman sat down, looking at her decimated tea trolley. 'I'll just have another little snack, perhaps, then have an early night. Safe journey in the arms of the Almighty.'

The Woman paused in the doorway for a moment, memories pouring over her like warm chocolate. Not all of them were good, but they were good enough. For now, good enough.

* * *

Back in the car, Harris had had enough. 'Look,' he said. 'I've really got to sort this out. I'm a Copper. The police.'

She looked at him before she turned the engine over. 'I know.'

'That line of yours,' he said. 'No names, no packdrill. I haven't got a clue what your name is and mine isn't Bobby. We've been traipsing around the countryside, visiting an assorted bunch of crackpots ...'

'My friends,' she corrected him.

'They may be your friends,' he said, 'but they're still crackpots. We've had a Bishop who's now a butler to a woman who was an actress but now seems to have joined a cult. We've had a gang of Ferals dealing in illegal, black market goods ...'

'And Gladys,' the Woman reminded him, smiling.

'Yes, all right, and Gladys. We've had a Nanny who didn't look any older than you.'

'Ah' she winked. 'Tricks of the light.'

'A woman who knits for England and likes codes. A drunk who used to be a singer and now this old girl who seems to work on and off for a third woman who ... Who *are* they all?'

Richard Denham

THE INNKEEPER

The car they had found waiting outside the Dresser's little cottage was not the one they had arrived in. This one, to his horror, was a black Railton, senior policemen for the use of. There was no two-way radio, thank God or whoever the Remnant prayed to, so that, at least, was something. The Woman had chuckled when she saw it – she liked it when her lads showed a humorous streak and also some acumen; they could spot a copper at a thousand paces, even when she told them otherwise. They also knew how to lift cars.

The inside of the vehicle was luxurious and Harris couldn't help stroking the fine leather of the bench seat in the front. The Woman spotted him.

'It *is* lovely, isn't it?' she asked him. 'So smooth and soft. Like a baby's bottom.'

Harris had been thinking of Gladys, but nevertheless twined his hands together in his lap. 'We must have a talk.' He wouldn't be sidelined.

'I don't know why,' she said, changing gear more smoothly than was her usual wont.

'Because ... because I don't know who you are. I don't know where we are. I don't know who the people are who we have been visiting. I don't know if you know Jack Jones or where he is or why he has gone off like this and ...' he stopped, aware he sounded like a petulant toddler.

'Have you quite finished?' she asked. 'No one knows

everything. That would be insane in the world we live in today. Has it not occurred to you that if all this goes totally wrong that the less you know, the better it will be for everyone? How can you tell what you don't know?'

'Tell? But who would be asking?'

The Woman slapped the wheel in frustration. 'I can't actually believe you are as innocent as you appear to be, Bobby, my boy. I am beginning to think that you are a very clever little policeboy who is out to find out about me and my … shall we call it business, because to call it anything else will be to put many people at risk and I am not going to do that just to satisfy your curiosity. It killed the cat, you know, and it might yet kill you.'

Kill? Like everyone else his age, Harris knew he was immortal. Dying was for old people and the terminally stupid.

The Woman went on. 'But perhaps you're right. Perhaps it is time you knew a bit more. We have found out more than I could possibly have hoped,' she said. 'We know that Jack Jones isn't alone. That's important.'

'Why?' Harris couldn't see the significance, other than perhaps that meant Jack Jones had just bunked off for a bit of a holiday with his Best Girl and would be back. Might indeed be walking into the studio as they spoke.

'I can't answer stupid questions and drive as well,' the Woman said. 'The Cow at Pasture is just up ahead. We'll stop there.'

Harris couldn't see how an ungulate could possibly help find Jack Jones, but the people they were asking seemed to be getting more and more tangential, so he went along with the plan. But for now, the leather was so smooth and he was really rather sleepy. It had probably been that fourth scone …

* * *

The Woman stood with her arms folded, looking in through the passenger window of the Railton at the sleeping Bobby. The man beside her was speaking in a low, conspiratorial voice.

'You gave me a bit of a turn there, I won't deny,' he said. 'What made you think of turning up here driving that?'

'Not my choice,' she said. 'My lads have got a bit of a funny bone, some of them.'

'I should think they have,' the Innkeeper said. 'Another minute and I would have been setting light to this place to hide the evidence.'

'Ooh, no, don't do that,' she said, leaning forward to wrench open the door. 'Bobby here is only a policeman by label, he doesn't have a policemanly bone in his whole body, I don't think. Although he does have a jolt from authority sometimes, he doesn't know where to go from there.' She poked the policeman in the arm. 'Rise and shine, Bobby, there's a lad. We're here.'

Harris sat up quickly – too quickly – and the world swam in his vision. His first thought was where was the cow, then realized almost at once that the Woman had been talking about a pub, because there was one, right in front of him. And who could mistake the man beside her for anything but a pub landlord – he was round, red faced and jolly but with a steely eye which brooked no nonsense.

'Hello,' he said. 'Sorry for falling asleep. It's the ...'

'I know,' the Woman said. 'It's the leather seats. Come on. Spit spot. We need to get this car under cover and ourselves inside before last orders.'

'Is it that late already?' Harris said, plaintively. Until a few days before, his time had been so predictable. Wake. Breakfast. Work. Tea. Sit staring at a wall. Sleep and repeat. But now it was all over the place and he found it hard to keep it all straight.

'Not quite,' the Innkeeper said. 'But best you come inside anyway. You're both a long way from home now and it might be hard to explain.'

'Where are we, exactly?' This was just the kind of information Harris wanted.

'Oh, you know,' the Woman said, waving a hand. 'Up and to the left.'

The Innkeeper guffawed. 'Up and to the left? Where did you learn geography?'

The Woman drew herself up. 'A very exclusive girls' school, actually, which needn't concern you. The main thing is where did *Bobby* learn his geography, because to be perfectly frank with you, his knowledge is woeful.'

The Innkeeper was a kind man and tried to see the best in everyone. 'I suppose things are different these days,' he said. 'These youngsters, they haven't had our education.'

'Remind me again where you went to school,' she said, handing the keys to a fresh-faced youngster who had suddenly appeared at her elbow. 'I forget.'

'Harrow,' the Innkeeper said, mildly. 'Followed by Magdalen. My doctorate was …'

'Yes, I remember,' she said and looked fondly at him. 'And yet, here you are …'

'Here I am,' he said. 'Alive and making a living. As opposed to my classmates. It is what it is.'

'Indeed.'

The Innkeeper opened his door with a flourish and they walked into a fug of stale beer and cigarette smoke but they didn't go through into the bar. Instead, a door dead ahead opened and the Innkeeper's wife stood there, beckoning them urgently.

'Come through, come through, quickly, quickly.'

She was a direct contrast to her husband. Tiny where he was huge, pale where he was rubicund. But she was endowed with a very archetypal barmaid's bust, which she flourished at Harris as she ushered them in.

'What's the rush, woman?' the Innkeeper said. 'Can't you see, she is gasping for a gasper?'

'Actually, I am all right,' the Woman said. She was indeed gasping for proper tobacco, but even with all her wiles she couldn't get much and had decided to eschew anything grown on the south slopes of Dartmoor or similar. Although it was true that afterwards, the real thing did taste extra nice. 'I've almost given up.'

'My word.' The Innkeeper was using his mixed company vocabulary. 'I never thought I'd live to see the day.'

The Woman turned her attention to his wife. 'What's the problem?' she asked. 'You seemed very anxious to get us under cover.'

'We've had a visit,' she said. 'I don't know who from, that's what's worrying me. I thought I knew all the locals, the police, the Home Guard from the town hall. Even the Remnant recruiters. But these were new. And scarier than all the rest.'

'What were they after?' The Innkeeper was flexing his jaw muscles and clenching his fists.

'They were very clever,' his wife told them all. 'They didn't say exactly. They certainly didn't describe you two. They just said I was to watch out for strangers.'

'They really don't know anything, then,' the Woman said. 'I'm here all the time.'

'I think it was just a generic term,' the Innkeeper said. 'Were they polite?' he demanded. 'Respectful?'

'Within their limits,' his wife said, calmly. 'They were fairly well spoken but none too bright. Could have been old school chums of yours, darling.' She treated her husband to a ravishing smile. 'Or one of the government, back Before.'

'Oh, as stupid as that,' the Woman said. 'Little to concern ourselves over, then, wouldn't you say?'

'They weren't very bright,' the Innkeeper's wife said. 'I didn't say stupid. They asked if we had seen strangers, then, they asked if we ever listened to Jack Jones. I thought that was an odd thing to ask, out of the blue.'

'What did you say?'

'The truth. We don't have time to listen to the wireless. We're always busy in the bar at that time, even if we wanted to.'

'You'd know him, though?' Harris was interested.

'I'm not sure I would. Would you?' She appealed to her husband.

He shrugged. 'Don't know as I would, actually. I'm not very good with faces. Not a good trait in Mine Host, I admit, but I get by. Blandish, is he? About this tall?' He held a hand out, significantly below his own six foot three.

'About that, yes,' the Woman said.

'So, you have met him, then?' the Innkeeper said. 'You're a dark horse.'

'Not lately,' she said, quietly. 'But we were friends, yes, back when I was younger.'

The Innkeeper's wife hadn't liked to say that the Woman was looking her age, but this was at least confirmation that she knew she had let herself go a bit.

'But why are they asking that?' the woman said. 'Surely they're not telling us what we can listen to now?'

'No more than they ever have, I don't think,' the Woman said. She was sitting in a chair at the table in the centre of the room and for the first time, her posture matched her wrinkled face. Harris suddenly realized that she was not as invulnerable as she seemed. She breathed out hard through her nose. 'This is not good, dears. Not good at all. Have you had any strangers stop by, just out of interest?'

The keepers of the Cow at Pasture looked at each other and shook their heads.

'Not to mention, really,' the Innkeeper said. 'Old George from the farm, he brought his nephew with him the other day. I was a bit suspicious, though.'

'Why?' Harris thought he should ask a question every now and again.

'Well, the lad was very well spoken and much cleaner than you'd expect, being related to George.'

His wife snorted. 'George has been known to make wallpaper peel when he's busy. He mucks out pigs and then goes to bed in his boots, so they say. He is quite … ripe, I think is a good word.'

'And his nephew was not smelly.'

'Smelled like a rose,' the Innkeeper said. 'And George said he wanted a bit of a baggin and the lad didn't know what he meant.'

'I don't know what it means,' Harris pointed out.

'Why should you?' the Innkeeper said. 'But the lad was supposed to be from round here, so he should have known.'

'What is it, in the interests of adding to my knowledge,' the Woman said.

'It's a snack, something to keep you going until tea time,' the Innkeeper's wife said. 'But I said to you,' she nodded at her husband, 'perhaps his parents are trying to bring him up a bit nicely. You know, not from round here, sort of thing.'

'And where is here?' Harris piped up.

'Good try, lad,' the Woman said, punching him lightly on the arm. 'But we're not going to fall for that.'

'So you thought ... what?' Harris changed tack slightly. 'That the nephew was a spy?'

'I don't see what he would be spying on,' the Innkeeper said. 'There's nothing round here to spy on. Well, apart from the contraband out the back ... oh, bugger!' He was grinning at Harris like a gargoyle caught in the headlights.

'That was it!' The Woman clicked her fingers. 'I knew I'd remember it − a doctorate in putting your bleeding foot in it.'

'Well ...' the innkeeper hadn't got much of a follow-up really.

'As it happens, young Bobby here is familiar with my little enterprises in aircraft hangars − well, one of them anyway. I think a little bit of Spivery in out of the way places is all right. After all, this,' and she waved her arm around, 'used to be smuggling country back in the day so there's a sort of precedent for it.'

'I haven't heard any gossip about the nephew visiting the other pubs around or anything like that,' the Innkeeper went on. 'No, I probably over reacted. He was just a bit of a posh relative, that's all.'

'What are we thinking?' his wife suddenly said, pretending that everything was right as rain. 'What would you both like to drink?'

Harris always hated that question. His preferred tipple, if he could be said to have one, was a nice port and lemon, but had always got the feeling that it wasn't a very policemanly choice. So he did as he usually did and asked for a pale ale. That was pretty tasteless being around 95% water these days and he could usually drink it without pulling a face. The Woman asked for a gin and tonic, heavy on the gin, with a twist and some ice. Harris was shocked. He had done the paperwork on a woman not that long ago who had been

Richard Denham

arrested for asking for a gin in a pub just like this one. She was finally locked up for a long time for displaying non-British tendencies.

'Oh, for goodness' sake, boy.' The Woman had read his expression. 'We're among friends here. And I know they have gin and tonic and lemons as well, come to that, because I sent a consignment only last week.'

The Innkeeper's wife looked at Harris fondly. It was good to know that there were still lads like this in the country, not fly, not ducking and diving, not on the make. Just a nice, old fashioned sort of lad, the sort of lad you could rely on to do the right thing. She hoped that whoever was looking for them didn't find them. This struck her as unlikely, so she changed her hope to if they found them, they were merciful and quick. She didn't want him to suffer. She put out a hand to pat his arm. She was always a woman to wear her heart on her sleeve.

'Don't worry,' she said. 'We don't give gin and tonic to just anyone. We won't get found out. And we've all sorts of alarms in place, haven't we, dear?' She appealed to her husband, who nodded. He loved his wife with every fibre of his being but for God's sake – the woman had a mouth on her; made him look like Silent Cal Coolidge. Some days, you might just as well print your secrets on leaflets and chuck them from the church steeple, so that the worshippers of the Remnant could chant them. He would have a word with her, later on.

* * *

The Woman didn't seem at all affected by her several rather generous gins and tonics but Harris could feel the floor tilting quite noticeably after his two Pale Ales. The Innkeeper and his wife watched them go.

'They're taking the car?' she said, mildly. Nothing much got her excited these days. A strange plant had grown from her discarded budgie seed a few years ago and she had been drawn to it in an almost supernatural way. She found a nibble on a leaf or, on special occasions, the inclusion of it in

162

a nice nourishing soup or some biscuits, took the edge off the world. She had had a nibble only that afternoon and its five-fingered goodness was still keeping her calm and happy, despite having had obvious fugitives in her house. And now they had taken the car. But never mind, they now had a nice black Railton to never go anywhere in, rather than the rather dented and bashed Morris to never go anywhere in. She waved, an extravagant finger wiggle, returned by Harris, slumped in the front seat.

'They needed to change, they have to be careful.' He tilted her face up to his and she pursed her lips, ready for a kiss. 'Are you all right? Your eyes look ... funny.'

'Thank you muchly,' she said, flouncing away. She had noticed that a nibble sometimes gave her eyes a funny look but had hoped he hadn't seen it.

'You will keep quiet, won't you?' he asked her, anxiously. 'They're looking for Jack Jones. He's a National Treasure, don't forget.'

'Yes, yes, I know. I know.' She closed the door and went down the hall towards the bar. 'It's last orders. I'll ring the bell, shall I?'

He nodded and watched her go. He had done his best. Now it was up to the Woman and Harris. He sighed. He just couldn't help but wonder how all this was going to turn out. And him with a PhD *and* an innkeeper's licence.

* * *

'Am I drunk, do you think?' Harris asked the Woman, who definitely was.

'What did you drink?' she asked.

'Pale Ale. Two Pale Ales.' He counted extravagantly on his fingers.

'Then in that case, no, you're not drunk.' She knew for a fact that there was more alcohol in the average jar of jam than in a dozen Pale Ales.

He held his hand up in the darkness of the car's interior and turned it this way and that. 'I think I am, you know,' he said, listening intently to his own voice and thinking how mellifluous it sounded. Like the Announcer's, but in a good way. 'Because I can see my hand in the dark. It's a kind of purply colour.' He twisted it around a few more times. 'Pretty.'

The Woman drove on, wondering whether the Innkeeper had perhaps played a joke on Harris and laced his drink and then had a thought. 'Did you eat anything?'

'No. I was still too full from tea. Although I am very hungry now, seeing as how you mention it. I … oh oh. Wait a minute.'

That sounded ominous and the Woman took him up. 'Oh oh? Oh oh what, exactly?'

'Well, it can't have any bearing, but I ate a biscuit. It was quite embarrassing, actually. It was down the side of the chair I was in and was clearly fresh. I didn't want the poor lady to find that she had sat me down on a snack, so I … I ate it. But that can't have had alcohol in it, can it?'

The Woman sighed. 'No, no it can't. But even so, I think it would be wise if, should we get stopped by anyone or anything, that you don't share these thoughts and for preference, you don't speak at all. Can we do the elective mute thing again?'

Harris was still watching his hand. 'Mmmm. Try my best. I am hungry, though. And sleepy. Suddenly, really sleepy.' He didn't remember this sudden overwhelming tiredness happening since he was a child.

'Well, you snuggle down and sleep, then,' the Woman advised. 'Then when you wake up in the morning, you'll be all fresh and ready to find Jack Jones. He's near. I feel it in my water.'

'Jack Jones. I'd be brown bread without you, Jack Jones. Brown bread. I'm hungry. Have we got any food?' Then, suddenly, he was asleep.

* * *

The Innkeeper liked being an innkeeper, as a rule. Given a choice, he would probably have preferred to be a Professor in some arcane subject but when he thought of all the other things he could have ended up as, well, innkeeper was not too bad. He liked his wife as well and he knew from keeping his eyes peeled that this was not necessarily a given. She had kept her figure remarkably well, knew how far to let the customers go and when to give them a quick tap to tell them to back off and generally ran the inn with charm and aplomb. But he knew about her guilty secret and had meant to talk to her about it but the right time never seemed to come. She got such pleasure from her little nibbles and it wasn't as if it was habit forming or anything. She didn't drink, she didn't smoke, she didn't take short breaks behind the lavatories with strange men like most other barmaids and a lot of wives with different jobs, so he let her keep her secret and her sanity. Because, whatever else he might be, the Innkeeper was a kind man and one who liked his peace and quiet.

He liked being an Innkeeper, that was true, but best of all he liked the time of day when the last drinker had gone, the teatowels were over the pumps and his wife was sitting in their private lounge with a cup of the Lapsang made from the bag of fragrant leaves always stowed between the gin and the lemons in their illicit packages. It was the highspot of a long and tiring day.

The second lot of boiling water had just been applied to the pot when the tap came on the door. Sometimes, when the night was fine and there was no moon, it was the Innkeeper's habit to let a few of his best customers in for a late drink, but tonight it was chilly with a moon you could read small print by, so it couldn't be one of them. Or, if it was, they would be given short shrift. He glanced at his wife.

'Don't answer it,' she said. The evening had been exciting enough as it was and she had been unable to find her half-eaten biscuit, forage though she might down the side of the chair. What she really wanted was another cuppa and then sleep, with possibly a short but pleasant interlude with the Innkeeper first.

'I think we should,' he said. 'We don't want to cause any suspicion.'

'Why should we?' she asked. 'We're hard-working people. We've gone to bed, that's all.' She knew the blackout,

165

kept up by habit, was intact and no one could know where they were.

The tap came again and they held their breath, their teacups halfway to their lips.

'I really should ...' The Innkeeper got to his feet and then stood there, irresolute. Sometimes, tucked up in bed, you could hear the tramp of feet and the grunt of laboured breathing as gangs ran through the village, trotting along in the age old Roman style, more dropping from foot to foot than running. They could keep it up for miles, he knew, and to hear it going past, intent on something nameless in another place, was not as funny as it had once been, watching the troops do it at the pictures, Before.

'Go on, then,' his wife said, taking his cup from him and sitting back, fingers laced together anxiously. 'See who it is.'

The Innkeeper opened the door and peered out into the dark. There were people there, he could hear them breathing, but he couldn't see a thing.

'Who's there?' he asked, trying to keep his voice even. 'What do you want? It's late. We're closed.'

One man stepped forward. 'I should hope you are,' he said, in a flat voice. 'Closing time was a while ago, after all.' He was still not in the light oozing from the hall and the Innkeeper stepped back, hoping to draw him forward. The man didn't fall for that old trick, staying in the shadows. All the Innkeeper could see was the edge of a trilby's brim and the shoulder of a trench coat. His heart almost stopped beating; the Agent had come for him. At last, after all his work to stay below the parapet, he was here, and with reinforcements.

The Agent chuckled and it was a sound that was a close relation to the snicker in the dark when you've locked the door, the growl in the throat of a lion on the veldt, the click of the hammer going back as you wait for the firing squad. The Innkeeper almost crumpled with the fear. 'Don't worry, Mr Innkeeper. I'm not here for you. I just would like a word with you and the missus, if that's all right. Could you dim the lights, though. I prefer ...' and again, that chuckle ...

'the shadows.'

He turned to the invisible crowd standing behind him.

'Wait for me, lads. I won't be long.' Then he turned back to the Innkeeper, who was standing rooted to the spot. 'Well, lead the way. I won't insult you by pretending I don't know every inch of this place, but it is your home after all and I am not an animal. Or at least, not yet.'

* * *

It was raining by the time Baker reached the crossroads. He had seen the Railton swing left and didn't think his old jalopy could keep up. There was a pub to the right – the Cow and Pasture – carefully showing regulation lighting and perhaps half full. He could see the Woman and Harris in the snug, chatting amiably to the man he assumed was mine host. Clearly, they knew each other. What was that the lad was drinking? Pale ale. All right; no cause for alarm there.

It was just trying to work out how to eavesdrop on the conversation when he heard the grunt of tyres on gravel. Dim headlit trucks turned up, two of them, and men tumbled out, in boots and carrying rifles. They weren't Home Guard that was for sure. And if not them, then who? It had to be Roundheads. He slid back into the shadows. The men fanned out in silence, forming a semi-circle around the inn. He heard the bell for last orders and saw the Woman and Harris come out, swaying a bit. Bugger! He couldn't break cover and reach his car. If these were Roundheads, in the shadows and out of sight of the revellers going their ways, such men opened fire first and asked questions later. And, of course, as he crouched in the rhododendrons by the downpipe, it started to rain even harder.

Richard Denham

THE AGENT

'Who was it, dear?' The Innkeeper's wife had raided the biscuit barrel while he was at the door so was feeling mellow. As long as the visitor had the requisite number of eyes – too few would be all right, too many perhaps not – and wasn't brandishing a weapon, she would be able to cope.

'It's only me,' the Agent said, sidling into the room and standing in the shadow cast by the door. 'If you could just turn some lights off ...'

The Innkeeper hurried to comply, while his wife sat glued to her chair with horror.

'I don't know what you people are thinking of,' the Agent said, making a note in a small notebook which had materialised in his hand. 'Don't you know that electricity has to be made, using precious resources? It isn't a bottomless pit, you know. Candles, they're the things to use. Tallow is cheapest, though I can see that perhaps the smell wouldn't enhance the place. Beeswax. Why not keep some bees? Lovely little chaps, bees. Honey, wax and in the end, used properly, a damned fine torture instrument. Excuse my language, ladies present. Black mark for me.' And he did indeed put a cross on the back page of his notebook. 'Ps and Qs, that's what I ought to be minding. But listen to me, going on when I am here to ask the questions, really. Do sit down.' He gestured to the Innkeeper. 'No. Over by the wife, please. I don't like having to look in more than one direction. Hard on

169

the neck.'

The Innkeeper and his wife sat side by side, watching as the man crept out of the shelter of the shadow and sat opposite them, the brim of his hat shading his face. His eyes were totally invisible and the only way they knew he even had a mouth was that occasionally a tooth would gleam in the darkness. The tip of his nose, damp and questing like a mole's, was the only feature that they could see clearly.

'Could you give us a clue as to what the problem is?' the Innkeeper said.

'Apart from your grasp of grammar, which seems tenuous at best?' The Agent made a note in another notebook. 'No, what I need to find out from you good people is who you have had as guests tonight.'

'This is a pub!' the Innkeeper said. 'We're meant to have guests!'

'Of course,' the Agent snapped. 'And you're meant to keep a list as well. Have you such a list?'

'It's in the bar.' The Innkeeper made to get up, but the Agent gestured him back to his seat with a peremptory hand. 'I can't *remember* them all, not off the top of my head.' The Innkeeper could see that staying calm was not going to be easy, important though it was.

'I'm not interested in old Ben from up at the forge or Mrs Chesney with her old trouble. I think really what I had in mind was the visitors you had here, in your private quarters.'

The Innkeeper looked at his wife and saw to his horror that her pupils were doing that thing again. He could only hope she would keep her trap shut. He dug his fingers into her arm just above the elbow.

'Ow! Why are you doing that? That *hurts.*'

So that answered that question.

'Don't hurt the little woman, now, sir, there's a good gentleman.' The Agent had once been a policeman and some verbal quirks were harder to lose than others. 'Let her say her piece. Now, dear,' he leaned forward and even the tip of his nose disappeared. 'Had any visitors, have we?'

The Innkeeper's wife giggled. 'We run a pub,' she said, echoing her husband. 'We've always got visitors.'

'In. This. Room.' The Agent's voice crawled out of his invisible mouth like some horrible miasma over a swamp and seemed to fill the room with its malevolence. 'Who were they?'

The woman was like a rabbit mesmerised by a particularly unpleasant stoat. She felt the words being dragged out of her and could see them dancing on the air, like mayflies doomed to die. 'A woman and a man. Well, a boy, really. I don't know their names. I don't know what they wanted. They weren't here long.'

'My goodness me.' The voice was now honey and light. 'Your wife seems to know a lot more than you do, sir,' the Agent said to the Innkeeper. 'Perhaps you weren't here when they visited. Could that be it?'

'I was probably busy in the bar,' the Innkeeper said, though it was hard for him to speak, his throat had closed over so much.

'No, dear, you were here,' his wife said, brightly. 'Don't you remember?'

'Oh, yes,' he said and thought to himself how much his voice sounded like the slamming of a cell door. 'I do remember now. A woman and a lad. Mother and son, perhaps ...'

'Oh, no,' his wife said. 'We know her, don't we? She's where we get our gin and that. We didn't know him, though.'

The Agent nearly stood up and cheered. This could hardly get any better. The visitor had been the Woman they had all been looking for for years. Martha. Lucie. Genevieve. Alice. She had an endless list of names, a clutter of addresses. As for her vehicles, the list went on and on. The Woman no one had ever seen, who never looked the same for two weeks together. Oh, hoo-bloody-ray. The Agent rarely swore and never laughed, but he felt like doing both, in copious abandon. Instead, he said, 'So, you don't know their names, then?'

The woman tapped the side of her nose. 'No names, no pack drill,' she said, proudly.

'No, indeed. Now, do you happen to know what car they were in? Or perhaps it was a van, was it? A lorry?'

The two faces in front of the Agent looked blank.

'Not a horse and cart, surely?'

The Innkeeper's wife giggled again. 'No, silly,' she said. 'They've got our car. They left a very nice Railton in exchange though, and it's not as if we go anywhere much.' She put her hand to her mouth as her husband groaned. 'What? What's the matter?' She suddenly realized that perhaps she had let her little nibble habit too free a rein. 'Oh. Oh, dear.' She looked at the Agent, who was jotting down a few bits and bobs in yet another notebook. 'Ignore me, I'm such a silly. I haven't been well. I imagine things. I hadn't even heard of Jack Jones, not really. They had to explain …'

The Agent dipped his head and made one final note in his notebook. The Innkeeper wanted to be sick. His wife sat there open-mouthed, wondering if it would be all right to mention that she was really, *really* hungry.

* * *

Outside the pub, the Agent lifted his head. The rain had stopped. His very ordinary face shone clearly in the moonlight.

'Gather round,' he said to his minions.

There was a shuffling as the men moved closer. Some of them, the ones who stayed towards the back of any crowd, were grinning in anticipation. They had been travelling for days and were ready for a bit of a ruckus.

'Now,' he said, when they were all more or less concentrating, 'I haven't got all the information I needed or wanted but I do have about one hundred per cent more than I thought I would get.'

'Urrggh!' A guttural sound from the back of his little crowd let him known that his most violent and irascible lieutenant was not happy. He had been looking forward to a little light dismemberment.

'I know, I know. You've all been very patient, but I am afraid I can't allow any extra rough stuff bearing in mind that the two of them were helpful, to a degree. We know the Woman and Harris were here.'

Rumbling cheers greeted his news.

'We know they have taken off in the pub car – I think …' the Agent looked out over the heads of his small mob '… one of you has the details of that, yes?'

A hand went up and waved.

'Good. Make sure that everyone knows what they are looking for. We know their approximate direction of course, allowing for the fact that they have been going in an almost straight line and I don't think they will change that much at this point. But, and this is the most important thing, is that we know that they are on the trail of Jack Jones.' He had expected this piece of news to be met with cheers, but in fact, he heard only silence. 'That's a good thing,' he reminded them. 'It means that all the small groups who have been hunting him can join us for the final push.'

'But won't that make it all a bit … unwieldy?' The owner of the voice of reason didn't speak often. He had often assumed that he was the only one in the mob who had even a small brain and he was right, by and large. He knew he was taking a risk, but it had to be said.

'Unwieldy? In what respect?' The Agent was ready to get quite testy.

'Well, everyone knows we've had trouble on the road already. We've lost, what, a dozen men. Injuries, boredom, some just plain old lost.'

'I still don't quite understand what you're getting at. Are you suggesting that I can't manage a larger horde?' The Agent was tapping his foot slowly, a sign which had some of his longer serving henchmen backing away nervously.

'Of course you can, of course you can.' The would-be Agent knew when he had gone too far. 'But you have to agree that some of these satellite mobs can be hard to handle.' He was on thin ice here and he knew it. 'They haven't had the discipline. They think they're above the law. They can all see that finding Jack Jones – or the Woman, come to think of it – will be a real feather in their caps and can see promotion and all sorts coming down the line.'

The Agent narrowed his already rather piggy eyes at the man and the horde on either side melted away as though choreographed. The would-be Agent suddenly felt very exposed and raised his chin and grinned in appeasement.

'So ...' The Agent was suddenly toe to toe with him and it wasn't a pleasant experience. 'So, you know this kind of thing, do you?'

'Well,' said the would-be, 'people talk, you know.'

'They do,' the Agent agreed. 'Indeed they do. If you could let me have a list of these talkers by,' he looked at his watch, 'shall we say one hour from now, then we'll say no more about it.'

The crowd melted further into the shadows.

'I don't have actual *names*,' the man protested. 'It's just ... scuttlebutt, you know. Gossip. Innuendo.'

'Scuttlebutt?' the Agent frowned. 'That's an American term, isn't it? I think we call all that lies, don't we, in this great country of ours?' The Agent's voice was a hiss.

'No, not lies.' The man's voice was high with panic. This was not how he foresaw this conversation going. 'Just ...'

No one saw the Webley until it was in the Agent's hand and its muzzle was against the man's forehead. They all heard the shot, though, as the bullet smashed through bone and brain and the man went down, flapping like a wet doll for a moment, then was still. The silence after it rang out was deafening. The Agent looked around and no one met his eye.

'Well, I hope it's all clear,' the Agent said, returning the revolver to the holster under his arm. 'You all have your jobs, assigned before we set off. We are now in Phase Four of Five, so I can't tell you – should not *have* to tell you – what to do now. You should know it as you know your own names. Which, as you are aware, we do not use.'

There was a small pause until some bright spark, a little quicker off the mark than the others, laughed, slightly hysterically it was true, but enough to make the rest realize that they had just heard a joke. The laughter spread outwards, rippling through the horde until they all realized that the Agent was no longer there. His trick of melting away still gave them the willies, even those who had worked with him from the Start. The laughter stuttered to a stop and one by one, the horde broke up and soon the night was full of the sound of revving engines, the smell of the countryside defiled by the smell of petrol and burning oil.

Baker had bitten his lip when he heard the shot and saw the man recoil. He'd seen men die before, but he didn't know the shooter or his circle of heavies. They were Home Guard, that was certain. Their webbing and lanyards in the moonlight made that obvious. Yet this lot seemed a little rogue, even by Home Guard standards. Yes, they shot people, but that was usually after a court martial and something that passed for the due process of the law.

Baker himself was unarmed. Even his truncheon lay across the yard in his car. And he was just pleased that the two trucks had grated and rattled off without anyone inspecting his vehicle. If *they* knew where the Woman and Harris were going, all he had to do was follow them.

The Agent's Driver went back to his car, to find it empty with a note on the windscreen. He got in the car and switched on the interior light. The Agent had possibly the worst writing the Driver had ever seen and he needed as much light as he could get, to make sure there was no mistake. Making a mistake when the Agent was involved could well mean it was the last mistake you would ever make. There was a dead man lying in the yard who would never be able to testify to that.

'Go on without me,' the note said. 'Have new car. First one to find Jack Jones is a cissy.'

The Driver furrowed his brow. Oh, God in heaven – the Driver still secretly believed he was there, waiting for all the stupidity to end – the Agent was feeling frivolous. The Driver had seen it only once before and then the death toll had been astronomic. He sighed and turned off the light. He had a choice, he knew that. He could carry on on the same path they had been treading for the last week or so, ever since Jack Jones had walked silently into the night. Or he could turn the car around and go and see if he could find where that nice little widow lived, the one he had got chatting to at a rally before all this nonsense about finding the National Treasure had kicked off. She had seemed quite … welcoming. The Driver was sure that he would be given a cushy billet there, assuming he could find her. He sat in the dark for what seemed to be many hours. He did one potato, two potato with himself. He told himself that if he heard an owl in the next half hour, he would go to the widow, if it was a nightjar, he would follow Jack Jones. If it was a nightingale … He bet himself that he couldn't recite the alphabet backwards in less than thirty seconds – if he lost, he would … oh, dammit. He banged the car into gear and spun it effortlessly round to face the way he had come. Jack Jones could go hang. It was time he had a little bit of rest and recuperation, widow-style.

* * *

As Baker kicked his car into gear to follow the trucks, the Innkeeper crept out into the night air. He saw the body near the path and feared the worst. No, not the worst. The worst would be that he was lying there, alongside his wife, high as a kite and nibbling biscuits. He knelt down and checked the body. Still warm, of course. The eyes were wide open, staring to the heavens not what the clouds had gone. There was a neat black hole in the centre of the forehead; he didn't want to think what the back of the skull would look like. He closed the man's eyes. He should bury him, somewhere quiet out in the fields, say a few words perhaps now there were no priests to do the honours.

On the other hand … He stood up, squaring his shoulders. He glanced back at his pub, the gently swinging sign of the Cow and Pasture. He'd miss the place, of course, but that went without saying. He hadn't planned to do what he'd suddenly decided, but the Agent and the dead Home Guard left him no choice. He'd grab a few belongings, tell his wife some mumbo jumbo and make for the Rendezvous. He had the coordinates, knew them off by heart – 'the beach the hun can't reach'.

He'd start again, do what he knew the Others were doing, build from scratch. Wherever it was, they'd need pubs there. The Cow and Pasture would rise again.

THE FARMER

For the first time since the Woman had found him sleeping on a bench, Harris was not spending the night in a bed. He had not always had linen sheets and goose down, but it had always been level and there was a reasonable chance of breakfast the next day. But now, he found himself sleeping in the front seat of a tiny Morris, complete with the smell of cigarette smoke, old beer and feet. The car had done stalwart service for a lot of years but Harris was suspecting it had just driven its last mile.

The Woman was beside him, her head pillowed on his shoulder, her breath coming in little snorts, unevenly spaced and sometimes quite worrying in the gaps between. He was reminded of the Bishop and realized that if anything happened to this person, he would be completely alone in the world, a world he had scarcely understood before but now realized he had no knowledge of at all. The world of the Station House and the Landlady seemed an eternity ago. And he wasn't PCv312 Harris any more, but Bobby, just a Christian name drifting in an alien world where no one had a name and no one was quite what they seemed. He suppressed a shiver and moved slowly to a less excruciating position – he refused to call it comfortable – leaned his head on hers and drifted back off into a fitful doze. City boy that he was he had no idea what information he could glean from the position of the moon in the sky, what time it might be or what weather tomorrow might bring. He smiled to himself and impaled himself briefly on a hairpin. He decided to be glad that ignorance was bliss and was finally asleep.

* * *

The Knitter hurtled into the Protector's room.

'Mother of God, Ireton, do you mind?' He sat bolt upright in bed.

'Sorry, Cromwell. Are you decent?'

'Of course I am,' he bridled. 'I went to a good school.' Even so, he glanced down to make sure all was safely tucked away in his jim-jams.

'I've got it.' The Knitter sat down on a little stool and cleared the dressing table in a single sweep, sending bay rum and balled socks flying. 'It's taken me all night, but I've got it. And I could kick myself I didn't get there sooner.'

Cromwell looked at the apparition in front of him. The knitting needles had gone from the hair and it hung around her shoulders like a shroud. She clearly hadn't been to bed and her rumpled clothes looked like she'd been wrestling in them. 'Purl. Plain, Fibonacci. It's none of these.'

'What are you talking about?' He was fumbling for his dressing gown, ready to murder a cup of coffee.

'Jack Jones. It's a code. And has been for some weeks.'

'What?'

'You know one of my little blessings – or is it a curse? – is that I have an eidetic memory.'

'If you say so.' The Knitter was only one of several Roundhead agents; Cromwell couldn't keep tabs on the strengths of a particular individual, especially when he had no idea what that individual was going on about.

'In weak, knitting moments, I used to listen to Jack Jones – well, there's nothing else on air, is there?'

'True.'

'I was revisiting it, letting his nonsense trickle through what I used, laughingly, to call my brain. You may remember some of it.'

'I doubt it, Ireton,' Cromwell sighed. 'I've got a cause

to fight.'

'Yes, yes, of course. But the devil's in the detail. What's his nasty little song? "Waiting on the beach, the beach the Hun can't reach".'

'So?'

'So, where's the enemy?'

'France,' Cromwell said, 'and the Low Countries. Norway. Probably Spain, too.'

'The *east*,' the Knitter nodded. 'Their war effort is concentrated in the east. That's why we've got our defences all over the east coast, right?'

'Of course.'

'Well, what's the beach the Hun can't reach? The West!'

'It may not have occurred to you, Ireton, that Fortress Britain is an island. There are beaches at every point of the compass.'

'Agreed. But the enemy aren't going to risk travelling around the island to reach the West. They can't be sure what Ireland would do, not to mention America.'

'Good God!' Cromwell's mouth hung open. 'Nobody's mentioned America for years.'

She spread out a rudimentary map. 'Jack Jones has. And he's been mentioning it for weeks, to all his followers up and down the country. Right under our bloody noses. Or via our ears, if I'm not mixing too many body parts there.'

'His followers?' Cromwell echoed. 'So you thing the theory's right, then, that he's smuggling people out. That's a hanging offence.'

'You know that. The Government knows that. I know that. So does everybody else. But freedom is a powerful motive, Cromwell.'

'I know,' he said. 'That's what we're fighting for.'

'*We're* fighting, yes. Jack Jones and his people aren't. They're getting out.'

'Desertion,' Cromwell said grimly. 'Those lily-livered …'

'Yes, yes,' she patted the air, 'words fail me too. But *that's* what Genevieve and her pet idiot are up to. They're going West to get the hell out. Leave these shores for good. God knows how many have gone already.'

'We've got to stop them,' Cromwell insisted. Then he frowned. 'But how …?'

'How do we pinpoint the leaving place? A lot of beaches in the West, aren't there? That's where the rest of the code comes in.'

'Say on.'

'The old Flanagan and Allen number – *Maybe It's Because I'm a Londoner*. The Jones version was 'Maybe it's because I'm from Lancashire, That I love London so.' We all chuckled, assuming it was a well-meaning jibe against Lancastrians. But it wasn't. it narrowed the beaches down to one area – the Lancashire coast.'

She pointed to her roughly-drawn map.

'From the Lune in the north to the Mersey in the south.'

'Liverpool!' Cromwell clicked his fingers. 'The docks.'

'Too obvious,' the Knitter shook her head. 'The docks are swarming with Government. Regulars, Home Guard, the Navy. Jones's people would be chancing their arms there. Somewhere quieter, I think. Then, there were the Two Leslies – *Umpa Umpa*.'

'God, yes.' Cromwell's teeth were gritted, 'Unforgettable in a Chinese torture sort of way.'

'I admit that threw me at first, despite the changed lyrics. Then it dawned. Ulpha in Cumbria. It must be some sort of way station, like the pilgrims' posts on the way to Compostella.'

'Anything else?'

'Jack Buchanan,' the Knitter said. '*Everything Stops for Tea.*'

'I don't remember the Jones version,' Cromwell said, 'if I ever heard it at all.'

'Tebay, Cumbria again. He's joining dots in the north of the county. Then there's that dreadful man George Formby – *I'm Leaning on a Lamppost*. It's not topographical this time; it's timing. The lyrics go, "I'm leaning on a lamppost at the corner of the street, In case a certain little lady comes by".

The certain little lady is Genevieve. When she knocks on your door – as she did on mine – it's time for all good men – and women – to come to the aid of the party.'

'This is damn'd clever.' Cromwell hated himself for having said it.

The Knitter winked at him. 'We were trained by the best,' she said. 'Oh, God, bloody Lupino Lane – *Doing the Lambeth Walk*.' To Cromwell's horror, the Knitter not only sang it, she did the steps as well. 'Any evening, any day,' she sang. 'It's a time frame. The exact day isn't clear, but they'll leave in the evening. Dusk would be my guess, before the searchlights come on. *Button Up Your Overcoat*. Jack Hylton. A little reminder to pack your clothes – remember when your mummy told you to take your hankie?'

Cromwell did, but he chose to forget it.

'They're going somewhere north. Canada would be my guess. *Umbrella Man*. Flanagan and Allen again ...'

'Has Jones got shares in them?'

'Same thing. They're all bloody Boy Scouts. Be prepared.'

'They'll be armed, I assume.'

'You can bank on it,' the Knitter said. '*Carrying Their Thingamabobs*.'

'God, not Gracie Fields!'

'She's a good old Lancashire lass, why not? Their thingamabobs will be hand grenades, sten-guns, Sykes-Fairburn knives, you name it.'

'I thought this lot were namby-pambies,' Cromwell said. 'Running away from it all.'

'They're running away from a world they don't like,' the Knitter said. 'The irony is they're prepared to die to make it happen. What's that line – "We believe in peace and we'll fight to the death for it"? That's the kind of nonsense we're all reduced to.'

She circled the room for a moment. 'It probably didn't need saying,' she added grimly, 'but the Andrews Sisters mickey-take must have been the most difficult of all.'

'What's that?' her boss asked.

'*Shoo-shoo Baby*,' she said. 'No children. The whole

venture's too risky. If things go wrong at the coast, anybody could be hit in the crossfire. That means that Jones's people have to leave their kids – grannies, aunties, the lady next door, who knows.'

'Yet more Ferals,' Cromwell tutted.

The Knitter nodded. 'I must admit I had to look the next song up, but it didn't need much extrapolating by dear old cryptic Jack – Leslie Sarony's *Why Build a Wall Around a Graveyard*?'

'What's that all about?'

'It's telling people to avoid the trap you nearly fell into. What's the biggest wall in Lancashire?'

'The one around Liverpool. Around the docks.'

'And the other one?'

'Er … Blackpool.'

'Precisely, so keep away from them. It hardly needed saying, really, but your average listener is none too bright. They'll all know *The Teddy Bears' Picnic*, though.'

'The Henry Hall version, of course,' Cromwell smiled.

'Why, Lord Protector, I do believe there's a little boy in there, after all, struggling to get out.'

He snorted.

'I will confess to always finding that song rather sinister. But leaving that aside, where do you get big surprises?' the Knitter said.

'Er … if you go down to the woods today?' he suggested.

She was back at the map again. 'Which takes us to here.' She pointed. 'Holmswood, north of Ormskirk. I believe that's the rendezvous point and then they head straight for the coast.'

Cromwell crossed to the OS map on his wall and he put his glasses on. 'That's still a big area,' he said. 'What's that, fifteen, twenty miles, depending on whether they go north or south.'

She crossed the room to him. 'They're going west, Cromwell,' she said. 'Always due west.' And she tapped the map where the coast curved outwards into the Atlantic. 'The irritating little ukulele player himself,' she said, in her Eureka moment. 'Formby Point.'

'When is this happening, though?' Cromwell always had to consider the costs involved and setting a watch on a whole stretch of coast in perpetuity was a little too much outlay for his parsimonious soul.

'That's the trouble,' the Knitter said. 'Soon, I'm sure, but exactly when I don't know. I'll go through the playlist again, see what jumps out at me. Can you wait a while?'

The Lord Protector nodded. He had waited ten years. What was another while or so?

* * *

The morning, when it finally came, also brought a moderately irate farmer with it. The Woman, in the dark, had made one of her rare errors and had driven the car into the middle of a field of cows which, the Farmer was informing her in a series of sharp barks, were of a very retiring and nervous disposition and would therefore not be giving their usual quota of milk by a long chalk. And as for the chickens, cooped up quite literally beyond the next hedge, if they laid another egg for a week he would be a monkey's uncle. Harris waited with bated breath for her to tell the Farmer his fortune and scare him into the middle of next week, but he was to be disappointed.

'I'm terribly sorry,' she said, looking and sounding contrite. 'But it was dark, you see, and I missed my turning. My ...' she turned to the car and made a curious gesture with twining fingers and twiddling toe '... friend and I had stayed out late and I daren't go back home.' She turned a tear-smudged face to the Farmer. 'My husband will b-b-beat me again.' She stifled an hysterical sob and buried her face in his jacket.

Harris was appalled. Her *friend*? Whatever would this bluff countryman think? He was just as likely to give them both a hiding and call the authorities.

'There, there.' To Harris's amazement, the Farmer had gathered the Woman to his manly tweed and was patting her on the back. 'The cows aren't that delicate, but I've had a lot of losses lately and it's made me rather testy. Come on, now, don't cry. That young man of yours and I won't let the beast hurt you.'

Harris looked around wildly. How on earth could the Farmer, innocent countryman or no, think that he and the Woman were a couple? She was old enough to be his grandmother. Then he saw it. The pot of cold cream on the dashboard, with the makeup-stained cloth beside it. There was almost a perfect print of a face, a face full of wrinkles, on the cloth. Thin strips of spirit gum were mixed in with the five and nine and on the floor there were little grey wisps of hair, each ending in a hair grip. The light began to dawn and Harris leaned forward to get a better look. Even the Woman's arse was smaller, he could swear. He could hardly believe that she had taken him in so thoroughly. Then he remembered – all her early stories were about being an actress. How could he have been so gullible? Then, self preservation kicked in and he swept the cloth and the cold cream into a rough bundle and stowed it under his seat.

Whoever this Woman really was, she *was* the Actress, she of the Bishop. The skeins of web were drawing closer.

He clambered out of the car and decided to do his best to keep the story going. He stretched extravagantly and walked over to where the Farmer was still patting the Woman on the back and murmuring the kind of endearments he usually reserved for his pigs when the farrowing was harrowing.

'Come on, now, old girl,' he said loudly, fetching her a smack on the backside. 'You're safe here with us two to look after you.'

The Farmer looked at him aghast. It was certainly true that some women really had no taste in men. Nice little filly like this – not in the first flush of youth, perhaps, but comely enough, what – jumps out of the frying pan into the fire if he was any judge. Knocking about with this young ruffian. He looked Harris up and down and didn't like what he saw. A bad 'un if ever he saw one, like as not been in quod more times than he had had hot dinners. 'If I see you lay a hand on a lady like that again,' he growled, 'I'll take my horse whip to you, no hesitation.'

'Yes, come on, Bobby,' the Woman murmured. 'Less of the handy stuff.'

'Bobby, eh?' the Farmer said, still staring as if he wanted to memorize every eyelash. 'You'll behave like a gentleman here or answer to me.' He looked down at the Woman's tear streaked face. 'Ask me, m'dear,' he said to her, 'You've made a bit of a mistake here. Wrong 'un, mark my words.' He looked Harris up and down and seemed to decide he was beneath his notice and started to lead the woman across to a gate in the corner of a field.

Harris trailed disconsolately in their wake and could hear snatches of their conversation.

'... m'dear, no offence but you're a bit old for him, aren't you ... no offence, you're a fine figure ... young whippersnapper ...'

'... of course, you are just so perceptive ... I just needed love and attention ... and he has got a very ...'

At this, Harris saw the Farmer's back straighten and the back of his neck turn red. 'Oh, I say,' he heard him say. 'Steady on, old girl. I don't need to know that kind of information.' But nevertheless, he glanced back and Harris tried to walk like a man with a very.

* * *

By the time the light was up, the trucks of the Home Guard had caught up with the Railton. Baker slammed on the brakes behind a spinney and waited. He saw the Agent get out and cross to his men who were tumbling out of their cramped quarters with gratitude. He couldn't catch much of the conversation, but it was clear that the Railton had run out of juice and they were all lost. A huge map was brought into play, spread over a truck's bonnet and fingers were pointed.

'You don't mean to tell me,' he couldn't miss the Agent bellow, 'that none of you buggers thought to bring a compass?' One of the more orienteering types squinted up to find the sun, but all he could see was grey skies from now on.

'I reckon we're here,' another said. 'Wigan.'

'Wigan, my arse,' his comrade grunted. 'That's gotta be St Helens.'

'I'm a monkey's uncle,' someone else added, by way of erudition.

'Shut up, all of you!' the Agent snapped. 'If this is Lancashire, they're making for the coast, which can't be Liverpool or Blackpool – too well guarded. Henshaw, you were in the lead truck; where did you see them last?'

'About two miles back, sir.' Henshaw was a little surprised – as well as a little concerned – to hear the Agent use his name; he'd almost forgotten what it was. 'We came to that crossroads and I couldn't see which way they went.'

'Right. We'll get back.'

Baker didn't hear the rest because he was staring down the barrel of a Lee-Enfield. One of the Guard had wandered off for a pee and the sight of a bloke crouching by a hedgerow had naturally piqued his curiosity. What it hadn't done was increase his speed or common sense. Before he could either fire or shout a warning, Baker had batted the rifle muzzle aside and swung it and its owner round and down. With the Guard on his knees, Baker rammed the rifle upwards with both hands and smothered the man's face with his chest. The Guard struggled and squirmed for what seemed forever, although Baker knew it was about four minutes. That's how long it takes to strangle a man. For minutes. When he felt the Guard go slack against his legs, he relaxed his grip and let him fall forward in the damp grass. He swung the rifle to his right, half expecting the rest of the truckload to be descending on him. But they were loading up, clambering aboard and snapping tailgates shut.

''Ere,' he heard somebody call, 'Where's Bert?'

But if there was an answer, it was drowned out by the revving engines as the trucks turned back to the road.

* * *

The farmhouse was a wonder of faded glory and Bobby, who was not usually much drawn to places for their own sake, was soon hoping that this would be the end of their travels, that the Farmer would open and door, reveal Jack Jones sitting there eating a cheese and onion sandwich and all would be well with the world. He knew this could not possibly be, but it didn't hurt to hope.

The Farmer lived with his sister, as bluff, red and tweed encrusted as he. After a whispered conversation in the hall, she had glared at Harris even more malevolently than her brother and had made it her business to always be between him and the Woman. Breakfast was served by the simple expedient of everyone sitting round a vast table in a kitchen so huge that from where he sat, Harris had difficulty focussing on the far end. The range was banked up to almost pulsing heat and the bacon, sausage and eggs all came from the farm, as the Farmer and his sister were at pains to make clear. Three places were set at one end of the table, one place, with the non-silver cutlery, was set at the other. Harris found that life as a pariah was not much fun. The food sizzled away to itself and everyone just took what they wanted, although whenever Harris was on his feet, the Farmer or his sister made sure that he couldn't see, let alone touch, the Woman.

From the length of the table, it wasn't easy to see much detail of the Woman's face, but Harris reckoned she was probably knocking forty, possibly more if she was well preserved, possibly less if her life had been hard – and whose life had not been hard? So best case, she could give him fifteen years, worse case more than twenty, so he had to applaud her chutzpah for claiming to be his lover. But – and he smiled to himself – he had his very to thank for that.

'Look at him,' the Farmer's sister hissed, 'grinning to himself like the cat that got the cream. Probably planning his next conquest. You poor, dear woman. You have had a lucky escape there, in my opinion. Jumped up little tyke. Been in more prison cells than enough, I wouldn't wonder.'

The Woman looked down the table fondly at Harris. She had bowled him some googlies since they had set off, but this was the worst and love the boy, he had come up trumps. He was stuffing bacon and sausage down him as if there was to be no tomorrow – and possibly, he was right. If she had done her calculations correctly, by tomorrow night they would have found Jack Jones and all would be right with the world, in one way or another. If she was wrong, it would scarcely matter, as they would be lying dead in a hail of bullets in the best case scenario, or would be being systematically tortured – she thought that, what with one thing and another, she would prefer the former.

The Farmer had taken umbrage. There she was, fine looking woman, still making sheep's eyes at that whippersnapper. 'Shouldn't waste your time on him,' he said, nastily. 'When we've had our breakfast, I'm sending the cowman down to the village, call for help.'

'Help?' The Woman was on high alert. 'Help? What for?'

The Farmer covered her hand with his own. It was like being fondled by a ham. 'Take the whippersnapper into quod,' he barked. Before, he had been a JP and still had some of the habits; unpleasantness, bigotry, lack of understanding.

'Why?' The Woman had not foreseen this.

'Broken the law,' the Farmer barked. 'Had carnal relations with a married woman. Laid a hand on a woman in a way likely to cause a breach of the peace.'

'Oh, no, no.' The Woman was truly contrite and for the first time, Harris heard her voice shorn of all cynicism. 'He's done nothing wrong. Really, he hasn't. Please, we don't need the cowman to get involved. Please.' She grabbed the Farmer's hand and worked her eyelashes for all she was worth.

'Whippersnapper,' was the Farmer's only response.

'You can't have someone taken to … where did you say you were taking him?'

'Quod!'

'Yes, well, quod, just because … look, we hadn't actually *done* anything, you know. He absolutely refused to break the law. Didn't you, Bobby?'

Harris shook his head. Then nodded. He wasn't sure whether the right answer was a yes or a no.

'But you said he had – cover your ears, Elspeth – a very …'

'I did, yes.' The Woman did a fair attempt at a simper.

'But I was just being ... well, to be honest with you, I've only *seen* it.'

'What, just lying about, was it?' The Farmer had withdrawn his hands from hers. 'Reading? Doing the ironing?'

His sister was very confused by now. A maiden lady, with the emphasis on the maiden, she had been under the impression they had been discussing the young man's penis. Now, she wasn't so sure.

'No. I happened to go into his room and he had kicked off his covers.'

'Decent man wears pyjamas,' the Farmer barked.

'And underpants, dear, don't forget.' Elspeth did the washing, so she knew.

'Of course.' The Woman was placating for all she was worth. 'But ... well, Bobby had just dropped in for a drink and he had too much to drive, so he stayed and of course had no pyjamas.' She blew out a breath. It didn't seem very likely, but these were simple folk.

'And your husband couldn't lend him a pair?' The Farmer was very suspicious. Whippersnapper!

Harris could see that she was beginning to struggle. 'Very tiny chap, her husband,' he called from his end of the table. 'Barely five foot wringing wet, very short legs. And of course, a commensurately short ...'

'That's *enough*!' the Farmer roared. 'I would remind you, sir, that there are ladies present.'

'Dick,' Harris muttered under his breath.

'What?' The Farmer had turned purple.

'Nothing,' Harris said. 'Just clearing my throat. That was a simply wonderful breakfast, but I think we ought to be thinking of getting on. My mother, the Countess of Arbroath, is expecting us.'

'The cheek of it!' The Farmer's sister was outraged. 'No one has used a title for years and for you to come here, bandying around talk of ... well, I thought you were talking about penises, but now I'm not so sure ... penises and ... and ... countesses, well, I never thought I would live to see the day.' She collapsed into her chair, her breath coming in a series of laboured squeals.

'Now see what you've done,' the Farmer bellowed. 'She'll be good for nothing for days now. *Whippersnapper!*' It seemed to be the most heinous slight he could manage, given the circumstances.

'Well, we'll be off then, shall we?' the Woman said, getting up. 'Come on, Bobby, time we weren't here.'

'Time your sort weren't allowed at all,' wheezed the Farmer's sister. 'Coming here with your smutty talk and aristocracy. You ought to be horsewhipped. Horsewhipped, I say!' She tried to get up but swayed alarmingly and the Farmer guided her back on to her seat.

The Woman and Harris took advantage of the Farmer's distraction and scuttled off out of the back door, standing ajar in a distant wall. Soon, they were running for their lives through the farmyard, past the perplexed cowman, while the Farmer's bellows followed them, underscored by the distinct click of a double-barrelled shotgun being cocked.

Eventually, they came to a stand of trees and hid there, each leaning on a mighty oak which could have sheltered most of the Agent's horde under its spreading branches. They leaned there, catching their breath. Finally, the Woman spoke.

'That was a bit exciting there, for a minute,' she said.

'I'm not sure I like exciting,' Harris said. 'Nice bacon, though.'

'That's what you get with farmers,' she agreed. 'All hand reared. But I wasn't talking about the breakfast.'

'Neither was I. But if I talk about the rest, I may have some kind of hysterical fit and although I am not in uniform, it wouldn't be becoming. He'll be on the blower, for sure. JPs are like that, Government to a man. I used to think I was a stickler for regulations, but his sort ...'

They rested for another few moments, the short exchanges having exhausted their breath.

'And what was all that about me having a very? And what about you wearing makeup? How old are you, really? And ...'

'I'm too breathless to answer more than one question,'

the Woman said. 'Which would you like?'

Harris was disgruntled. He really needed to know the answer to them all. The issue of the very was simple – she had made it up, because he was almost certain his came well within the normal range. The makeup and the age was almost the same issue – it was really the why that was important.

'All right. The makeup.'

'That is so simple and obvious I wonder you ask it. I am a wanted woman, you must have noticed that. And a bit of slap is the easiest way to hide and of course, no one notices an old lady.'

'It's funny, that,' Harris said. 'I had never thought of you as an old lady. You're too ...' he was stuck for the word, but what he wanted to say was vibrant, alive, something like that. It seemed too intimate, though, and although he had only been her lover in a story, it was a step too far, somehow. Too cheeky. Too impertinent.

'Thank you,' she said. 'I think I know what you're trying to say. But don't worry, I don't have designs on you; despite not being old, I am far too old for you. As well as being taken.'

'Oh.'

'Oh and?'

'I don't know what you mean.'

'I fell in love one day a lifetime ago and so – I'm taken.'

'But you said it didn't work that way.'

'My goodness,' she laughed. 'Mr Elephant Memory. Don't do as I do, do as I tell you, that's my advice. But we can't stay here. We need to move on.'

'Where is the car from here?' Harris's geographical shortcomings were not improving with time.

'We can't use the car any more,' the Woman said. 'That oaf of a farmer meant what he said. That cowman will be in the village by now, rounding up a posse, unless I miss my guess. No, we'll have to think again. Have you got your breath back now?'

'I think so.'

'Then let's be off. The farm is that way,' she pointed, 'and the village is that way. So we go this way. Come on. Follow me.'

And they headed off, up a bit and to the left.

THE END OF THE BEGINNING ...

Or the Beginning of the End ...

As they set off at a very determined pace, Harris couldn't help comparing his current situation to the one he was enjoying when he first stepped out to find Jack Jones. He would have been lying to himself if he had pretended that he had expected anything more than a short stroll across London taking a couple of hours at most. And now here he was, he couldn't work out how many days later, jogging across open country, following the Woman, who appeared to be completely calm despite having been stripped of her support system, cars, people and, presumably, money.

'You're fit at least,' the Woman said, glancing at him. 'The last time I did this, I was with someone in far worse shape than you.'

'Last time?' Harris couldn't imagine how anyone would do this more than once. Angry mobs he had seen; running from them on a regular basis seemed unnecessarily risky. 'You mean you've done this before?'

She looked at him in surprise. 'Of course. Surely you have things that you have done more than once.'

'Well, of course. Breakfast. Going to work. Not ... not running for my life.'

'Oh,' she flapped a hand at him. 'Don't exaggerate.

We're not running for our lives. In my experience, mobs don't chase anyone for long. And besides, can you hear a mob?' She stopped and listened extravagantly, her hand cupped round her ear. 'No. That's because they are still in the village, working out who's in charge, how far they are going to chase us, whether anyone is going to stump up for out of pocket expenses. You know, the usual British way. So don't worry.'

'So ... why are we hurrying, then?'

'To catch the tide, Bobby, my boy. To catch the tide. Do you know what day it is?'

'Not a clue,' he said. 'Thursday?'

'It's the thirtieth of April,' she said. 'Tomorrow's the first of May.'

* * *

The Farmer's sister flinched at the hammering at the door. Her brother had gone out to send the cowman down to the village as promised and she could still hear him out in the yard, mobilizing the remaining farm workers to fetch that bloody Woman's car in, get it in the barn so she couldn't use it. He was sending men out to scour the hedges and ditches, under the hedges, probably, where he was convinced the Woman would be taking advantage of the boy she had with her. He was cursing the day they'd cut his phone off, when they'd told him he wasn't a JP any more. She, Elspeth, had never been privy to anything of that nature, but she was quite sure that her brother's belief that it was a constant preoccupation was probably not that accurate – she had just never dared to tell him. She hunkered down in her chair and counted the picot edging on her handkerchief, a habit she had had since a child, when her father would rampage around the farm in just the way her brother was doing now. She shut her eyes and waited for the noise to stop.

It stopped with a splintering crash and suddenly, the room was full of men in khaki uniforms, bristling with guns. They trampled the carpets and upset the tables of knickknacks which were her only comfort and one of them, his hat shading his face even in the daylight, was leaning over her suddenly, his mouth opening and closing, but she couldn't understand what he was saying. She cowered and counted and squeezed her eyes shut and waited for it all to go away. He wasn't wearing khaki; he was in funereal black.

'Ignore her, Boss,' one of the Men said, giving her ankle a savage kick. 'She's as mad as all get out, look at her. She's drooling. All these country types, they're all the same.'

The Agent looked down at the quivering wreck in the chair and was inclined to agree. He shouted at her once again but this time she didn't even flinch. 'You'd think she'd at least deny they were here, wouldn't you?' he muttered. 'Simple enough thing. Then we could … well, we could persuade her.'

Some of the Men had wondered for some while whether the Agent was perfectly sane. He seemed to prefer winkling things out with a pin or other painful measure, rather than clever words, which had once been his stock in trade. The Man who had spoken first kicked the woman again, but she didn't even blink. He reached down and pulled an eyelid up. Her eye didn't move, just kept its fixed gaze on his shoes.

'Er … Boss,' he said, 'I think she's dead. A gonner.'

'Of course she isn't.' The Agent hated it when this happened. 'She was looking at me just a second ago.'

'Well, she ain't now,' the Man said. 'She's as dead as mutton. Look.' This time he rolled both eyelids up and it was undeniable. Elspeth, the maiden sister of the Farmer, was indeed as dead as a nit.

'Bugger.' The Agent tried not to swear – it demeaned him in front of the Men. But this really was a proper bugger. He hated the paperwork, for one thing, when they had a death in … well, he didn't like to call it custody. 'You, Men,' he said, raising his voice. 'Was this woman alive when we came in?'

'Yes.' Several voices murmured from various corners of the room.

'What?' The Agent cupped his ear.

'No.' A more definite reply this time.

'Good. In that case, we don't need to log it. Do we know who else lives here?'

'Her brother, apparently,' the one with the ledger said. 'It's a family place. Lucky to keep it, really, but they run it well enough, and all his beef and mutton goes to Headquarters. So ...' he shrugged. It was no good arguing with Headquarters.

'Right, then,' the Agent said. 'Let's go and look for the grieving brother. Outside, everyone.'

With a clatter of boots, the Men left the room and it was soon silent, with just the occasional shout from outside breaking the stillness. The Farmer's sister lay in her chair, already beginning to cool imperceptibly. Her dead eyes, frozen in their dying stare, looked blindly at the devastation wrought by the Men, broken tables, shattered mirrors and nothing of value left behind. But she didn't care. The small smile on her dead mouth said more eloquently than words that nothing could hurt her now. Nothing.

* * *

In the yard, the Agent and his horde watched as a strange cavalcade came around the corner of a half-demolished hayrick. Six men were pulling on ropes which were attached to an old and battered Morris, and behind them came the Farmer, shouting instructions and curses in approximately equal quantities. The men pulling the car had been ignoring him for the last quarter of a mile and in this way had avoided going into the duckpond and running over the prize bull. He was waving his arms around and was even more purple than usual. He stopped when he saw the Agent and the horde.

'Help you?' the Farmer barked. He was beginning to get a bit fed up with today.

'I don't know,' the Agent said. 'I haven't asked you anything yet.'

'Not for you to be doing the asking, is it?' The Farmer was on his own land, no matter what he was told to the contrary. As it happened, there were a few rather unfortunate government lackeys buried in the slurry pit, but that was for him to know and hopefully no one else to find out. But there were rather a lot of them, this time. A quick count suggested that he and his men were outnumbered at least three to one. And all the bastards were armed. The Farmer nevertheless struck a militant attitude, though keeping safely behind his men, who had dropped the ropes. The Morris had come to an ungainly stop, half through the rickyard gate.

'Hmmm. We'll see,' the Agent said. 'My first question would obviously be where did you get that car?'

'In my field,' the Farmer snapped. 'Mine, therefore.'

'Stealing,' the Agent snapped back. 'can still see you behind bars, if my memory serves.'

One of the horde stepped forward and whispered in his ear.

'My apologies,' the Agent said. 'Apparently as of the fifteenth inst., the punishment is rather more severe.' He looked at the Man who had spoken to him, who nodded. 'A little too draconian, perhaps but ... well, in these days, we must all expect to be kept in check with perhaps more zeal than formerly. So, I repeat, where did you get that car?'

The Farmer set his mouth and folded his arms. 'My field. My business.'

With the speed of a cobra, one of the Men suddenly had one of the Farmer's workers round the neck with a deathly hold. The man scrabbled with his hands at the rock hard forearm that was crushing his windpipe.

'Where did you get that car?' The Agent's tone had not changed.

'My field,' the Farmer said, looking straight at the Agent. 'My business.'

'Have you known that man long?' the Agent said, with a flick of the hand towards the struggling farm worker

'All his life, I suppose. His father worked for my father, that's how things work around here.'

'In that case,' the Agent said, 'and because I am a sentimental man at heart, I will ask you one last time. Where did you get that car?'

'For the love of God!' One of the workers broke ranks and ran forward. 'Let him go. It was in the field down there.

It belonged to some woman or other, travelling with a lad. I saw them walking up to the house with him.' He pointed at the Farmer, who was so angry he went white before he went magenta on his way to purple. 'They've gone now. I saw them crossing the fields there.' He pointed up and to the left. 'Now, please, let him go!'

The Agent nodded to the Man who dropped his prey like a stone. He lay on the ground, threshing like a landed fish, gasping for air.

'With luck, he should recover,' the Agent said. He clicked his fingers to his men. 'Half of you, I don't care which, follow them across the fields. The others, back to the trucks.' He looked with contempt at the Farmer, still standing at bay behind his remaining workers. 'As I said, he should recover,' the Agent said. 'Unlike your sister.'

The Farmer goggled at him, beyond words.

'She's in the sitting room,' the Agent said. 'I should hurry if I were you. It's a bugger when they stiffen up in a funny position.' He turned to his nearest minion. 'Do you remember that chap? Doncaster, the other day?'

'Oh, yes,' the minion said and made a very realistic snapping noise. 'Messy.'

'Messy. That's the word,' the Agent said, with an icy smile at the Farmer. 'Anyway, can't stop here chatting with you, delightful though it is. Traitors to catch, you know how it is.'

And in a hail of gravel and mud, the trucks accelerated down the farm track, back on the hunt.

For a moment, Baker toyed with going over to the huddled group and their car, to check on the old girl he'd just heard had died in the house, but time was pressing; he felt sure of that. And however elusive and resourceful the Woman was, she and the lad would be no match for the Home Guard.

* * *

'The tide?' Harris was confused. 'Are we near the sea, then?' He was looking left and right and all he saw was fields.

She risked stopping for a moment and grabbed his arm, turning him to the left. 'Can't you *smell* it?' she asked. 'Come on, Bobby, there's a good chap. Breathe in, go on, right down into the lungs. There. Smell that?'

Harris inhaled until his ears rang. He wanted to be helpful, but he didn't know what he was smelling for. 'I can smell ... grass,' he said, hopefully.

'Of course you can, you idiot,' she said. 'We're standing in acres of the stuff. Try again.'

'Cow shit?'

'Ditto. *Concentrate*! Breathe!'

'All right.' He tried a more dignified sniff, the sort of sniff he always imagined a wine connoisseur would use, should there still be any wine worth sniffing. 'Ooh, hang on. I think ... does it smell a bit like ... a bit metallic?'

'Possibly. A little bit. Do another.'

'It smells like ... lightning?'

'Lightning! Bobby, you've got it. You're smelling the ozone off the water. If you could stand here sniffing all day, you would get the iodine from the seaweed, the salt from the sand, the smell of little crabs waiting to be snatched up by a gull, the smell of tar from boats. Then, Bobby, you will know the smell of the sea. But meanwhile, we need to be on our way.' She stiffened. 'What's that sound?'

Harris, still standing with eyes closed, nostrils extended, said, 'Is it the waves?'

'No.' She punched his shoulder. 'I'm not talking about the sea any more. I mean that *sound*. Trucks, at least two. Coming up the road.' Instinctively, they both crouched down, eyeball to eyeball with the gorse.

He spun round, eyes wide. 'Yes,' he said. 'I can hear them.'

Ever since they had left the farm, they had been climbing steadily and now they were on the brow of a hill, down which a road snaked at a cruel angle. He could hear the cars struggling as their drivers tried to find the right gear before they stalled and rolled back.

'They are having trouble on the hill,' he said. He might not be able to drive, but he could tell the sound of an engine in trouble just the same.

'You need to know the roads around here.' The Woman grabbed his sleeve and pulled him across the road and over the verge on the other side. There was a drop of about ten feet, where the land had slipped some time in the last hundred years. The grass on the lower piece was cropped by rabbits just the same as the patch they stood on, but it also was studded with sea pinks and a giant tree lupin leaned out of the low cliff at a rakish angle. But Harris had no eyes for the grass upon which he would soon land – all he could comprehend was a huge grey-blue mass, quivering and heaving under the sun.

'What … what's *that*?' He was about to point but before he could, he was pulled off the grass by the Woman and seconds later was spreadeagled on the grass below. He grunted as the breath left his body and gulped several times as he tried to force air back into his lungs. He grabbed handfuls of grass and bucked and writhed as he struggled to breathe. The Woman sat him up and thumped him between the shoulderblades and suddenly, he had oxygen and his eyes stopped spinning.

'What *is* that?' he wheezed.

'It's the sea, you fool,' she said. 'Surely, everyone knows what the sea looks like.'

'How could I?' he said. And at that point he realized for good and all that he and the Woman came from different worlds. 'It's not allowed. Only fishermen are allowed and they have to sign all sorts of things.'

'Don't quote the rules at me,' the Woman said. 'I wrote most of them. Surely, you must have seen pictures.'

'I've seen some pictures of boats,' he said. 'When I was at school. But I don't really remember …'

'Didn't you go on holiday when you were little?' The Woman put her finger to her lip suddenly. 'Sssh. The trucks are making the hill. Shuffle back here, under this underhang. If they find us here, it will be like shooting fish in a barrel.'

'Who are they?'

'Home Guard. They'll have an Agent with them, just to make sure they all behave.'

'Do they?'

She shook her head. 'God, Bobby, what are we going to do with your generation? Look down there. See that?'

'It's a wood.' He hoped he had followed her pointing finger correctly.

'Holmeswood,' she nodded. 'See where the road snakes through it? That's where we're heading, at least for the night. You can't see it from here but there's a pub, the Jack-in-the-Green. They should all be there by now, those of them who made it.'

'They?' He blinked. 'Who do you mean?'

She clapped her hand over his mouth as they crouched under the cliff and the trucks rattled by above their heads. When the last labouring engine was gone, they leaned back with their legs outstretched on the cropped grass, the afternoon sun warm on their faces. Harris still couldn't take his eyes off the sea. Every now and again, a larger than normal wave broke the surface in a flourish of white. Far on the horizon, a lone fishing boat patrolled its beat. Suddenly, a spout of water made Harris cry out and point.

'What's that? That there!'

'My word,' The Woman was quite moved. 'Mother Nature is putting on quite the display for you today, Bobby, my lad. That's a school of dolphins. You don't get them that often off this coast. That really is something. Your first view of the sea and of dolphins, all in the same ten minutes. Some people go their whole lives and don't see a dolphin. Perhaps it's an omen.' She watched his face as he glowed with pleasure. She had seen dolphins off almost every coast the world had to offer, so his face was a greater pleasure for her than the grey mammals doing what they did best out to sea.

Finally, the dolphins moved off, down and to the left, and Harris tore his eyes away from the sea. 'How did people feel, who had lived by the sea, when they were told they couldn't?'

'That's a very perceptive question,' the Woman said. 'I think the ones who moved were the ones who could bear it. The ones who couldn't – well, they waited to be taken away, because how could that be worse?'

'I think I'm beginning to see why you ...' Harris stopped. He didn't want to be rude.

'Why I screw the system wherever I can? Thank you for understanding that. It will set us in good stead for the next few hours.'

'What's going to happen?' Harris sat up straight and looked at her. 'I still don't really know.'

'Who does?' She shrugged.

'Do you mean that? You really don't know?'

'I thought I had made that clear. Haven't you been listening?'

'Well, of course. But you have said so many things that I don't know whether they are true or not.'

'Name one.' The Woman delved into a pocket and pulled out a compact and made repairs to her face. Another pocket provided lipstick and a comb.

'Well, to start with, Nanny being your nanny.'

'Absolutely true. Why wouldn't it be?'

'When I thought you were old it seemed to make sense. But now I know you are ...'

She cocked an eyebrow at him and waited.

'... not so old, I wonder. She would have already been well over sixty when she was your nanny.'

'Anything wrong with that? Anyway, Nanny doesn't really count birthdays in the conventional sense. Any more than I do, in fact. Next.'

'Why did the knitting lady call you Genevieve?'

'Why do I call you Bobby?' she countered. 'It was how she knew me Before. We were colleagues, young, impressionable, doing our bit in a man's world and having a whale of a time. I could tell you more,' she suddenly laughed, 'but of course I'd have to kill you.'

He tried to laugh, but that didn't really work. The Copper in him had seen something dark and steel in her handbag and he really hoped it wasn't what he thought it was.

'How old are you?'

'How old do you think?'

He always hated this. Occasionally, little old ladies

with missing dogs or cats would come in to the station and when he asked their date of birth for the records, they often said 'Guess'. And although he often took a good twenty years off, they were still almost always affronted when he actually aged them by ten years. He was just no good at this. 'I don't … oh, go on, then. Shot in the dark. Thirty-seven.'

'Perfect. Spot on.' She was outlining her eyes with a liner that had appeared from nowhere. 'Sorry, did you want to borrow my comb?'

'Not really.' He was feeling that piss was being taken, but wasn't sure how or why.

She looked at him. 'I think you should, you know. Also, look, pull one of those teasels.'

'Those what?'

She sighed. 'You're such a townie. One of those spikey jobs over there. Brush yourself down. You're all over fluff and cat hair. You have looked like a lint factory ever since we visited the Knitter, to be honest. Yes, there you are. Look, give it to me. I'll give you a brush.'

Harris stood and waited patiently while the Woman brushed him down and then let her comb his hair. He closed his eyes when she licked her handkerchief and wiped around his mouth. 'Bacon grease,' she explained. 'We can't meet Jack Jones with you looking like a chimney sweep.'

'But … where is he? When will we meet him?'

She laughed and cuffed him round the head. 'Just because I have combed your hair for you and given your face a lick and a promise doesn't mean you have to behave like a toddler. It is by no means a given, we still have to get there and hope that Agent and his mob don't get to Jack or us first.'

'Agent? How do you know?'

'Because he's been behind you since you stepped out of the police station. Just because you didn't see him doesn't mean he wasn't there. But now he's close, very close, and he will soon realize that he has overshot. So we have, I would estimate, about half an hour before it's all too late.'

'What will happen if it is too late?' Harris was trying not to sound like a toddler, but sometimes it didn't work too well.

'If it's too late, well … I suppose the world ends or something. It wasn't in my orders. But let's hope we don't have to wait around to find out.'

'Your orders? But … but you're …'

'I'm no one, Bobby. I'm just the Woman.'

'I know you're a woman, but …'

'No, Bobby. Not *a* woman. The Woman. You'll understand. Or you'll be dead. Either way, I've got to get to that pub. Now, follow me and do exactly as I do, all right. Don't question. Don't try and do it a better way, an easier way. Just follow me.' She grabbed his chin in her hand and made him look her in the eye. '*Capisci?*'

'*Capisco.*' Harris opened his eyes in surprise.

'My word,' the Woman said. 'It seems you speak Italian.'

'That's twenty years hard, I think,' he said, with a smile.

'I think it is. We'll see. Now, come on, follow me and put your feet where I put mine. No exceptions. Do you promise?'

'I do.'

'Then let's go.'

* * *

The trucks had rattled through the wood and had not so much as slowed down by the pub. That was good. The Woman wasn't running now, bit striding steadily along the hedgerows. It was a dull, miserable day, approaching dusk and the weather had nothing of the joys of spring about it. The dim lights of the Jack-in-the-Green twinkled among the foliage of Holmeswood. There were one or two vehicles outside, but the licensing laws meant that the place was shut. The Woman sneaked around the back and tapped on the leaded windowpane. She put her face nearer the glass. 'I heard the running grave tonight,' she said softly.

'I know the song,' a voice answered and the door grated open. 'Hello, dearie,' the woman who had opened the door said. 'I hope I got that right, did I, the code? I don't know, I get so forgetful, these days.'

'You did,' the Woman smiled, 'but how did you get here ahead of us?'

A man's voice answered. '*We* didn't have to keep making detours. No price on our heads, yet.' And he hugged the Woman to him.

Harris was astonished. It was the Innkeeper and his wife from the Cow and Pasture.

'We've only just arrived, to be fair. There seems to be some sort of Remnant gathering in Formby. We stayed wide of them.'

'Very wise,' the Woman said. 'You didn't fancy a philosophical conversation with them, then, trying to reconvert the converted?'

The Innkeeper laughed. 'I know a waste of time when I see one,' he said. 'Come in. The gang's all here.'

He led the way through a darkened passageway into a large snug at the back. Harris stood open-mouthed. Scattered around the room, with appropriate drinks in front of them, were most of the motley rabble he had been introduced to in the past few days. The Singer, looking as suave as he was ever likely to, was predictably nearest the bar. He raised a gin and tonic to the lad. 'Hello, dear boy.'

'It's time for introductions, I think.'

'Names?' the Innkeeper said. 'Is that wise?'

'It's now or never, Greg,' she said. 'Everybody, this is Bobby, as I think you know. Actually, he is PC Robert Harris.'

'PC?' The Singer's face fell. 'That's even less wise than names.'

'Relax, Grant. He's one of us now.'

She half turned to Harris. 'You probably recognized Mr Golden Tonsils there from Before,' she said. 'His face was everywhere, back in the day. I give you Mr Grant Anstruther.' There was a ripple of applause and the Singer half-bowed. 'Actually,' the Woman whispered in Harris's ear, 'he's Alfie Herring from Chester-le-Street, but don't burst his bubble.' She led Harris around the room. 'Mine host for this evening, now he's taken over behind the bar again,' there were jeers and laughter, 'is Greg Embleton, PhD and Bar – excuse the pun – and his good lady, Mattie.'

The little woman grinned at the boy and mine host raised a glass he was polishing.

'My dear old Nanny,' the Woman hugged her and gave her a kiss. '*So* glad you're here.'

'I'm delighted to be included,' the old girl said. 'Are we the last cohort?'

'For now,' the Woman said. 'Nanny's name …'

'No, no,' the old lady held up her hand. 'I've been Nanny now for so long, anything else wouldn't sound right. Now, spit spot, on with the introductions.'

'Delighted to meet you again, sir.' An old man held out his hand. It was the Bishop – or was it the Butler? He wasn't wearing purple and he didn't carry a tray either. Harris couldn't put his finger on it but the Jack-in-the-Green seemed to have re-energized him and his joints didn't click any more.

'My Lord,' Harris said.

'Dear boy,' the Bishop wiped a tear from his eye.

Harris and the Woman had net everybody ow and stood together at the bar. 'There's no Dresser, of course,' the Woman said. 'Not now she's joined the Remnant. I must admit, I wasn't expecting that. There'll be no Duchess, for the same reason. What a pity.' She was looking round the snug. 'No Knitter either, which is odd. Anybody seen Marjorie?'

There were shakings of heads and grunts all round.

'Well, I expect she's been held up,' the Woman said, taking a large gin and tonic from the Innkeeper and passing another to Harris.

'What about you?' he asked. 'You haven't introduced yourself.'

She laughed. 'The name wouldn't mean anything to you,' she said. 'I'll settle for Genevieve. Gen.'

'And you *are* the Actress?'

'I am,' she bowed with a flourish, 'but, hang on, where are my manners? There's one person you've been dying to meet.' And she led him along the bar to a recessed corner.

A nondescript man sat at a table there. His height was

average, his hair ... so. His eyes, a curious green-grey. Nothing about him was remarkable at all. You'd pass him in the street any day.

'Hello,' he stood up. 'I'm Jack Jones.'

For a moment, Harris didn't know whether to laugh or cry. The voice on the wireless he seemed to have heard all his life had a face and a presence.

'Jack,' the Woman said, 'this is Robert.'

'I prefer Bobby,' Harris said, and he shook the man's hand.

* * *

The next day – *the* day that everybody had been waiting for – dawned bright and clear. Harris had slept in a little bed in an attic room with a sloping roof, the wallpaper a ghastly Twenties thing with grapes and vines. He got dressed and wandered down the stairs to find the Woman and Jack Jones deep in conversation. He remembered the poster – just before the Amazing Maurice – Jack and Jill and their novelty act. The childhood friends who were ... what now? Lovers? Fellow travellers? Comrades in arms?'

'There's breakfast in the kitchen,' the Woman told Harris. 'Nothing lavish, I'm afraid. It's five miles to the Point and it'll be the longest five miles of the journey.'

He looked at her. 'You knew, didn't you?' he asked. 'You knew exactly where Jack Jones was all along. All that stuff about up and bit and left a bit. And asking people if they knew his whereabouts.'

'I am sitting right here, you know,' Jones smiled.

'Sorry,' Harris said. 'You've been a shadow for so long I wasn't always sure that you were real.'

'Ah,' Jones said. 'The Holy Grail of broadcasters. You have to be a bit will o' the wisp in my line, the blur you see disappear around the corner before you realize you've seen anything. Have you told him?' he asked the Woman.

'Not yet,' she said. 'It'll keep. Bobby, we have a problem.'

'No, really?' Harris looked pained and sat on a bar

stool. The Bishop or even the Scoutmaster might have been philosopher enough to make the point that all life was a problem, certainly now, if not Before; but perhaps that was a glimpse of the bleeding obvious.

'The Remnant,' she said. 'We hadn't factored in May Day.'

'I don't follow,' Harris said.

'We chose the First of May so I could broadcast it in my shows,' Jones told him. 'There aren't too many songs with dates in them, so Gen came up with today as a clear instruction over the airwaves.'

'But you've done this before,' Harris reasoned.

'But this is the last of us,' the Woman went on. 'The inner circle and of course,' she held her arms wide like a circus ring-master, 'the legendary Jack Jones himself.'

'Unaccustomed as I am …' Jones wiped his hand over his face like Rob Wilton.

'But it was getting more difficult all the time. The Government are cracking down in a way they haven't done before. As you've noticed, there are Home Guard everywhere.

'And the Roundheads are gathering, too,' Jones nodded. 'If they're not recruiting for active service, they're setting up firing squads for a little bit of lesson-teaching. Behave or die's the motto of both lots now. Which brings us back to the Church Remnant,' Jones said. 'We knew they have their big days, the First of May being one of them. What we didn't know was that they'd hold a rally here, at Formby. The town's crawling with them, sobbing and wailing like the lunatics they are. They're making for the sea, just like us.'

'To start a new life?' Harris asked.

'No,' the Woman chuckled. 'They're happy, poor deluded bastards, with what they've got. Have you ever wondered what they believe in?'

Harris shrugged. 'God, I suppose.'

'God's a grey area,' Jones said, 'a side issue. Like every cult throughout history, it's really about the here and now not the hereafter. Today, they'll be up to their waists in water, evoking the spirit of the sea. Tomorrow they'll be hugging trees for all I know. It'll all end with their kit off and a bit of mild orgying.'

The Woman tutted and shook her head. 'Jack, you old cynic,' she said.

'But,' Jones reached for the cup of tea on the bar, 'if we can't beat 'em, we might as well join 'em.'

'How do you mean?' Harris asked.

'One man's problem is another man's solution,' the Woman said. 'The Remnant, according to our information, are beginning their procession at four o'clock, when, Before …' and she and Jones broke into song. '"Everything stops for tea",' they all laughed.

'They're setting off from the old Post Office in the High Street. Others will join them on the road,' Jones said.

'Those others,' the Woman murmured, 'will be us. A bit like the other day, Bobby, when you suddenly became my son and lost your voice, all in one tricky afternoon. Do as we do, blend in and maybe, just maybe, we'll all get away with this.'

* * *

There was only so much sleeping in a car a man could do. Baker stretched in the cramped rear seats and heard more bones click than he knew he had. He peered out of the window. The Jack-in-the-Green looked quiet, almost deserted and the May Day sun meant that there was no need for lights inside. He didn't know what made him abandon his surveillance of the trucks when they'd gone on to Formby and the coast. Perhaps it was a sixth sense; perhaps he'd got used to the Woman's sneaky ways by now. His throat was bricky dry and he couldn't remember when he'd had a square meal last. And don't get him started on pissing and shitting in the hedgerows …

The Agent and his men had commandeered the Douglas View tea-rooms and hotel. They'd put their 'Keep Out' signs around the little car park and placed armed guards at the entrance. The family staying in Room 21 were kicked out, bag and baggage, despite the sobbing of the woman and the attitude of the husband. Oddly enough, that attitude disappeared in the face of a Lee-Enfield rifle butt, bullying moron, for the use of. They'd gone quietly.

The Agent was annoyed by all this distraction. He knew in his water that the Woman and her boy would be making for the coast, a mile and a half away. He got up to the roof balcony of the Douglas View and trained his binoculars on the coast ahead. Barbed wire, rotting traps, deserted pillboxes, silent in their cement. Away in the distance, as the mist lifted, he could make out the grey lump that was the Isle the Man to the north. Ireland he couldn't see. But then, why would he want to? He let his binoculars angle down to the beach again and the single road that ran from the town. In the streets below, the Church of the Remnant were forming up with floats fluttering with flowers and excited children screaming around then, getting in everybody's way. The Agent had no time for any of that; he had no children of his own and couldn't remember being a child himself.

He clicked his fingers to a minion who stood to attention at his side. 'Find out when these religious maniacs are going to set off and where they're going.' He gripped the man's sleeve. 'And put that lanyard straight. Where do you think you are, man?'

'Yessir,' the lad did as he was told. 'Sorry, sir.'

Waiting. That's what the Agent hated about his job. He was always waiting for somebody else.

* * *

One of the people who had slid by under the gaze of the Agent's binoculars was the Dresser. She'd been looking forward to this outing for a while now and hoped she might meet up with the Duchess again, but there was no sign. She sat on a bench, along with other adherents of the faith, all driven to this by desperation and the need of most people to belong to the herd, the tribe. She nibbled her cheese sandwich and sipped the tea from her Thermos. The ride in the charabanc had been lovely, if a little tiring, what with the potholes and the community hymn singing. She hadn't been a Remnant convert all that long and she kept trying to sing the old Anglican words to the hymn tunes the Remnant had pinched. 'Lord of all hopefulness, Lord of all calm, Whose voice is contentment, whose presence is balm' still secretly meant more to her than 'Here in our darkness, now all light is gone, The Remnant will save us, the Remnant lives on'. Hmm, she had thought to herself; needs work.

She couldn't help but notice, as she sat there, the breeze from the distant sea blowing its fragrance into her face, that those nasty Government men from the Home Guard were prowling in pairs up and down the Front. They stopped by some people and prodded a couple with their rifle muzzles. Then they came for her.

'How old are you, mother?' one of them asked.

She peered up at him, squinting into the sun. 'That's none of your business, sonny,' she said.

He loomed over her. 'I'll make it my business, bitch,' he growled.

'Let it go, Arnold,' his oppo said. 'The old cow ain't worth a bullet.'

The first man straightened. 'S'pose,' he said, 'if you're gonna march with these herberts,' he said to the Dresser, 'don't get under my feet, all right?'

The Dresser smiled at him. As he walked away, she called, 'I'm sixty-four. No chance of a threesome, I suppose?'

And the guard's oppo was already dragging him away before anybody saw the steam coming out of his ears.

* * *

In the snug of the Jack-in-the-Green, the little cohort of leavers was forming up. Some of them weren't as sprightly as they'd once been, but they knew the procession would be slow, so there was no rush. They left in ones or twos so as not to attract too much attention along the road through the woods, each of them with a plausible story in their heads should they be stopped.

In the end, only Jack Jones, the Woman and Harris sat waiting. The little clock in the corner ticked to itself and the chimes rang for half past three. The Actress in the Woman made a bid for freedom. She had never really believed in playing against type and especially against gender, but you couldn't beat a nice bit of Henry Vee. 'We are time's subjects, and time bids be gone.' They all got to their feet.

'No, not you, Bobby,' she said. 'Three of us on the road is chancing our arm. Give us five minutes by the clock. You're making for the Town Hall in the High Street; that's the Remnants' setting off point.'

'Oh. All right.'

Jack Jones bent his arm and made a half-bow. 'Ready, Jill?'

'Ready, Jack,' she said and linked her arm with his.

Then they were gone. And Harris had never felt so alone in his life. Sometimes, in his little room at the Landlady's, he had lain in the dusk on his hard, narrow bed and listened to the murmurings from below, some singing, even, sometimes, and had felt so lonely he could have cried. But that feeling had nothing on this, that the entire world had just gone out, shutting the door softly as it went. He listened to the clock, to those thousand little clicks that happened in every building in the land, which everyday life usually drowned out; the shifting of the foundations, the creak of timbers, the groan of glass.

'Hello, Bobby,' a voice made him spin round. 'We'd better be off.'

He couldn't believe it. At the bottom of the stairs, no longer in the boiler suit but with the same red hair and gorgeous smile was Gladys. *His* Gladys. The girl he thought he'd never see again. He wanted to hold her, kiss her, never let her go. But they had both been caught up in the magic that was Jack Jones now and they just linked arms and slipped out of the door, following in the footsteps of Jack and Jill.

In the way that people meant for each other sometimes will, they broke into song, under their breath, at the same time.

'Follow the yellow brick road,' murmured Gladys.

'Follow the yellow brick road.' Bobby had always had an ear for a tune.

'Follow, follow, follow, follow, follow the yellow brick road.'

But were they off to see the wizard, or something much darker? Arm in arm, on a glorious spring afternoon, they hardly cared.

* * *

'The sea be with us!'
   'Amen.'
   'The sky be with us!'
   'Amen.'
   'Keep us safe from the dark.'
   'The dark! The dark!'

Harris had never heard anything quite like it. He'd seen gatherings of the Remnant before, circling Hyde Park, tramping round the Aldwych. They'd always been watched by the police who would move in now and then to pick ringleaders and troublemakers out of the crowd. He had no idea how many were here – three hundred? Four? Quite a few were the old and infirm, hobbling on sticks or being pushed in wheelchairs. He didn't recognize any of the faces at the front, the people in robes with flags and icons raised high. Oddly, there were no crosses, nothing he recognized from the churches Before at all.

They all swayed from side to side as though dragging some huge weight behind them, lased by ropes and leather. A single drum kept time, not a military drum which the army had used back in the day, but something out of Africa, with a boom and a thud that sank to the bottom of your soul.

Gladys walked alongside him and he was careful to keep Jack Jones and the Woman in view. He knew the Bishop was behind him, but couldn't, as yet, see the others. They left the street outside the Town Hall, fanning out along the Front where the floats were lined up. There was a long delay while these got in line and everybody shuffled around to accommodate them. He saw the Dresser hobble to her feet from a bench, her hands clasped in prayer and her lips moving. Some salvation, this.

The sun had gone now, masked by gathering clouds and it was still the best part of a mile to the water's edge. Again and again, despite the swaying, praying, groaning tide of humanity around him, he was drawn to the sea; he who had never seen it. He chuckled to himself as he remembered his Sunday School in the years Before, that the saviour Jesus could walk on water. He knew now, if he didn't know it before, that that wasn't possible. Then he saw the Woman, shoulders back, head high and knew that she could. Walk on water? Ain't it like her.

Then, a movement on the cliff caught his eye. A man in black with his hat pulled down was leading a column of Home Guard along the ridge. Their rifles were slung over their backs, but they had their battle bowlers on, ready for action. He tried to catch the Woman's attention, Jack Jones's, anybody's, but they marched on regardless, swaying, singing now the stolen hymns of Before.

He caught Gladys's hand and squeezed it, closing in to her. 'Home Guards,' he muttered.

He saw her blink. 'What are they doing?'

He looked left and right. 'Forming a firing squad. Move to the right,' and, still swaying to the drum, he pushed her gently to the centre of the procession. They were at the Front now and fanning out as the floats were hauled onto the sand. He felt the ground soft and moving under his feet and read the fear in Gladys's eyes. The column had become a line, a scattering of people between the floats, garlands floating madly in the rising wind. To the right, the beach fell away to hidden depths. The red flags warning the bathers of Before had long gone and barbed wire lay half buried in the sand. At the edge of the line, one of the floats lurched, the tide hitting it and rocking it to a standstill.

It was then that he saw them, a line of soldiers on the other cliff, the lower one to the right. He felt Gladys's hand clutch his, because she had seen them too. 'Home Guard?' she mouthed.

Harris was shaking his head. 'No,' he said. 'Roundheads.'

'They're going to kill us,' she hissed, fighting the terror

inside her. 'Catch us between them like rats in a trap.'

'No,' Harris said. 'The Government and the Roundheads don't exactly sing from the same hymn book. They're both after us, it's true, but, with a bit of luck ...' He pulled her back into the centre as he felt the water hit his feet. It was just a trickle at first, that first wave. The second was harder, faster, circling his ankles with froth and spume, pulling the sand from beneath his feet. The third hit his knees and rocked him backwards. Dear God, was Nature against them too?

'Bobby!' Gladys's skirt had ballooned up on the water's thrust.

'Hang on,' he shouted over the rising roar of the wind. 'Hang on to me. It can't be long now, surely.'

He remembered the plan was to reach a boat at dusk, to disappear in the confusion of twilight, but it was still broad daylight and it wouldn't be dark for hours. The procession of the Remnant had advanced too quickly, longing for their salvation in the sea as they were. The water was shallower now where Harris and Gladys stood, the beach firmer under their tread. Even so, they were nearly up to their waists in water and the cold was numbing.

He couldn't hear the snick of the rifle bolts on both sides of the beach, but he could see the Home Guard taking up positions, the front rank kneeling, the rear standing. He counted thirty-two guns; they would decimate the unarmed mass in the water, trailing their hands in the stuff and throwing it over themselves, laughing hysterically as the cold took hold. At the front, in the centre, someone lit a flare and the sky turned pink-purple as though God himself had loosed a lightning bolt. There was a roar from the Remnant and when it subsided, a single voice was bellowing over a loudhailer.

'Church of the Remnant. Stay where you are. Stand still and no one will get hurt.'

Harris tried to identify the hailer. It was the Agent, standing like an ox in the furrow, commanding the Red Sea not to part, whatever analogy flooded the minds of both men.

No one knew who fired first. Some said it was the

Home Guard; some, the Roundheads. Somebody said it was one of the crowd, a madman among madmen, a renegade in the Remnant. It didn't matter. The rattle of rifles shattered the afternoon at what was once a peaceful seaside village where the gulls wheeled and soared, minding their own business. People were running, screaming, floundering in the water now stained red. Here and there, people leapt from the floats, others fell, dropped by a bullet.

Whatever the Agent's plan had been, he'd abandoned it now, screaming at his men to carry on shooting. On the other side, the Roundheads were firing too, creating as much carnage as the Guard.

'Down!' It was Jack Jones, shouting orders. 'Everybody down!' Those nearest to him dropped to their hands and knees, spitting out salt water and sand. Others dithered, racing backwards and forwards, wrestling with each other, fighting the water as best they could. Harris cradled Gladys in his arms, on his knees as he was, trying to work out what was happening. One or two of the Home Guard went down, hit by bullets from the other side of the beach. Suddenly, Jack Jones was at the boy's elbow, crouching in the crimson froth. 'Can you use one of these?' He was holding out a Webley.

'I can try,' Harris said.

'Good. Get as close as you can to the left. That bastard in black, he's the ringleader. Take him out.' He patted the gun and smiled at the boy. 'But take the safety catch off first.' And then he was gone. Harris glanced round. He saw the Woman wading through the shallows, making for the right cliff, for the Roundhead line. He could see a gun in her hand. He grabbed Gladys's arm and pulled her to him, kissing her hard on the lips. 'Stay here,' he said. 'I'll be back.'

'No!' she screamed, but he didn't listen to anyone. Or he knew he'd never leave.

A woman died in front of him, her head shattered and her blood eddying on the tide. He shoved a screaming toddler into somebody's arms and made his way to the left, to the low cliff with its deadly line of fire. There. There was the Agent. All Harris had to do ... A large Home Guardsman had leapt from his position, blocking his path, his rifle muzzle pointing

216

at him. Harris didn't have time to think. He jerked his revolver upwards and fired. The gun kicked in his hand and he saw the Guard reel back, blood spurting from his nose and mouth. Harris grabbed the rifle, but lost it immediately in the scrabble at the cliff's foot. He fired at the nearest Guardsman, who was aiming his rifle at the handful still struggling on the floats. The man spun sideways, then pitched forwards into the water. The firing line had seen Harris now and were half-turning to face him. A scatter of shots took down two of them and Harris turned to see the Innkeeper, up to his waist in water, grinning at him.

As he spun back to find his real target, he realized that the target had found him. The Agent was kneeling in the dunes, an automatic cocked in his hand, the muzzle pointing at Harris's head. There was a crash of rifle fire in the lad's left ear and he saw the Agent look down disbelievingly as the crimson stain spread over his coat. Harris looked up, eyes wild, heart thumping.

'You picked a hell of a day to take a paddle, lad' the rifleman said.

'Sarge?' Harris was lost for words.

The man looked him up and down. 'You do know you've lost a button there, don't you?'

* * *

Cromwell checked his revolver, if only to stop the damn thing sticking into his armpit. Alongside him, Fairfax had already had enough.

'Sir, we're killing people. They're unarmed civilians. There are kids down there.'

'*We* aren't killing them, Fairfax,' his commander said. 'Those Home Guard bastards are. And anyway, Jack Jones is in that melee somewhere and he's not getting away with it. Good God!'

Fairfax followed Cromwell's pointing finger out to sea. A dinghy, dangling with floats and bobs was arcing its way towards the beach.

'The getaway boat!' Fairfax said, 'You were right.

How many would it carry, do you think?'

'Enough,' Cromwell grunted. 'But we don't know how many we're after, do we? Jones, Genevieve and that idiot lad we know about. But there must be others. Pym!'

Another minion scuttled over. 'Yes, sir?'

'Have your men concentrate their fire on that boat.'

'It's out of range, sir.'

'Well, wait until it isn't, man!' Cromwell bellowed. He needn't have shouted so loudly because Pym couldn't hear him. He fell poleaxed at Cromwell's feet, blood oozing from his temple. 'Bugger,' Cromwell growled.

Ireton watched Pym die. She checked his pulse, but there was nothing she could do for him. She glanced up to where the boat was idling in the shallows, engine roaring, bubbles bouncing off the stern. A knot of people were wading out to it, as bullets pinged the water around them. She didn't recognize them all, not any of them, actually. Wait, there was the Bishop, silly old fart. The Innkeeper and his wife. God almighty, not the Singer? How was he still on his feet? But one who wasn't there …

'Hello, it's Ireton, isn't it?' The voice made her turn. Below the low headland, under the guns of the Roundheads, the Woman stood there, pistol level.

'I wondered if you'd realized,' the Knitter said.

'I didn't,' the Woman admitted, 'but I knew all the Roundhead high command, by sight and reputation. Cromwell, Fairfax, Pym … the only one I couldn't place was Ireton. As soon as I saw your people on the cliff, I knew. Only you could have cracked Jack Jones's codes. Miss Purl. Miss Plain. Miss Fibonacci. Tell me, Sis, did you hear the running grave tonight?' And she fired.

She fired. And nothing happened. 'Damn.'

'It's all the excitement,' the Knitter said. 'That's the trouble with Webleys, isn't it? Six shots and that's your lot. But this,' she held up her pistol, 'has eleven shots.' For a long moment, the sisters stared into each other's eyes. Then the Knitter fired, but she'd turned the gun sideways, at arm's length, and the bullet thudded harmlessly into the sand.

'You'd be brown bread without Jack Jones,' the

Knitter murmured, and jerked her head towards the boat. The Woman smiled and hurtled back down the beach, struggling through the bodies and the debris of the floats.

Without the Agent, the Home Guard were falling back, unnerved, shaky, leaderless.

'Cease fire!' Cromwell ordered and his ranks obeyed, shouldering their arms and listening to the crying of the Remnant and the sobbing of the sea. The dinghy engine roared into life as those on board hauled the Woman out of the water. Cromwell caught the Knitter's eye.

'I must be slipping,' she smiled, 'missed her. Me!'

'Fairfax,' Cromwell said, 'take Ireton into custody, will you? Maximum security. I have a few questions …'

Richard Denham

HOME

It was a while before anyone spoke. They sat there as darkness fell, sipping the welcome cocoa the dinghy's crew had brought. They knew it would be tough, all of them, they just didn't know how tough.

'Where are we going?' Harris asked the Woman.

'There,' she said, pointing beyond the bobbing bows. A ship loomed out of the darkness over them. No noise. No lights. Like the Flying Dutchman transported into Now from Before. 'And beyond that, home.'

Other titles by BLKDOG Publishing for your consideration:

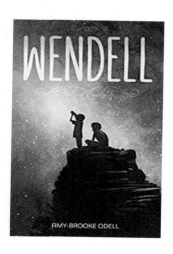

Wendell
By Amy-Brooke Odell

Wendell and his friends, both human and animal, embark on a journey to discover the truth about the Wind Folk and where his mother really is. His world of baseball, camp-outs, and fishing is rocked when he discovers that the adults in town know a lot more than they say, and sometimes those tales told around a campfire are true.

And, when it comes to the Wind Folk; it is said if you see one, you become one.

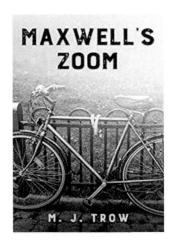

Maxwell's Zoom
By M. J. Trow

When asked about when it all began, Peter Maxwell would always say that it was at breakfast one day, when his son said, 'It says in the news that bats are giving people colds.' At that point, that was all anyone thought, if they thought anything at all. Nolan was worried about the Count and Bismarck but of course, as everyone would soon know, it was more than that – much more.

What was perhaps not quite so obvious as the world started to pull together to halt the spread of the pandemic, was that it would also restart a killing spree, one that had been halted for decades. Old memories rising to the surface, old enmities and slights recalled and suddenly, in masked and socially distanced Leighford someone is prowling with a hammer raised to create mayhem.

As an historian, Maxwell is keeping his head while most people are running round like chickens minus theirs – loss and tragedy stalk the land, closer to home than anyone thought possible. In a world where death is striking everywhere, how can anyone hope to bring a murderer to book?

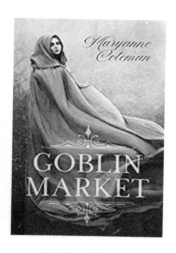

Goblin Market
By Maryanne Coleman

Have you ever wondered what happened to the faeries you used to believe in? They lived at the bottom of the garden and left rings in the grass and sparkling glamour in the air to remind you where they were. But that was then – now you might find them in places you might not think to look. They might be stacking shelves, delivering milk or weighing babies at the clinic. Open your eyes and keep your wits about you and you might see them.

But no one is looking any more and that is hard for a Faerie Queen to bear and Titania has had enough. When Titania stamps her foot, everyone in Faerieland jumps; publicity is what they need. Television, magazines. But that sort of thing is much more the remit of the bad boys of the Unseelie Court, the ones who weave a new kind of magic; the World Wide Web. Here is Puck re-learning how to fly; Leanne the agent who really is a vampire; Oberon's Boys playing cards behind the wainscoting; Black Annis, the bag-lady from Hainault, all gathered in a Restoration comedy that is strictly twenty-first century.

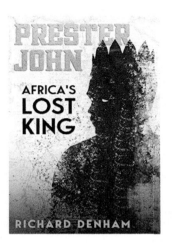

Prester John: Africa's Lost King
By Richard Denham

He sits on his jewelled throne on the Horn of Africa in the maps of the sixteenth century. He can see his whole empire reflected in a mirror outside his palace. He carries three crosses into battle and each cross is guarded by one hundred thousand men. He was with St Thomas in the third century when he set up a Christian church in India. He came like a thunderbolt out of the far East eight centuries later, to rescue the crusaders clinging on to Jerusalem. And he was still there when Portuguese explorers went looking for him in the fifteenth century.

Was he real? Did he ever exist? This book will take you on a journey of a lifetime, to worlds that might have been, but never were. It will take you, if you are brave enough, into the world of Prester John.

Fade
By Bethan White

There is nothing extraordinary about Chris Rowan. Each day he wakes to the same faces, has the same breakfast, the same commute, the same sort of homes he tries to rent out to unsuspecting tenants.

There is nothing extraordinary about Chris Rowan. That is apart from the black dog that haunts his nightmares and an unexpected encounter with a long forgotten demon from his past. A nudge that will send Chris on his own downward spiral, from which there may be no escape.

There is nothing extraordinary about Chris Rowan...

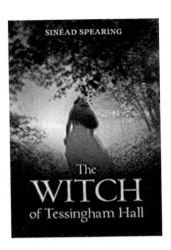

The Witch of Tessingham Hall
By Sinéad Spearing.

England 1657.

Alison, a folk- healer, stands falsely accused of murder by witchcraft, an allegation that sets in motion a powerful curse — "May your women forever wane!" — the spell haunting generations of her accuser's family, sending their women early to their graves.

London 2022.

Eden Flynn – an anxiety-ridden academic of Old English magic is invited for a job interview in the crypt of Southwark Cathedral, where her interviewer, the dashingly handsome geneticist Lord James Fabian, pulls her into the midst of his family secret: his sister is sick, and his daughter is showing signs of the same mental affliction.

Can Eden fulfil her part in the web which has been woven stronger and stronger over hundreds of years? Can she find the strength to break the bonds that bind her and Lord Fabian to the past? And can she live with the changes she will unleash?

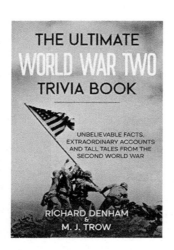

The Ultimate World War Two Trivia Book
By Richard Denham & M. J. Trow

The Second World War ended over seventy-five years ago and yet it holds a lasting fascination for millions. Most school children worldwide have studied it but it is unlikely that they would have learned any of the fascinating facts to be found in The Ultimate World War Two Trivia Book.

Funny, heart-breaking and downright borderline unbelievable, the snippets in this book are perfect for dropping into conversations to amaze and amuse your friends. You might also find yourself becoming the king or queen of the pub trivia quiz when you have knowledge of Winkie the Pigeon, the Battle of the Tennis Court and the Bee Bombs of Prester John. One thing to be careful of - never, ever lend this book to anyone; it is totally addictive and you will never see it again!

www.blkdogpublishing.com

Printed in Great Britain
by Amazon

28584122R00138